29
DATES

**Books by Melissa de la Cruz
available from Inkyard Press**

Something in Between
Someone to Love
29 Dates

MELISSA DE LA CRUZ

Recycling programs
for this product may
not exist in your area.

ISBN-13: 978-1-335-99471-4

29 Dates

Copyright © 2018 by Melissa de la Cruz

This edition published by arrangement with Harlequin Books S.A.

For questions and comments about the quality of this book, please contact us at CustomerService@Harlequin.com.

Inkyard Press
22 Adelaide St. West, 40th Floor
Toronto, Ontario M5H 4E3, Canada
www.InkyardPress.com

Printed in U.S.A.

With so much love, this book is dedicated to
the Korean side of my family:

Francis de la Cruz and Ji Young (Christina) Hwang
Sebastian Francis Hyunhu Hwang de la Cruz
and Marie Christina Huyoung Hwang de la Cruz

In Korean culture, there is a common belief that any number that ends in nine, or "plus nine" as it's called there, is bad luck and leads to more hardship and problems than usual.

PROLOGUE

JISU: Hey, I'm Jisu.

DAEHYUN: I'm Daehyun.

JISU: Korean name! But you're born and raised here?

DAEHYUN: Yup, and you moved from Seoul not that long ago?

JISU: Yeah, my parents decided it would be a good idea for me to become a last-minute international student and sent me across the Pacific to San Francisco. And here we are now.

DAEHYUN: I'm not even going to try to relate. I can't imagine moving to a whole new country.

JISU: It hasn't been the easiest. But I've met people along the way who've made it worth it.

DAEHYUN: This is gonna sound silly, but I actually feel a little nervous right now.

JISU: For real? It's like we're just hanging out!

DAEHYUN: I know, but it's my first seon. Even just saying that makes it sound official and formal. And you're making me nervous. I even asked some friends for dating tips.

JISU: And what did they tell you?

DAEHYUN: That kindness is underrated. And common likes and dislikes are key. Heavy emphasis on the common dislikes. So, you've been on a lot of seons, both here and in Seoul?

JISU: Yeah, but none of them have worked out…clearly. I did meet some cool guys and I'm actually friends with some of them. But there was never really that chemistry with anyone, you know? I love meeting new people, but I'm kind of over seons, to be honest.

DAEHYUN: I bet the right guy could be the end of all seons for you. You seem to know what you want.

JISU: What do you want? What are you trying to get out of these seons?

DAEHYUN: Actually, I have a girlfriend, which might really screw me up in the long run if I keep sneaking out. I'm only going on these dates to appease my mother. She kinda hates my girlfriend.

JISU: Oh, that's too bad. I actually thought this might go somewhere.

DAEHYUN: Well, it was nice knowing ya, Jees.

JISU: Did you just call me Jees? I hate nicknames. Especially when someone you just met assigns you one.

1

The big red 79 percent circled at the top of Kim Jisu's history exam wasn't what worried her. It wasn't the fact that she had actually studied hard. It wasn't Mrs. Han's look of concern that made her anxious either. No, it was the disappointment on her parents' faces that Jisu could so clearly imagine that made her want to crumple up the exam, crawl under her desk and curl into a ball. She didn't want to let them down.

So, this is how you're going to start the school year? Don't you know how important senior year of high school is? How do you plan on getting accepted into a top school here, or any university in America for that matter? Even if you want to move halfway across the world, your grades still have to be strong. Jisu could practically hear her parents' endless nagging, their *jansori*.

There it was in bloodred, mocking her. Only 79 percent. A solid C+! Couldn't Mrs. Han have bumped her over by just one point so that she could squeak by with a B-? The number nine was truly the worst. Anything ending in nine for her was the height of unlucky. Close, but no cigar—almost there, but not good enough. She would've felt equally miserable if she'd gotten 59 percent, 69 percent or even 89 percent. *Actually if I got 89 percent, I would be really happy*, Jisu thought. *Except that it's just one point shy of getting a 90 percent. And anything in the nineties is close enough to 100 percent, but still not perfect! Ugh.*

Her parents were the type to question even a 100 percent grade by asking why she didn't get 110 percent—wasn't there extra credit?

"Dae-bak!" Park Minjung exclaimed, smiling as she looked at her exam. "I didn't even study," she bragged.

Jisu peered at Min's test. An 86 percent—a solid B. You didn't need perfect scores to become a pop star, which was Min's dream. How could Jisu have done worse than a girl whose life was dedicated to selfies and singing classes?

Jisu slid her exam into her notebook so that no one could see. If only she could retake the exam, restart the year and redo all of high school.

"Jisu, don't tell me you failed the first exam of the year," Min said as she reapplied her lip gloss.

"I didn't fail," Jisu muttered. And technically she hadn't. One could even argue that she'd scored several points *above* passing. This argument, of course, would never fly with her parents.

"Then how did you do? Why won't you say what you got?" Min never did know when to shut up.

"Oh, Min, mind your own business," Euni chimed from behind them.

For as long as Jisu could remember, Hong Eunice had always had her back. Euni was born seven days before Jisu and, aside from that one week, the two girls had always been in each other's lives, growing up on the same street in Daechi-dong, taking the same classes at Daewon Foreign Language

High School and enduring every extracurricular activity that their parents pushed onto them. Painting, archery, French, ballet—they were privileged to be exposed to an array of arts and cultures, but more often than not, it felt too deliberate, like they were being groomed to replace their parents in society. Like a boot camp for the upper class. Academics came naturally for Euni, but not so much for Jisu. Still, every time Jisu fell behind, Euni was there to help her catch up. She was also there for her whenever Min got a little too out of hand, which was often.

"This test was actually really hard," Euni said. "I didn't think I would even finish in time." She was lying through her teeth. All three of them knew that she'd gotten the highest score in the class, as she always did. Euni was a great student but a terrible liar, and Jisu loved her for it.

Jisu thought about the weekend she had wasted sitting at hagwon like a prisoner, doing her school homework and then chipping away at all the additional readings and exercises from her hagwon tutors. She could've walked around Gangnam alongside the Han River and taken photos on her brand new DSLR. But no, this would've disappointed her parents. *If you spent the same amount of time studying as you do with your camera, your class ranking would be much higher.* If Jisu knew anything about herself, it was that she was definitely not the academic type.

"Euni, you're lucky I don't actually try," Min said as she checked her reflection in her compact. "You would have serious competition if I ever opened one of these books."

"No one would want you to." Jisu pushed the eraser end of her pencil into Min's contoured forehead. "You might grow wrinkles from thinking too much. Then you'd look like Euni and me, and no record label would ever sign you."

Euni laughed and even Min couldn't help cracking a smile. Jisu felt better immediately. Wasn't this how you were supposed to spend your time in high school? Enjoying time with your friends, instead of getting caught up in your anxious thoughts about the future?

"Class, settle down." Mrs. Han's booming voice cut through the chatter. "This exam was a tough one, but I don't want you to be discouraged. Senior year is the most important year. I cannot emphasize this enough. College, your career, your future—the beginning of a great new chapter is about to start. Isn't that exciting?"

It was not exciting.

It was absolutely terrifying. Jisu looked at her classmates and could imagine everyone's future but hers. As annoying as Min could be, she was talented. Eventually her perfectly symmetrical face, with her expressive eyes and natural pout, would be plastered over every bus and subway stop in Seoul as part of a major ad campaign for her hit album. It was only a matter of time. Euni's perfect grades meant Harvard or Seoul National University for sure. Then there was the rest of them—there were rumors that Lee Taeyang would follow his brothers' footsteps to Oxford. Choi Sungmi was a shoo-in for Yonsei, one of the top universities in Seoul, while Kang Joowon had spent the last three summers playing cello at the prestigious Interlochen Arts Program, making strides with his fellow camp members in securing admission to Juilliard. And everyone knew Kim Heechan was flunking, but he was from a chaebol family, so a generous donation would get him into Seoul National University and he'd eventually take over the family business.

But Jisu? What was next for her?

Her phone buzzed, alerting her to an email from Ms. Moon, the Matchmaker. Aka the Matseon Queen. Ms. Moon came from a family of matchmakers. It could easily be argued that Ms. Moon, her mother and her aunt were collectively responsible for the social infrastructure of Seoul's upper class.

Ms. Moon was well into her sixties, but her excellent psychological profiling skills, along with the consistent pulse she had on pop culture and trending topics, had made her successful in pairing off couples in their late twenties and thirties left and right, for several decades and counting.

After a long streak of success, Ms. Moon had recently turned her attention to a slightly younger crowd. Rumor had it that a certain matriarchal head of a chaebol family was behind this additional business venture. Ms. Moon had found the perfect match for her son, a fairly easy task given that he was one of the most eligible bachelors of Seoul: handsome, charming and heir to the lucrative family business. But the concern was with the beautiful but painfully shy and introverted daughter. She was a senior in high school, the baby of the family and a target for suitors whose sole intention was to seduce their way into the family business.

If you asked her, Ms. Moon would probably agree that the end of high school and start of college was too early a time to look for a life partner, but she'd also tell you that it was never too late to get yourself acquainted with the right crowd, which really translated to the crowd approved by socialite and social-climbing parents.

As long as the status-obsessed parents of Seoul were willing to pay for someone to keep tabs on their children's social lives, Ms. Moon was willing to provide that service.

Dear Jisu,

This is a courtesy reminder of your seon with Lee Taemin tonight at 7:00 p.m. at the 10 Corso Como Café. Taemin's one-sheet is attached again for your review. Please confirm receipt of this email. I hope the two of you have a wonderful time.

Warm wishes,

Ms. Moon

Ughhhh. Another seon.

Earlier in the year Mrs. Kim had heard whisperings from her friends about Ms. Moon expanding her clientele. Mrs. Kim was unlike the other mothers in that she was still working full-time even though, as her socialite peers would say, their family didn't necessarily *have* to be a two-income household. Working as a head data analyst at the Han Group wasn't quite the same as taking three-hour lunches and planning elaborate charity functions, but she loved her job and that was reason enough to stay. Still, Mrs. Kim subscribed to all the other rules of society, especially ones that concerned the raising of her only child, and signed Jisu up for Ms. Moon's matchmaking service.

Sure, it was icky to so blatantly climb up and maintain your place in society, especially through your own child, but no one was above such gestures if they worked. Even Jisu's lifelong friendship with Euni had started with each of their parents cautiously eyeing and inquiring about the others. This was the world that they lived in. And so Mrs. Kim sent Jisu on seons all summer in the hopes that she might snatch a promising boyfriend who would fit in with her promising friends, who would turn into a promising fiancé, who would then become a promising husband and complete every Korean mother's idea of a picture-perfect life for her daughter.

But summer had come to an end and Jisu had not made a love match. Another flop.

Socializing with the right people is just as important as getting into a top university. Her mother's nagging jansori was inescapable. Her parents' voices were like buzzing mosquitos that wouldn't leave her alone. But she had no choice other than to comply.

The Matseon Matchmaker was highly selective about which clients she took on and certainly not cheap. With Jisu's not-so-promising high school transcript, her parents likely had pulled some strings to get her on the exclusive client list. Jisu hadn't asked for any of this; her parents were doing it all for her. And if she did want anything, it was to be a good daughter. To make all their efforts worth it.

"You have another date?" Euni asked. "I thought your mom said the seons were just for the summer."

"Yeah, but none of them turned into anything, which was definitely not my mother's plan." Jisu opened the email attachment.

LEE TAEMIN. Occupation: Studio art student with focus in sculpture. Education: Seoul Institute of the Arts (full scholarship; first solo art exhibit to happen early next year).

It was impressive, like the others, and went on and on with a list of his accomplishments. Jisu cringed at the thought of whatever overload of information her mother had sent to Ms. Moon so she could put together her profile.

Kim Jisu. Average student. Pretty enough (Min's makeup lessons helped). No real accomplishments (she is seventeen—give her a break).

The truth was she was just an ordinary, average teen. She liked all the things many girls her age liked—selfies, slime videos on Instagram, rom-coms, candy. And disliked the same things everyone disliked—acne, rude people, Instagram ads for ugly clothes emblazoned with "empowering" statements. (Seriously, who were they kidding with the $800 *The Future is Female* T-shirts?)

Cute boys were in the plus column for sure, but some of the seon guys she met were so serious that, even if they were cute, it almost didn't matter. Her father liked to joke that any guy with an expensive car was handsome, after which her mother would quip that it wasn't so much about a guy with an expensive car as it was about a guy who could afford a car as expensive as yours.

"Are you sure you're just not being picky?" Euni teased. "What happened to the one with the restaurateur parents?"

"Oh, I remember that one. He was cute!" Min said. "If you didn't like him, you should've set him up with me. A nationally beloved songstress and the heir to Korea's top restaurants—we'd be an amazing power couple."

"I don't know, Min. He was kind of full of himself and kept checking out his reflection. But that's something you guys have in common, so maybe it would work out!" Jisu laughed.

"What does the guy you're seeing tonight look like?" Euni reached for Jisu's phone. "Isn't there a photo that comes with the résumé?"

"Wait, the date is tonight?" Min asked. "I got us those tickets to this week's *Music Bank* taping. You guys said you were coming with me!" She rolled her eyes and let out a dramatic, heavy sigh.

Jisu and Euni exchanged a guilty glance. They *had* promised. And unlike the poorly attended open mics and over-crowded celebrity meet-and-greets that Min usually dragged her friends to, *Music Bank* was actually an exciting show that Euni and Jisu looked forward to. Many of their favorite pop stars would be performing back-to-back. Jisu always watched it on TV, but the thought of being at the studio, right there with her favorite artists, filled her with excitement.

"Oh, yeah, that's right. Jisu, can't you just reschedule?" Euni tapped Jisu's phone and enlarged the attached headshot. "Or cancel?" Euni frowned. "He's not that cute anyway."

Jisu grabbed her phone back and looked at the picture on the screen. She wished for a reaction—her heart beating faster, a tiny stomach flip, anything. But her body remained static.

There was nothing. He wasn't *not* cute. He just looked like every other squeaky-clean, accomplished, coiffed son of a well-off family.

Sorry, Ms. Moon. I need to reschedule. I have hagwon until late in the evening today.

Jisu hit Send and felt a wave of relief. She had spent the whole summer going on dead-end dates and had wasted last weekend studying for a test she would've never aced. One night of fun couldn't hurt.

When Jisu stepped out of the elevator and into her family's apartment, she was relieved to see that all the lights were out. She carefully removed her shoes in the foyer and slid into her house slippers. From the top floor of their apartment in Daechi-dong, Jisu could see the rest of the Gangnam neighborhood below her. A stream of traffic lit up the Dongbu Expressway. The red-and-white lights of buses, trucks and cars ambled alongside the shimmering waters of the Tancheon.

It was way too late to say that she was coming home from hagwon. She had texted out a full, elaborate lie five different ways before simply letting her parents know she was seeing a late movie with her friends. That was all it took for them to believe her.

Jisu's ears were still ringing from the concert, which only exaggerated the complete silence surrounding her. Every creak of the wooden floor loudly announced her presence. She held her breath, crept into the living room and peeked at the white leather couch to make sure her father hadn't fallen asleep there while waiting for her to come home. She exhaled quietly. He wasn't there, slouched on one side like he was sometimes. As she made her way into the kitchen, she imagined her mother seated at one of the high stools with her arms crossed atop the cold marble island top. *Don't be awake. Please don't be awake.* But there was no night-light left on, and neither parent was waiting for her. *Thank god.*

Jisu grabbed a sheet mask from the fridge and scurried to her room. *Finally.* After placing her phone and camera on her nightstand and changing into pajamas, she crawled into her bed and sprawled her limbs out, as if to stretch and rid her body of the entire weight of the day.

Her phone vibrated. It was a text from Min.

Jisu!! Did you get home safe?

Usually Euni was the one who checked to make sure everyone safely returned home.

Also don't forget to send me the photos from tonight!

Jisu smiled. Of course. Min really just wanted the photos. Jisu sat up, ripped open the sheet mask package and then aligned the mask on her face so that she could properly see and breath out of the eye and nose cutouts. The refreshing smell of cucumber and aloe almost immediately put Jisu at ease. The mask was nice and cold and would reduce any puffiness in her features, eliminating evidence of how late she'd stayed out. She caught her reflection in the mirror and laughed. Looking like a wide-eyed and extremely innocent killer from *Friday the 13th* was never not hilarious.

She lay down again so that the sheet mask wouldn't slide off her face. Holding her camera directly over her head, Jisu scrolled through her photos. Min dancing, Euni laughing. All the shots of Min were perfectly posed, but somehow still looked candid. How many selfies did it take for her to figure out her best angles? Euni, the stay-home-and-watch-a-movie type, looked like she'd had fun, too. And of course there were the shameless selfies. The three of them cheesing hard, having a good time. Why did having a fun night with friends have to feel so illicit? What was the point of killing yourself to have a "happy, successful life"—whatever that meant—if you couldn't relax once in a while?

And who got to define what a "happy and successful" future looked like?

There was no greater failure than being a senior at Daewon High School and not knowing your five-year plan.

Jisu's eyelids grew heavy. She took off her sheet mask, pressed the cold cucumber and aloe goo into her skin and fell fast asleep.

When Jisu stepped into the kitchen the next morning and found her parents seated at the dining table with stern looks on their faces, every drop of euphoria from the night before evaporated into thin air. Her limbs grew heavy, and making her way to the table felt like dragging a ton of bricks. She was caught. Of course they knew. How could she have thought for a second that she'd get away with it? Jisu seated herself at the table and braced for impact.

"I hope the *Music Bank* concert was fun, because that is the last one you will be going to," Mrs. Kim said as she dipped a spoon into her cup and stirred the tea. Straight to the point. As always. Had Jisu's parents had her followed? It honestly wouldn't be surprising if they had.

"Min wants to be a silly pop star, so at least it makes sense for her to go." Mrs. Kim turned to her husband, talking to him as if their daughter wasn't sitting right in front of them. "I'm surprised Euni went. Usually she is good about these things. Her mother will not be happy to hear about this."

Jisu gritted her teeth. She could take her mother's endless jansori, but she couldn't stand it when she dared to talk about her friends.

"Oh, so *now* you're upset?" Mrs. Kim stared at Jisu, whose clenched jaw was probably telegraphing "attitude problem" to her mother. "Now that you've been caught ignoring your responsibilities and coming home late, but not when you barely passed your first exam of the school year?" Jisu's exam was still in her backpack, which she'd had with her all night. Her mother must have called Mrs. Han.

"Umma, please. I wasn't happy with my score either," Jisu protested. She looked down at her folded hands. "But it wasn't that low of a score. I am really trying. I'll do better on the next one. I'm sorry I can't be perfect."

"Perfect?" Her mother sighed. "No one is asking you to be perfect. It would be more than enough for you to score higher than your class average. But apparently even that is too much to ask."

Her father placed a hand on her mother's shoulder as if putting a brake on his wife's anger. Jisu's father was the calm, rational one between the two of them. These were the roles they played: Mrs. Kim as the mother whose standards were as high as her emotions were strong, Mr. Kim as the father whose disappointment was quiet, but just as devastating, and of course Jisu as the disappointing daughter.

"And the seon that you missed…" Mrs. Kim sighed again. "A lot of time and energy goes into preparing these meetings. When you blow one off, it's disrespectful to Ms. Moon. It's disrespectful to your date. It's disrespectful to us."

Jisu's chest tightened, and all of a sudden it felt hard to breathe. Her arms tensed as if they were wrapped up in a straitjacket. Doing well in school, getting into a good college… Jisu could understand why her parents put pressure on her with academics. But orchestrating her love life was taking their obsessive parenting to the next level. She wanted to scream, but frustration paralyzed her. She could only muster a few words.

"Umma, I spent the whole summer going to every single seon. I only asked to reschedule yesterday's." Jisu dared to look at her mother. "What if I don't *want* to meet anyone through some arranged matchmaker?"

"You want a perfect romance to fall into your lap?"

"Isn't that what happened with you and Appa? That's literally the story of how you guys met," Jisu shot back.

She was right. Her mother had been walking across campus when she was knocked over by a group of students protesting the bloody outcome of the Gwangju Uprising. The protest was led by none other than Mr. Kim. Jisu's mother had just checked out an armful of books on the Medici family for her research on the birth of entrepreneurship in art, and they were strewn about on the ground. By the time Jisu's father picked up each one, he'd gathered enough courage to ask her on a date.

But that was a long time ago. Mrs. Kim was no longer an art-history scholar, and Mr. Kim's protesting days were long behind him. Jisu wondered if her parents ever remembered their past selves. She saw glimpses when her mother would take her to the latest gallery opening and actually observe and talk to her about the art instead of eyeing each person who entered the space. But those were only glimpses; her parents were entirely different people now.

Mrs. Kim furrowed her brows and placed her hands on her temples. "Finding a partner today holds the same kind of importance as finding a job. Do you think meeting someone who comes from a good family and has a great education just like you is as easy as bumping into them on the street?" Mrs. Kim cupped Jisu's face in her hands. "Jisu-ya, listen to me. Nothing happens if you sit around and wait. Nothing will work until you do. Every decision you make now affects your future. With school, even with the seons."

"Jisu, we are supporting you in every way we can," Mr.

Kim chimed in, making his best diplomatic effort. He was always the olive branch between Jisu and her mother. Jisu knew in her heart that her parents wanted her to be happy. She knew that her own optimism and faith in the world were things her parents loved about her, but they worried that she would be hurt by what they saw as her naivete. Still, at the end of the day, both her parents were going to be supportive of whatever she wanted to do with her life…so long as she was first accepted by the best college she could get into. This logic probably had its roots in her mother and father having studied in not-so-lucrative fields—art history and philosophy respectively—but having done so at Seoul National University, the top school in South Korea. The reputation of their alma mater had helped them as they'd both made their way to become head analysts at the Han Group, one of the most reputable conglomerates in the country.

Mr. Kim looked at his daughter with sympathy, as if he too felt the very growing pains he was putting his daughter through. "If your grades aren't improving and you're skipping out on your seons—you can see how we might get upset. We're just asking you to try."

"But I am trying!" Jisu cried. "I'm doing my best!"

"Exactly," Mrs. Kim snapped. "Your best at Daewon is not good enough, which is why your Appa and I are sending you to Wick-Helmering High School in San Francisco."

Jisu stared at her mother in disbelief. Surely she had to be joking. An empty threat to scare her. But her mother's perfectly unwrinkled porcelain face remained stoic.

"San Francisco? *America?* Why?"

Mr. Kim slid a folder across the dining table. The logo on the front showed a roaring tiger perched above the letters *WHHS*, all outlined in gold.

"What is this?" Jisu asked, genuinely confused.

"After the start of the semester last March, your father and

I looked into applying for you to potentially attend a school in the States," Mrs. Kim explained.

"We know and understand how tough it is to stand out at a competitive school like Daewon." Mr. Kim looked at his daughter with kind, encouraging eyes but didn't help to dilute Jisu's confusion. "It isn't too late for you to spend your final year at a somewhat easier but still highly reputable school in the States."

"When we received your midsemester review in May, we went ahead with the application. And it's a good thing we did, given your scores at the end of the term," Mrs. Kim said.

"My scores weren't *that* bad last semester," Jisu said. But she quickly saw the bigger picture, the grand scheme her parents had been cooking up. And the forms. Her parents had made her fill out a bunch of paperwork, citing that it wouldn't hurt to get the process started if she got accepted to a university in the States, as she hoped.

Her scores truly hadn't been so bad last term. They were barely above her class average, which was an issue. At any other high school in Seoul, her scores would be great, but at Daewon, where only the best were admitted, she was struggling to stand out as a promising college candidate. And Jisu had always been interested in going to a university abroad, particularly in the States, so if she were to transfer out of Daewon she might as well make the early jump overseas.

This explained the high volume of seons that Mrs. Kim had made Jisu attend. Ms. Moon really had been working over-time in setting her up on as many dates as possible during the few weeks of summer break in July and August. Clearly it had been a last-ditch attempt to pair her up with someone before her pending school year abroad.

"Why didn't you tell me any of this?" The thumping in Jisu's chest seemed to grow louder. Her head throbbed, as if someone had hit her with a large steel hammer. How could her parents betray her like this?

"Jisu, we don't want you to leave Seoul." Mrs. Kim placed a hand on her daughter's. "We didn't want it so much that we kept holding off in case you might be able to pull yourself up. But I don't think we have much of a choice now, and this is the last window of opportunity to make the transfer to Wick."

Mr. Kim opened the brochure like a salesman would to a potential customer. "Their academic year doesn't start until September, so you'll arrive just in time for the first day of school and the change won't feel so abrupt."

"I don't know how this could feel anything but abrupt, Appa." Jisu crossed her arms. She felt so dizzy that she could pass out.

Being grounded, no allowance, having her phone taken away—Jisu was willing to endure any of those punishments. But being exiled halfway around the world by her own parents was so unnecessarily harsh. Jisu placed a hand on the school brochure. It didn't disappear into thin air. This wasn't a bad dream. It was really happening. She tried to keep a straight face, but her eyes started to well up.

"Don't cry," Mrs. Kim said. "Your face will get red and swollen. You don't want to look like a mess walking through the airport."

"*What?*" Jisu pulled her hand away. She let the hot tears fall down her face. When exactly was the first day of school at Wick? How soon were her parents going to kick her out of the country?

"Jisu-ya, this is painful for us, too." Mrs. Kim sighed. "But your Appa and I are doing it for you."

For you. Each time her parents said those two words, Jisu's guilt doubled. It weighed on her shoulders and sank to the bottom of her stomach. The burden of expectation was already too much to bear, but now she had to carry it across the ocean to San Francisco. Sisyphus had nothing on Jisu. Or was it Prometheus? Ugh. At least with the last-minute continent move, Jisu wouldn't have to take the classics exam next week.

Mr. Kim ushered his daughter out of her seat. "I was able to get you on a flight this afternoon, so get your things together."

"Appa, please don't do this," Jisu begged. "I'm sorry! I'll do better, I promise. What about my friends? I can't even say goodbye?"

"Jisu-ya, calm down. You'll see them during winter break." Mrs. Kim stood and smoothed the wrinkles from her tweed skirt. "Until then, you can think fondly about all the fun you had with them last night."

Jisu dragged herself to her room, each step feeling infinitely heavier than the last. On her desk was the Korean-to-English dictionary she used at school. Like her friends at Daewon, she was fluent in English, so she wasn't worried about being able to communicate at her new school so much as she was upset about leaving everything she knew.

A long slip of paper was tucked inside the book.

ICN to SFO. Her boarding pass.

This was actually happening.

Jisu had always wanted to visit sunny California, but not like this.

DATE NO. 1

NAME: Cha Myungbo aka Boz

INTERESTS:
Mathematics, Basketball, Horror Movies

PARENT OCCUPATIONS:
Online Games CEO; Tourism director

BOZ: It's actually Myungbo, but you can call me Boz.

JISU: Boz? I haven't heard that one before—is there any special meaning behind it?

BOZ: No, I just like the way it sounds.

JISU: Oh…okay. I guess it does sound unique. I've certainly never met anyone with that name!

BOZ: Yeah…that's why I picked it.

JISU: So, have you seen any movies lately? I saw you listed movies in your one-sheet.

BOZ: You actually read those? I never do. But yeah, I love horror movies.

JISU: Cool. Did you see *It* yet? It looks so scary and I'm terrified of clowns, but I heard it's good!

BOZ: No, American horror movies are a joke. They're never scary and are always so predictable. Don't you know that *we* make the best horror movies?

JISU: We do? I actually don't watch too many because I get scared so easily.

BOZ: That's the thing though. A good horror movie isn't about the blood or gore or any of that physically scary stuff. Those are all cheap thrills. The best horror movies mess with your brain and haunt you for days after. Like *A Tale of Two Sisters.* You saw that one, right?

JISU: No. Like I said, I don't really do scary movies.

BOZ: What? That one was a huge hit. Literally everyone saw that. You might be the first person I've met in Seoul who hasn't seen it.

JISU: *shrugs*

BOZ: Anyway, it's based on the Janghwa and Hongryeon story—you do know that story, right?

JISU: Actually, I do. With the gwisin sisters and the evil step-mom, right? My mom tells me those scary folklore stories all the time. They're actually why I don't even go to the movies. The stories alone are so terrifying!

BOZ: Really? What other stories has she told you?

JISU: Well, there was the one about my great-great-grandmother…

BOZ: Wait, you have horror stories within your family? That's so dope.

JISU: Um, I wouldn't say it's dope. It's actually really terrifying. When I was a kid, I couldn't even go to bed because I was so scared.

BOZ: So…what's the story? You can't just say you have a scary family legend and not tell the story!

JISU: It's really not that interesting.

BOZ: C'mon, Jisu. Don't tell me you still stay up at night, scared like a little kid.

JISU: To be fair, my mom is a really good storyteller and scared the crap out of me when I was little.

BOZ: Do I have to ask Mrs. Kim for story time, then? What happened? I wanna know!

JISU: Okay, fine. My great-great-grandmother lived in the shigol, in the deep neck of the woods. But my family has said that she was cursed by her own mother.

BOZ: A curse! What was the curse?

JISU: Her mother had an unhappy marriage. Her father cheated on her mother all the time. But he stopped when she got pregnant. They wanted a boy so badly to carry on the family name. But they had my great-great-grandmother, and her mother was devastated.

BOZ: Geez.

JISU: Right? I can't even imagine being a woman back then. And even though we've made so much progress, I still think we see obvious traces of it in society today and—

BOZ: Wait, so what was the curse put on your great-great-grandmother?

JISU: Well, her mother died shortly after giving birth to her. And she was so bitter and so broken by that point. Her marriage had long been dead. She knew she was dying to give birth to a child that couldn't even win her husband's love back. So she cursed her daughter so that she would be hyperaware of suffering and forever be haunted by all the wronged, betrayed, starved spirits that still roamed the land. Apparently, until the day my great-great-grandmother died, she claimed to always be bothered by these spirits.

BOZ: Wow. That's messed up.

JISU: Gee, thanks. My family is clearly *so* messed up.

BOZ: No, I didn't mean it like that! That's actually a really cool story. Have you heard about people seeing ghosts on the subways?

JISU: I heard one of my classmates mention it, but I didn't really listen. I take the subway all the time and I don't want to get creeped out—

BOZ: This wasn't even in Seoul. Remember the Daegu subway fire that happened when we were kids?

JISU: Of course. That was awful. So many people died.

BOZ: Apparently, every year on the anniversary of the fire, multiple people report seeing the ghosts of the victims on the subway when they get close to Jungangno Station.

JISU: Oh, my god. I don't know if that's more sad or terrifying.

BOZ: Right? My friend's aunt who lives in Daegu apparently had a full-on conversation with a ghost who sat next to her. When the subway pulled up to Jungangno, the ghost apparently said, "Ah, finally I can go home." When she stepped out to the platform and turned around, he was gone. She looked inside the car and it was empty. The doors closed, and when she peered through the window again, she saw the guy sitting right where he was before! That's when she realized she had been talking to a ghost.

JISU: So the ghosts of the victims haunt the subway station where they died because they never got to leave? That is so heartbreaking.

BOZ: Isn't that an amazing story though?

JISU: Amazing? I guess. But, Boz, those were real victims. It's not just another fictional horror story. Real people died.

BOZ: All horror stories have roots in reality though. And they reflect the most tragic, ugliest parts of humanity. At least the good ones do.

JISU: And that's why you like it so much?

BOZ: Yeah, it's compelling stuff. Look, Jisu, I get it if horror is not really your thing. But you have to admit it's fascinating, right?

JISU: To be honest, I just don't think it's for me.

2

When the Korean Air flight attendants walked up and down first class, handing out hot towels, Jisu immediately pressed one to her tearstained face. It released a hot steam that smelled of eucalyptus and jasmine. Despite her best efforts to heed her mother's advice, Jisu had sobbed and sniffled her way through Incheon Airport. The last time she'd been at Incheon, she was flying back with her parents from a relaxing vacation at Jeju Island. But now she was being sent out of the country against her will.

"Please turn off all electronics as we prepare for departure."

Oh, god. It was really happening. She was really leaving. This wasn't an elaborate prank conducted by her enemies. *My own parents!* So this was what betrayal felt like.

Jisu took her phone out of her pocket. She tapped the yellow Kakao icon to open the app. There was an unread text message from Eunice.

Jisu! What are you doing today? Wanna come over to do homework? And then maybe go shopping as a reward?

A loud sob escaped from Jisu's mouth and startled her fellow passengers. The flight attendant instantly reappeared and slipped Jisu a bottle of Fiji water and another hot towel.

Euni-ya—I can't believe I'm writing this. My psycho parents put me on a one-way flight to San Francisco. They're making me go to a new school and I won't be back until winter. Please don't hate me. I love you. Promise to Kakao me every day, okay?

Eunice replied instantly.

What? How could they do that? Of course I don't hate you. I can't believe this.

The seat belt light above Jisu's head turned on. Jisu strapped herself down. Then she answered Eunice.

Maybe you can just transfer to my new school? Can you take the next flight out of Incheon? My life would be better if you were here with me.

Jisu could barely see her phone screen through the tears in her eyes.

Jisu-ya be strong. You will be okay. More than okay. I know it. Just promise me this. Do YOU. I love your parents, but they are way too controlling. Honestly, sometimes I think they look out for me more than my own parents do hahah.

But seriously, think about this as a vacation from them. Do the things you really want to do.

The flight attendant appeared again, but this time her wide smile was a touch menacing and her gaze was locked on Jisu's phone.

Ugh. Can't a girl at least text her best friend a proper goodbye?

Jisu switched her phone to airplane mode and took deep breaths. As the plane raced down the runway, she braced herself. This was her least favorite part of any flight. The deafening white noise blaring in her ears, the turbulence rattling her bones and the crushing pressure from being thrust upward against gravity that weighed down every fiber of her being.

And then, at thirty thousand feet, there was a silence and a ding. The seat belt light above Jisu's head turned off.

She stretched her legs across her sleeper pod and emptied the contents of her bag. The Wick-Helmering pamphlet mocked her beneath the scattered mess of her carry-on makeup and travel-size face creams. Jisu opened the pamphlet and started reading. This was her future now. Might as well get familiar.

Her eyes glazed over as she took in the rambling, self-congratulatory text about quality academia and high percentage rates of students accepted to Ivy League schools. Then came the endless list of clubs. Daewon offered every standard sport and activity you could imagine, but Wick-Helmering went above and beyond: a man-made river for sailing, fully serviced stables for horseback riding, studios for ballet, jazz, *and* modern dance, and shuttles that took students to the nearby mountains during the skiing season.

Everyone in the photos looked aggressively happy. Their taut smiles insisted they were having the best time. There were but a handful of Asians among the faces, but that was to be expected. Daewon had its small share of international students, but it was nothing like the diverse student body at Wick-

Helmering. It looked more and more like the CW American high school dramas that Jisu and her friends would download and watch on weekends, late into the night.

Jisu gulped the rest of her Fiji water and took more deep breaths. She dug out her rose-infused face cream and smoothed it across her face. Personal crisis aside, staying hydrated at thirty thousand feet was important. She rummaged through her assortment of lip stains and applied each one as if she were following one of her favorite beauty vlogger's tutorials. A little makeup break always distracted her from the daily stress of being a teenager who was held to impossible standards, but no amount of liquid liner could distract Jisu from the fact that she was en route to a place where she had no friends and knew no one.

A San Francisco travel guide peeked out from Jisu's bag. Her dad had handed it to her right before they parted ways.

Make sure you visit the Golden Gate Bridge and send us photos, he had told her at security as he wiped the tears from his daughter's face.

Jisu is going to California to study, not to play, her mother had retorted. *But yes, if you do take pictures make sure you send them to us. You know I love seeing what you capture. And that's if you have extra time after your studies and your seons.*

The seons. Of course there was no stopping them. Mrs. Kim fully intended to keep paying Ms. Moon to set her daughter up as she settled into San Francisco. With her high success rate and rapid word-of-mouth, Ms. Moon's matchmaking empire had gained international reach.

What good was moving across the entire Pacific Ocean if your parents still managed to keep their leash tight around you?

Jisu-ya, I know you're sad now. But when you land, you will forget all that and be excited to be in a new city. Mrs. Kim had held her daughter's face in her hands. *Just remember, this is not a vacation.*

No one knew and felt that more than Jisu. It pained her.

But she could tell it pained her mother, too. It would be a long three months before Mrs. Kim saw her daughter again—the longest she had been away from her only child. Still, sending Jisu off to Wick-Helmering was a last resort and final hope.

"Here you go, miss." A flight attendant handed Jisu a glass of pineapple juice.

"Sorry. I didn't ask for this."

"We noticed from your last flights with Korean Air that you like a glass of pineapple juice before your meal. If you'd prefer not to have it, I can take it back."

"Oh, no, that's fine. This is actually great, thank you."

The flight attendant looked at her knowingly, having clearly sensed that Jisu was going through a tough time. Jisu took a sip and her face scrunched up. It was more sour than sweet. The tangy flavor transported her back to the past few Korean Air flights she had taken. There was the big summer vacation trip to Macau with Euni and Min and their families, the quick spring visit to Jeju Island with her parents and, before that, the winter trip to London. All pleasant trips with only good memories.

This was the polar opposite.

"And here is the menu for the on-flight meal." The menu was written in gold ink and inscribed onto a black matte cardboard. Food was being provided by La Yeon, Jisu's favorite restaurant in Seoul. But looking at the entrée selections only made her miss her city more. She was going to miss everything, from trying out a new non-Korean restaurant in Itaewon with her friends and shopping in the streets of Cheongdam-dong with her mother and aunt, to simply taking a stroll down the Garosu-gil and wandering in and out of the smaller boutiques and quiet galleries. None of the trappings of first class mattered. Jisu could have everything in the world delivered straight to her sleeper pod and presented to her on a silver platter, but it wouldn't change the fact that, within a few hours, she would be landing in a new city, all alone.

"*Psst.* Hey!"

From the corner of her eye, Jisu could see that the passenger in the pod across from her was waving her arm. A girl maybe a few years older than her, dressed stylishly in all-black athleisure, smiled at Jisu.

"You okay? Looks like you might need some reading to keep you distracted."

Her English was perfect, with zero hint of an accent, just like an actress in a Hollywood movie. She must be a Korean-American girl going back home. Jisu could tell by the way she sat in her seat, by her demeanor. You could always tell the Korean Americans from the Koreans.

The girl pointed to Jisu's clutter of lip gloss, highlighter sticks and school pamphlets and handed her a stack of her own magazines. *Cosmo, Allure, Vogue, Glamour.* "I've skimmed these already. Plus I just took my melatonin pills, so you can have them. Enjoy!"

Before Jisu could thank her, the girl hopped back into her pod, slid on her sleeping mask and snuggled into her blanket.

"FALL INTO COLOR! Twenty Perfect Transitional Pieces to Settle You into Fall."

The beaming model on the cover wore a burgundy sweaterdress and patterned tights. Her smile and soft-blown hair beckoned Jisu to flip through the pages.

"The 10 Rules of Dating & Non-Dating."

Non-dating? Was there an entirely new set of rules in America that Jisu would have to follow? Maybe Ms. Moon had a separate guidebook for dating in the States. Not that Jisu cared. She had a bunch of cramming and college applications to worry about first. Jisu browsed through countless ads and perfume samples until she finally got to the article.

In the current age of nonstop swiping on apps and sliding into one's DMs, you might find yourself with a potential bae and ask yourself, "Is this a date? Or a non-date?" These ten easy indicators will clear up any confusion between you and your maybe-bae.

Non-dates, sliding into DMs and maybe-baes? After nine years of English classes, Jisu was fluent in the language, but the words used in the world of print magazines were like a separate dialect.

If he asks you simply to "hang out"—it's a non-date.

If he takes you somewhere specific, say the movies or a new restaurant downtown—it's a date.

If he sees you with a group of friends—it's a non-date.

If he officially introduces you to his friends—congrats, you are fully practicing the art of dating.

If the only time you see each other is in your bedrooms—you are fully practicing the art of non-dating.

The list went all the way down the page. Thinking about each of these scenarios made Jisu's head spin. For the first time, she felt grateful to have the Matseon Matchmaker to fall back on. More formalities and less mind games. Maybe her mother was onto something.

Jisu read the rest of the magazines and tried to absorb every headline, tip and piece of advice. Fashion and beauty were no problem. Popsicle-tinted lips, dewy skin, athleisure—all of these trends that were just catching on in the States had already come and gone in Seoul. But the so-called rules and guidelines of dating got more confusing the more she read about them.

At least cramming on how to be an American teenage girl was more fun than cramming for US history or math.

On the screen in front of her, the icon of the Korean Air plane slowly trudged across the map. A red dotted line stretched across the Pacific Ocean, from Korea to California. Ten hours remained. Each second dragged on, and each minute felt like an eternity. Jisu sighed. Until she was back in Seoul, every moment leading up to her return would feel infinitely longer.

Euni's words lingered in Jisu's mind. *Do YOU.*

DATE NO. 2

NAME: **Yu Jinwoo**

INTERESTS:
Squash, Young Investor's Club

PARENT OCCUPATIONS:
Retired surgeon; Cardiologist

JINWOO: What do you think of this place? Great, isn't it?

JISU: It's beautiful! I know hotel lobbies can get fancy, but this might be the fanciest place I've gone just to get coffee!

JINWOO: Not just any coffee, Jisu. The coffee beans they use here are overnighted straight from Colombia. Apparently the Park Hyatt is the only other hotel in Seoul that gets them.

JISU: Oh, wow. Are you really into coffee?

JINWOO: I'm into anything that's good quality. I don't know why people would have it any other way, really.

JISU: I mean, I could think of a few reasons why—like not having the means for the fanciest coffee beans in the world.

JINWOO: Fair, I guess. But you and I—we have the means. Might as well live it up, right?

JISU: Right...

JINWOO: Are you hungry? Maybe we can get some of those finger sandwiches. I'll ask for a menu—you ord whatever you want.

JISU: I'm good with my cappuccino for now. But thanks.

JINWOO: You sure? The caviar spread is pretty good here.

JISU: No, thanks. I don't really like caviar anyway.

JINWOO: C'mon. Years down the line, your future grandkids are asking about how you met your husband. High tea at the Shilla Hotel sounds better than coffee at a Starbucks, no?

JISU: Husband? Grandkids? You're thinking an awful far lot ahead. Also, wait, does this mean you get caviar on every seon you go on?

JINWOO: I'm not saying that I don't.

JISU: Jinwoo, if you have nice things all the time, that kinda takes away from them being nice in the first place. Don't you think?

JINWOO: If you're not hungry, we can at least get some biscotti, right?

JISU: Sure, biscotti is fine. Were you playing tennis before you came here?

JINWOO: Oh, these? These are actually squash rackets. There are a few courts around this neighborhood and I played a game today at the one that they have here.

JISU: That's cool—are you part of your school team?

JINWOO: No, no. I don't play at school. I'm part of this small league. Everyone's a member of the Apgujeong Social Club. We have matches once a week.

JISU: Apgujeong Social Club? That's that all-male club, right? That's so old-school.

JINWOO: I know, old-school is the best.

JISU: I meant old-school, like in a stuffy way. You're participating in a literal boys' club.

JINWOO: Well, it's a good way to meet people and network. The person you play squash with might end up being the next president or the wealthiest man in the country.

JISU: It's just squash. It's just a sport. Jinwoo, do you ever do anything for the sake of doing it? And not for any other reason?

JINWOO: Hmm. Probably not, but c'mon. That doesn't make me a bad person.

JISU: I never said it did. It's just that not everything needs to be related to who you are and how much money your family has. Not everything has to be shallow.

JINWOO: Ah, yes. And that must have been exactly what you thought when you got my one-sheet from Ms. Moon, looked at how much my parents earn, where I go to school, and didn't immediately turn it down and cancel your services with Ms. Moon in the name of "not being shallow."

JISU: Hey, that's not fair. My parents are forcing me to go on these seons.

JINWOO: Forcing you! Wow, I'm *so* terribly sorry you are being held up against your will to hang out with me. I hope my materialistic tendencies don't taint your oh-so-altruistic ways.

JISU: Jinwoo, please. That's not what I meant.

JINWOO: I'm just teasing you, Jisu. Lighten up! Life's unfair, which means it's also very lucky for some—like us.

JISU: Can we start over?

JINWOO: Yes—hi, my name is Jinwoo. That is a lovely trench coat you have on—I'm assuming it's Burberry? It goes so well with your boundless humility.

JISU: Jinwoo!

JINWOO: I'm sorry. I don't mean to laugh. It's just too easy to get you riled up. I've never met anyone who was so uncomfortable about their money.

JISU: It's not that I'm uncomfortable with it. I just think it's silly to spend all your money on stuff that screams "I have money!" One day you might end up with nothing but those worthless things.

JINWOO: Well, if you're spending your money right on things that are actually nice, it's not worthless. You know, Birkins are supposed to be an excellent investment?

JISU: I did hear that…

JINWOO: I bet if a guy gave you a Birkin, you'd melt. And you'd bring it everywhere. And whenever anyone complimented you on it, you'd say, "Oh, this? My boyfriend got it for me," because let's be honest, that is next-level social currency.

JISU: Actually, I don't even really like Birkins. They're so stiff and boring-looking. I think I'm more of a shapeless-tote-bag kinda gal.

JINWOO: Really? I thought all girls liked Birkins.

JISU: Not all girls are the same, Jinwoo.

JINWOO: Of course. I don't mean to generalize. To each his own, I guess.

JISU: Yes, to each his own.

3

They spotted her before Jisu could even rub the sleep from her eyes.

WELCOME Jisu KIM!

The neon-pink poster was hard to miss. A petite blond-haired woman waved it around enthusiastically. *This must be my mother's newest spy, Linda Murray, reporting for duty.* She was wearing a white turtleneck, blue jeans and a Patagonia fleece. Simple and polished. The young girl standing next to Mrs. Murray had her arms crossed and looked less than enthused. She kept her headphones in and rolled her eyes as Jisu approached them. *And this must be her thirteen-year-old daughter, Mandy.*

Jisu did her best to shake off the flight fatigue. Sunshine spilled through the glass windows and into the airport. All the small coffee shops lined up along the arrivals area were brimming with customers. It looked and felt like morning.

Was it morning? You could never really tell the time of day at an airport.

"Hi, Mrs. Murray! And you must be Mandy," Jisu said. Mandy remained still, with her arms still crossed. *The bratty teen wants nothing to do with me. Noted.*

"Please, call me Linda! And my goodness, a ten-hour flight! I can't imagine being on a plane for that long." Linda grabbed one of Jisu's bags. "You must be exhausted."

"Oh, it wasn't so bad," Jisu lied and thought about all the packets of tissues she'd gone through as she cried across the Pacific. "I watched a few movies until I fell asleep."

"Well, I had to miss a very important livestream to come here," Mandy quipped.

"Mandy! Don't be rude to our new guest," Linda snapped at her daughter and handed her Jisu's other duffel bag. "My husband, Jeff, would've joined us but he's away on a business trip. You'll meet him in a couple weeks, when he's back."

"Next week, when I'll miss another Jake & Jimmy livestream," Mandy huffed.

"Jake & Jimmy? I didn't realize they were having one today. Did I miss their fall look tutorial?"

Jake & Jimmy were one of YouTube's top makeup vloggers. The sixteen-year-old twins from upstate New York had been constantly bullied at school but found a safe space and huge audience online, where they channeled their passion for makeup into fun, hilarious tutorials. Within months, they had achieved global fame, even reaching viewers in Korea, like Jisu, who sought their help to learn how to properly apply highlighter.

Mandy's eyes grew wide.

"You know about Jake & Jimmy?"

"Um, yes, of course I do! How else do you think I was able to learn how to do my makeup? My brows were a tragedy before I watched their videos."

Linda looked relieved, as if thanking her lucky stars the girls had quickly found something in common. No doubt having two incompatible feuding teenagers in the house would be a total nightmare. Jisu followed her new host family out of the airport.

It was hardly noon when they finally arrived at the house, but Jisu was ready to collapse into bed—any bed—and sleep until she felt like a normal human being again.

"You need to stay awake for at least another eight hours if you want to shake off that jet lag," Linda warned. Did all mothers have hawk eyes and a hyperactive sixth sense? Or maybe Jisu did look that exhausted.

"I won't fall asleep." Jisu fought back a yawn.

"Why don't I give you a tour of the house? And then you and Mandy can catch up on Jake & Jimmy to keep you awake."

"I'll be in my room!" Mandy shouted as she ran up the stairs and disappeared.

Linda motioned Jisu into the living room. They sat on a chic blue velvet couch in front of a massive marble fireplace. Above it, framed photos of Mandy, Linda and Jeff lined the mantel. A large mirror above the fireplace reflected the bright sunshine into the rest of the house.

"First, a few house rules," Linda started as she adjusted some of the framed photos so that they were all angled in the same direction.

"School starts at 8:30 a.m. sharp, so you and Mandy will be waking up at 7:00 a.m. every morning. Since the Wick-Helmering High School building is right next to the middle school, you'll have rides to school. But if you have any club meetings or activities after school, you're responsible for getting back home."

Jisu's eyelids grew heavier and heavier. She sat up straight and resisted the urge to slump into the plush couch.

"Of course, we'll provide food—I pack Mandy's lunch each

morning and can put something together for you also. You'll get the guest bathroom to yourself, and I do expect you to keep your space cleaned routinely. We are welcoming you into our home and family, but this is not a hotel." Linda paced left and right as she spoke, as if she had run a boardinghouse in a past life.

"Any questions?" Linda smiled. Clearly she ran a tight ship. There wasn't a speck of dust to be seen on any surface, and everything from the furniture to the art and fashion books on the coffee table were neatly arranged.

Of all things, the stark cleanliness and organization made Jisu feel her first pang of homesickness. Mrs. Kim probably would welcome an international student into their home with the same semi-confusing mix of wide-open arms and strict rules and expectations. Sure, there was a lot to be bitter about—her parents *had* shipped her across the ocean to an entirely different country without warning—but they were her parents, and Jisu was already starting to miss them dearly.

After the rundown of the house rules, Linda showed Jisu the downstairs and then brought her to her new room and left her to unpack. Jisu gingerly lifted her camera and equipment from her suitcase and carefully removed the bubble wrap. No cracks or smudges. Phew.

If there was anything good about this sudden uprooting, it was the fact that she now had a whole new city to explore and so many pictures to take. Her parents were thousands of miles away and couldn't breathe down her neck like they used to. Although who knew how closely they were having Linda watch her? Parents could always conspire among themselves. You never knew.

Jisu's phone buzzed. It was an early-morning group text from her parents in Seoul. Of course they were already up and checking on her.

APPA: Did our Jisu land safely in San Francisco?

JISU: Hi, Umma & Appa. Landed safely, met with Mrs. Murray and I'm now in my new room, unpacking.

UMMA: Don't fall asleep until it's nighttime! You need to get rid of jet lag before school starts. And make sure to review your class schedule and ask Ms. Murray any questions you have...

The list of reminders went on and on. At least now that she was in San Francisco, Jisu could shut her parents out simply by muting the group chat.

Meanwhile, the group chat with Eunice and Minjung had been flooded with sad, teary, crying, bawling emojis. Jisu laughed at the ridiculous display as she scrolled down, but the sadness quickly returned when the reality of their separation set in.

MIN: Jisu-ya, Euni & I promise to video chat you every week and fill you in on school gossip. I can't promise that we won't have fun without you just because you're gone, but we will definitely tell you everything that happens!

EUNI: What Min is trying to say is that she's going to miss you a lot...

MIN: Eunice—that is what I said! Jisu, we are devastated. Please flunk out of Wick-whatever school you're attending and maybe your parents will move you back.

EUNI: Okay, definitely don't purposely flunk out. Min, how do you only have terrible ideas...

MIN: Well, the smoky eye I practiced on you last week wasn't such a bad idea, was it? You loved it!

EUNI: Anyway. Jisu—what we're trying to say is we love you and know you will be great! Fighting!

It was almost more painful to have a constant virtual connection with your dearest friends if you couldn't actually be with them.

And then there was an email from the matchmaker.

Dear Jisu,

Please let me know when you have settled into your new home. Our global services extend to eight major cities in the US, including San Francisco and the general Bay Area. We can be ready to set you up as early as next Monday. Wishing you a smooth transition.

Warmly,

Ms. Moon

That was quick. Clearly Mrs. Kim had wasted no time and was getting every cent's worth of Ms. Moon's pricey services.

"You literally just landed in America. Who is already texting you?"

Jisu hadn't noticed Mandy standing by her bedroom door. She quickly closed out of her email and messages and tossed her phone onto the bed.

"Oh, just my friends back home and my stupid matchmaker."

"You have a *matchmaker*? Like a real professional? Is that

what people in Korea do?" Mandy plopped herself onto Jisu's chair.

Ugh, why did I slip and mention the matchmaker? Now I have to explain the whole thing.

"No, not everyone. My parents hired this matchmaker to send me off on seons, which basically means arranged dates in Korean."

"So, is that what everyone in your school did?" Mandy asked.

"Honestly, there are just a few people in my class whose parents are well-off and also crazy enough to pay as much as they do to get their kids set up. That includes my parents. They want me to find a boyfriend that I can become serious with throughout college and then settle down with. It's like having a five-year plan but for love and partnership."

"Hmm," Mandy pondered. "Honestly, that sounds kinda nice."

"Really? You don't think it's weird? It felt too forced to me initially. And it still does to me a bit. The process just feels so... clinical. And once you go on date after date, it gets tiresome. I'd rather meet someone organically, you know?"

"Okay, but just because you meet someone you like doesn't guarantee you get a date with them. At least your dates are actually happening with all these different guys."

"Trust me, Mandy, I've gone on seons all summer. After the fifth one, they start to blur into the same person. I swear, if I have to chitchat with another boy about the weather or college applications, I'm going to stab my eyes out."

"They can't *all* be bad. And you must have *some* good stories."

Jisu laughed. What did this middle schooler know about boys and dating?

"Well, you're not wrong. And I've actually become friends with some of them. They're not all romantic matches, but I realized that once you stop obsessing over your life plans, it really is just nice to get to know someone."

"Okay, so these seons…" Mandy said. "Does that mean that every dude you've gone on a seon with is your boyfriend? Since it's so serious?"

"Oh, my god, no. Not at all! *Boyfriend* is way too serious a term. I've had zero boyfriends. The seons are just dates."

"But the dates sound really intense. Plus, a handful of dates makes a boyfriend."

"Says who?"

Mandy scurried out of the room and returned with a pile of her own magazines. "Says everyone." She spread them on the ground and rummaged through them until she found the one she was looking for. "Look, this one has a quiz that's literally titled, 'So You've Been Dating—Is He Your Boyfriend?'"

"Those quizzes are silly. They don't really mean anything."

Mandy ignored Jisu and started reading the questions.

"'Do your parents know about him and vice versa? Have you guys talked about your future plans—career, children, etc.? Have you discussed politics?'"

"Okay, so technically, my answers for those questions are yes—"

"For each guy you dated?"

"Yes, but—"

"Okay, so how many seons have you gone on this summer?"

"Not that many…" Jisu stammered. "More than ten, I think? No more than fifteen."

"At least *ten*? That means you've had at least ten boyfriends, Jisu! Wow. And none of them were good enough for you. Queen." A mischievous grin stretched across Mandy's face.

"Okay, no. It's not like that at all. And it's different here! I'm not going to walk into school as the new girl and tell everyone I'm looking for my fifteenth boyfriend."

"Well, thirteen is an unlucky number, so you wouldn't want that anyway," Mandy said.

"Four is the most unlucky number in Korea. It means death. And nine is unlucky, too, but for me personally, it's the unluckiest," Jisu said.

"Why nine? Was boyfriend number nine the one that got away?" Mandy giggled.

"No, Mandy! It's not all about boys. Also, you're thirteen—how would you even know what 'the one that got away' means?"

Mandy shrugged and pointed to the magazine in her hand. "At least I know how many boyfriends I've had," she said.

"Oh, do you? And how many would that be?"

"Just one." Mandy smiled sheepishly. "But he's not my boyfriend anymore. And don't tell my mom! She says I can't date until I'm in high school. Dad says I can't date until I'm thirty, but then Mom will tell him that's sexist and I have my own autonomy—but just not until high school."

Mandy gathered her magazines from the floor.

"Anyway, Mom and I are going shopping tomorrow. She promised to get me a new bag for the school year. You should come with us!"

"Maybe I can bring these guys with me." Jisu placed a hand on her cameras. She closed her eyes and imagined herself shooting the streets of San Francisco.

"Jisu, you're going to fall asleep any second. I can tell." Mandy grabbed her shoulders and shook her awake. "Mom said to make sure you don't."

"It's still so early. A little nap couldn't hurt…"

"No! You're coming to my room. We're going to watch every Jake & Jimmy tutorial." Mandy grabbed Jisu's hand and dragged her out of the room. And although sleep was the only thing on Jisu's mind, she found she didn't mind at all.

DATE NO. 3

NAME: **Kim Heesoo**

INTERESTS:
Anime, Cats, Pop Music

ACCOMPLISHMENTS:
Olympic Gold Medal for Archery

HEESOO: Hey, I've got a confession to make.

JISU: What's up?

HEESOO: This is my first seon. And I think I'm actually kinda nervous.

JISU: Oh, my goodness, don't be! You've been doing great so far. I honestly wouldn't have known until you told me. You're lucky your first one is with a dork like me.

HEESOO: Your one-sheet said you were an award-winning photographer. That sounds very non-dork-like to me.

JISU: It said *what?* I entered one random local contest and won. I'm not like a *National Geographic* photojournalist.

HEESOO: That's still pretty cool.

JISU: I can't believe that's what it says on my one-sheet. Ms. Moon would be the type to take poetic license and exaggerate.

HEESOO: It also said that you've adopted and raised five abandoned puppies as if they were your own children.

JISU: It so did not!!

HEESOO: Nah, I'm just kidding.

JISU: Wait, back up. *Your* one-sheet said that you were an Olympic gold medalist for archery. Does this mean that you've shot an arrow with a bow maybe more than once in gym class?

HEESOO: No, no. I actually have a gold medal, I swear!

JISU: Wow, and between the two of us, *you're* the one nervous about this seon?

HEESOO: Well, I'm no Son Heungmin. Archery is cool, but not as cool as soccer. I literally stand in place and pull and release a taut string. Nobody is giving me cool sponsorships.

JISU: Okay, that may be true, but it must at least feel good to be the best in the world at something, no? It's more than I can say for myself.

HEESOO: I guess that's true.

JISU: Heesoo, I have to be honest, for an Olympic gold medalist, your lack of vanity is pretty shocking.

HEESOO: It's really not that big of a deal.

JISU: You deserve another gold medal. For self-deprecation.

HEESOO: Ms. Moon should include how funny you are in your one-sheet.

JISU: I never want to see what mine looks like. I can't even begin to imagine what alternate, fake version of me she is putting out there.

HEESOO: Yeah, I wouldn't want to see mine either. It must be like listening to a recording of your own voice. What did mine say, aside from the gold medal bit? Do you remember?

JISU: Hmm. I think there was some mention of cats under interests. Do you have a cat?

HEESOO: I do! His name is Simba. He's an orange tabby.

JISU: Aw, those are cute!

HEESOO: They are! He does this thing where he'll rub his head against your leg and push you in the direction of the kitchen so you can feed him. Oh, god, now I'm telling you too much about my silly cat. No one wants to hear that.

JISU: No, not at all. Simba sounds so cute. I love that name.

HEESOO: My younger brother named him. He was going through his *Lion King* phase when we got Simba.

JISU: Honestly, is the world ever not in a *Lion King* phase? That's probably my favorite Disney movie.

HEESOO: Mine, too. My younger brother and I are twelve years apart, so I've been rewatching them all with him lately. Most of them actually hold up.

JISU: Really? Even the ones where the princesses are literally not conscious when their Prince Charming kisses them awake?

HEESOO: Oh, yeah. Those definitely don't hold up. Wow, I must sound like a jerk.

JISU: You really don't. Heesoo, you have literally no reason to be nervous. Just think of these seons as a super-watered-down version of job interviews.

HEESOO: But what if I've never been on a job interview?

JISU: What do you mean?

HEESOO: The whole archery thing has just been my whole life, you know?

JISU: Oh, right. And I bet there's not much socializing in archery.

HEESOO: Yeah, my teammates are my bow, my arrow and my hands.

JISU: You're hilarious. Do you know that?

HEESOO: You really think so? Is this how seons work? Should I be expecting nice compliments each time?

JISU: I don't want to set the bar too high, but trust me. I think you'll do fine and only go on a few before finding your match.

HEESOO: And you? How many of these before you find your match?

JISU: To be honest, I'm just going through the motions for my parents' sake. I don't really want to be in a relationship. There are.too many other things going on!

HEESOO: Well, I hope you link up with someone nice. You're a good person, Jisu.

JISU: Aw, thanks, Heesoo. I want the same thing for you, too.

4

Jisu was cleaning her dishes and finishing her cup of morning coffee when Linda and Mandy came downstairs. If there were any benefits to jet lag, it was that waking up early now felt effortless.

"Up bright and early, I see!" Linda exclaimed as she poured coffee into her travel mug. "Mandy—can you grab the keys? I left them on my desk in the study."

"Are we taking the car?" Jisu asked. "I could always just take the BART and meet you at the mall. I want to learn how to find my way around the city anyway."

"Don't be silly, Jisu. A car will get us there quicker. We'll get what we need and get out. You need to prepare for your first day at school. And you'll have plenty of time to see the city. You don't need...all that." Linda motioned to Jisu's camera bag.

It was fascinating how Jisu could hear traces of her mother's jansori in Linda's voice. She buttoned up her jacket and kept her camera slung around her neck.

"Maybe if we have some extra time after shopping, we could walk around a bit?" she said, hopeful.

"Yeah, Mom. What's the rush?" Mandy said. "Ooh, and can we have lunch at the Rotunda? We have to show her!"

"All right, all right. Let's make sure we get everything we need first."

The major mall in the middle of San Francisco wasn't quite as tall, clean or expansive as Seoul malls, but it was similar enough to remind Jisu of home. The winding escalators that stretched from the basement to the eleventh floor reminded Jisu of Shinsegae and Lotte department stores. Fashion, shopping, supply-and-demand—it was essentially the same at the root of it all, no matter what country you were in.

Jisu was browsing aimlessly through a rack of coats when she heard a group of middle-aged women laughing and chatting among themselves in Korean. The familiarity made her ears perk up.

"Aigoo—another Michael Kors purse? If you saved up and didn't buy the last three Michael Kors bags, you could've gotten yourself one nice Chanel one."

"I don't care about Chanel anymore. Michael Kors is what the younger agashis are wearing now."

"You're about three decades from having once been agashi. Give the Kors to your daughter-in-law and you stick with the Chanel."

"Omo, omo! Come here and look at this one! Valentino—so chic!"

Ajummas. They were the same everywhere. Fawning over designer bags, making endless comparisons and talking about their daughters and daughters-in-law.

To Jisu, their Korean chatter was like being wrapped in a

fuzzy blanket. A wave of homesickness hit her in the stomach as she watched the women trot away to the next section of the department store.

Jisu took a quick picture, then texted her mom in English.

Just overheard a bunch of ajummas talking about purses. Reminded me of you. Miss you lots.

Before she could put her phone back in her bag, it dinged. Her mother had already replied.

So funny! I went shopping with your gomo today! Ajummas really are the same no matter where you go.

The message was followed by a laughing cat emoji and a photo of a new handbag with the tags still on it.

Jisu, what do you think of this? I bought it today. Should I keep or return?

Jisu smiled. She had always preferred to hang with Euni and Min whenever her mother and aunt dragged her to the department stores with them. But now she ached to be in a fitting room in a shop in Gangnam, giving them her opinions in person.

Gomo also bought some sweaters she's going to send you even though I told her she didn't have to! Make sure you call her and thank her when you get it in the mail.

Thanks, Umma. I will! Don't spend too much time with Gomo or Appa will get lonely.

Mrs. Kim replied with a laughing emoji, accompanied by a

photo of Mr. Kim. He was seated on the opposite end of the couch and intently reading the newspaper.

You mean this old man? I can't even get him to look up from the paper. I don't think he would notice if I spent the whole day with your gomo!

If Jisu could dive headfirst into her phone and emerge in her parents' living room on the other side and crash in between them on their white couch, she would have. Jisu looked around for the ajummas and wished they had lingered longer.

"But, Mom, you promised I could get a new bag for school!"

Jisu moved through some clothing racks and saw that Mandy and Linda were arguing.

"Mandy, this is a very nice but very expensive bag. This can be your Christmas present, but you can't just use it as a backpack for school. How many students carry their notebooks in Celine? Honey, be realistic." Linda looked exasperated.

"The girls at school have much more ridiculous bags than this! I would use this bag forever. And if I don't get it now, everyone will already have it by Christmas and people will think I'm just a copycat. You don't even get it!" Mandy whined.

Jisu froze. Every mother and daughter butted heads while shopping, but that was always between you and your mother. It felt awkward to encounter and witness someone else doing that. She picked up a sweater and looked at it with much more interest than she actually had, hoping Mandy and Linda wouldn't call her over and get her involved. She could turn around and wander to the other side of the store until they simmered down. But before she could walk away, Linda looked up and beckoned her over.

Nooo, Linda. Please don't involve me in your drama.

"Jisu, do the girls at your old high school traipse around with their fancy Celine and Louis bags?"

Jisu could feel intense gazes from both Linda and Mandy. It was as if rope was wrapped around her body and they were on opposite sides, playing tug-of-war. She wasn't budging to either end, but the rope grew tighter with each pull and paralyzed her.

Side with Linda and you stay in her good graces and continue to stay under her roof. Side with Mandy and she won't ice you out...

"Daewon was uniform only, so we all had the same backpacks."

Phew. That was close.

"But don't you think it would be a bit ridiculous for an eighth grader to be carrying around a designer bag from Spanish to social studies?"

Linda, why are you doing this to me?

"Well, it *is* a gorgeous bag. Mandy, I can see why you love it," Jisu started and looked to Mandy with assurance. "But it is pricey. So I would just save it for special occasions? And even if you got it later, no one would think that you're just trying to fit in."

"Who says I'm trying to fit in with anyone?" Mandy glared.

Yikes. I was so close. Ugh, teenagers.

"Are you saying I'm some loser follower? Mom, is she calling me a follower?" Mandy groaned. "This is the newest bag, from the latest line. If I bring this to school, everyone will try to copy *me*."

"Mandy, honey, that's not what Jisu was saying." Linda looked at Jisu as if trying to get her to say something—anything—to calm her daughter down.

"Yeah, sorry, Mandy. Not what I meant at all. You clearly have good taste. But what's the rush? Wouldn't you rather go for maximum impact and wow your classmates every now and then instead of hitting them with your style on the daily?"

Mandy pondered this for a moment.

"You know what—you're right," she said. Mandy calmly put the bag back on the display table.

Thank you, Linda quietly mouthed to Jisu.

Note to self: don't ever get involved in mommy-daughter drama.

Jisu let out a deep breath, as if she had held her head underwater for too long. She walked behind Linda and Mandy at a safe distance as they walked out of the department store and headed to the Rotunda for lunch.

The Rotunda was located at the top of the department store. Jisu marveled at the vast dome of colored glass above their heads. It was held up by gigantic pillars with ornate gold accents. Bright afternoon sunshine spilled in through the surrounding floor-to-ceiling glass windows. Linda ordered a selection of dainty finger sandwiches, a pot of tea and an assortment of pastries. Jisu felt like she had ascended from the women's accessories section straight into heaven to have high tea with the angels. She took her camera out and snapped a few pictures of the stunning glass.

"Can I see the photos you took today?" Mandy asked. Jisu leaned across the table and showed her how to scroll through the images on her DSLR.

"Is this street photography?" Mandy pointed to a photo of a woman standing at the curb with her skirt billowing in the wind.

"Technically, yeah, I guess?" Jisu wasn't really aware of proper photography terminology. She simply took a photo if she saw something worth capturing.

Mandy hit the right arrow. The next image was a blurry one of a man on a bike, zipping down the street. Next. A child holding his mother's hand as they crossed the street. Next. A candid of Linda and Mandy walking through the parking lot, arms linked. Next. A group of middle-aged Korean women, chatting and laughing by a display of designer handbags.

"Jisu, how do you even know how to properly work that thing?" Linda peered over Mandy's shoulder to look at the pictures.

"I mostly taught myself. Whenever I couldn't figure something out, I'd just look it up on YouTube," Jisu said.

"You know, Wick-Helmering has a fantastic photography club. You should join. I bet you'd love it."

Jisu knew this already. The extensive list of clubs was sitting on her desk back at the house. She had circled Photography Club, along with Debate Club, Model UN, Intermural Volleyball and Drawing, and intended to check them all out. Wick was a good school, with a great reputation, so being active with extracurriculars was probably important. But really, how ambitious was the average Wick student? Jisu shuddered. Pondering the differences between Daewon and Wick made her dread her first day of school. At the very least, she could try to avoid thinking about it until she was forced to face it.

"I don't know if my parents would be too crazy about that. They want me to stay focused on my studies—I'm here to cram in as much as I can for the year."

"If they're so obsessed with you studying, how are they okay with sending you on dates with hundreds of boys?" Mandy asked.

"Dates? Hundreds of boys? Did I miss something?" Linda asked.

"Mandy's exaggerating," Jisu said. "On top of college applications, my mother is adamant that I find the perfect boyfriend, from the right family, who's going to the right school. She makes me go on some dates."

"Sweetie, I don't know that you'll have time to even find a boy like that, or even if a boy like that exists," Linda said.

"Apparently they do!" Mandy said. "There's this professional matchmaker. She's like Jisu's fairy godmother. She puts together the future power couples of South Korea. And it starts with these fancy seons and—"

"It really isn't as glamorous or as crazy as it sounds." Jisu laughed nervously. She felt like a complete alien. A date was a date—there wasn't anything so weird about a matchmaker, was there? "It's like going on a boring job interview over and over again."

"Well, maybe you'll meet someone at school. The old-fashioned way—like how I met Mandy's dad." Linda smiled and put her hand on Mandy's arm. Mandy squirmed. "Mandy, what would you say is the best way for Jisu to present herself to Wick society?"

"You don't have to do much, honestly." Mandy shrugged. "You're already going to be the new girl. Everyone will notice you and be watching no matter what!"

DATE NO. 4

NAME: **Yoon Sejun**

INTERESTS:
EDM, Media Club, Music Promotions

PARENT OCCUPATIONS:
Soap opera actor; Wedding planner

SEJUN: So, tell me, Jisu—what do you like to actually do outside of the boring school stuff?

JISU: I recently got into photography, which—*I know*—are there any seventeen-year-olds with an Instagram account who don't call themselves a photographer?

SEJUN: Well, I can be the judge of that. Right now! Here, put in your Instagram handle.

JISU: You're really going to put me on the spot like that? Okay, here. Let me know what you think.

SEJUN: These are actually really cool. People can put up basic landscape shots, but I like your eye. Like this one of the Namsan Tower. I feel like everyone takes the same boring photo, but I haven't seen it from this angle. This is cool stuff.

JISU: Wow, thanks! That's really nice of you to say.

SEJUN: Also this one. Is this Jeju Island?

JISU: Yup! I was there last spring for vacation with my parents to see the canola flowers bloom.

SEJUN: This photo reminds me so much of that Andrew Wyeth painting. I just learned it in my art-history class. It's this painting of a woman in a field, but this is like the bright, happy version of it.

JISU: *Christina's World?*

SEJUN: Yes! That's the name. How did you know?

JISU: I was actually thinking about it when I was shooting and trying different poses.

SEJUN: So, that's you in the photo? And you took it, too?

JISU: Yeah, this was when I was first trying out self-portraits with my camera. I'm really just learning as I go.

SEJUN: That's impressive. Honestly. But wait, how are there only fifty-seven likes on this photo?

JISU: Really? I feel like that's a lot… It's definitely been one of my more popular posts.

SEJUN: That's because you only have 259 followers.

JISU: Only? I couldn't think of 259 people to invite to a party, so it's a lot, at least for me... How many followers do you have?

SEJUN: I just hit ten.

JISU: Ten...?

SEJUN: Ten thousand. My goal is to hit fifty before the year's end. I'm already getting lots of good free stuff to advertise.

JISU: How do you have so many followers? Do you have a blog?

SEJUN: No, people just like my face.

JISU: That's hilarious.

SEJUN: No, I'm serious. Any post with my face in it gets three times more likes than a post of the crowds at a music festival, my car or my morning coffee.

JISU: That's good...I guess?

SEJUN: Hey, do you ever take portraits or headshots? I was just thinking of getting some done.

JISU: No, I haven't really done that...

SEJUN: I bet you'd do a good job. All your posts have a good sense of composition and lighting.

JISU: Why do I feel like I'm being interviewed for a photography job?

SEJUN: No, no. I don't mean it to be like that. You're just so obviously talented.

JISU: Are you trying to act also, or...?

SEJUN: Nah, I don't need, like, those cheesy headshots or anything. Just figured it would be good to have some photos taken. At least while we're still young and before the wrinkles and gray hairs set in, right?

JISU: Yeah...totally. I bet your followers would eat it up.

SEJUN: Exactly! Now you're getting in the spirit. Okay, I'm going to regram your Wyeth self-portrait, and when you take my portrait, I'll tag you. I can guarantee you that your following will triple.

JISU: Thanks...I guess? Photography is really just a hobby for me right now. My parents are always saying I get too distracted and need to focus on school.

SEJUN: My parents say the same thing, too. Keep telling me I spend too much time on my phone.

JISU: Yeah...it's like staring into a lake at your reflection.

SEJUN: Yeah...wait...what?

JISU: Nothing! So, where would you want to do these photos?

SEJUN: Hmm, nowhere obvious like the Namsan Tower. Actually, do you have your camera on you?

JISU: You want your photo taken now?

SEJUN: Oh, ha. No! Not at all. That was a joke. Totally a joke.

JISU: Here. Let me take one now with your phone. It doesn't have to be a whole shoot to be Instagram-worthy.

SEJUN: Are you…sure?

JISU: Yeah, just don't pose. Be natural. Look that way. Now take a sip of your coffee.

SEJUN: I've never had this happen on a date before.

JISU: You don't say. Here, what do you think?

SEJUN: Wow—even these are really good. None of my friends are good at taking photos. I should introduce you to my mom.

JISU: Your *mom*? Sejun, we literally just met.

SEJUN: No! Not in any serious way like that. Sorry. She's a wedding planner and she could probably hook you up with her clients. Could be super profitable, and you can get more cameras and cool equipment.

JISU: That's actually not a bad idea. I'll think about it! What does your dad do?

SEJUN: He's a retired soap opera actor. Everyone says I look just like him.

JISU: Must be how you have all those Instagram followers.

SEJUN: Yeah, actually. Half of the comments on my pages are middle-aged ladies, who are his biggest fans.

JISU: I was just joking...but I guess I'm not surprised.

SEJUN: These portraits are actually so good, Jisu. I'm glad we met!

JISU: I'm glad you like the photos, Sejun.

5

*T*o say that Wick-Helmering looked exactly as it did in the pamphlets would be an understatement. Somehow, every patch of grass was just as lush and green as depicted, every modern glass building as sleek as advertised and every student as impeccably dressed as expected. Seeing everyone in normal individual outfits was a nice change of pace and made people-watching all the more interesting. Like most private schools, Daewon had its students wear uniforms to school. Theirs was better than the uniforms at some of the other private schools in Seoul—well-tailored white polos, sharp navy blazers and simple khaki pants and skirts—but all the expressive individuality here was much more visually stimulating than Jisu had anticipated.

Euni—I have no idea how I'm going to make new friends here. Is it even worth the effort if I'm here for only one year?

Jisu typed away on her phone. Due to the time difference, her conversations with Euni sometimes had a delay, but it was better than nothing. It still felt good to send her a message, knowing it would be waiting to be opened on Euni's phone.

How had friendships or any relationships survived before texting and video chat?

"Hey! You must be Jisu Kim." A bright-eyed, bushy-tailed girl appeared before Jisu.

"I'm Kaylee Andrews—your assigned class buddy. It's so nice to meet you!" Kaylee gave Jisu a hug as big as her smile. She had fair, pale skin, light brown eyes and long auburn hair that was braided into a fishtail and tied at the end with black-and-gold ribbon—the Wick-Helmering school colors. She wore a sweatshirt with the WH letters and was carrying a water bottle branded with the school logo. Kaylee was dressed like a sponsored ad for the school.

The international students had had a separate orientation in the days leading up to the first day of school. Each student had been paired with an WH student who would show them around the school grounds and help them get settled in. Technically, Jisu wasn't behind on Wick's academic calendar, but she wasn't quite settled in like the others either. They had found their people and were all buzzing with excitement and comparing class schedules. Jisu was the only incoming senior this year, and the usual excitement of starting a new chapter in life was replaced with dread. Jisu's only hope was that the semester would go as fast as possible.

"I'm terrible with maps and have no idea where my first class is. Can you show me where to go?" Jisu asked Kaylee.

"Of course! Let's see—English is going to be at the Scribner Building, which is across campus. I have a different class, but it's in that same building, so I'll just walk with you. Plus I can give you an unofficial tour of the school!"

Kaylee and Jisu made their way through the student

grounds. What should've been a short walk across campus became an extended stroll, with Kaylee stopping to say hi to every other person they encountered.

"This is the Harding Building, which is where all the math and science classes are. Mrs. Sullivan's office is in this building, and she always has her adorable German shepherd chilling with her during office hours. He's a service dog."

Kaylee pointed to a field of green. "This is the main lawn where everybody eats lunch when it's nice out. In the winter we all just cram in the auditorium. Sometimes if I need my space from everyone, I'll sneak into the computer room and eat there while I scroll through Twitter. It's super quiet and no one will bother you.

"Those trailers over there are temporary study hall spots while the school works on construction, but it's really just a glorified makeout spot. I once saw Jimmy Chow and Angela Sarinas sneak out of one, all red in the face."

Jisu nodded and smiled, a bit confused at all the information being thrown at her.

"Oh, of course those names don't mean anything to you." Kaylee laughed. "Jimmy has been Karina Bahari's boyfriend since the sixth grade. But not anymore since he was caught making out with Angela!"

Kaylee continued to rattle on, giving Jisu all the insight into which teachers were strict and which ones were nice and always offered extra credit. And for each school fact Kaylee gave, she also doled out a bit of social intel on every classmate they ran into.

"*Kelly! Oh, my god, hi, how was your family trip to Morocco? All your pics on Insta were amaze… Dana! I just binge-watched the rest of* Scandal *with Molly. We have to talk about it… Um, Sam? Please don't tell me all you did this summer was grow a man bun. You really need a haircut… Brittany! I'm obsessed with your skirt. You should buy it in every color.*"

It seemed that Kaylee had an endless, accurate inventory of all her classmates. She laid out a map for Jisu of all the friends, lovers, enemies and frenemies.

"Madison stabs everyone in the back and changes her friend group every other month. Stay away from her. If you have any classes with Jayson, he will definitely be flirty and then immediately ask if he can copy your homework. Ignore him."

Jisu stopped trying to keep up. If she had any questions, she could always consult Kaylee's social dossier.

"Wait, don't look, but the guy by the statue over there is Austin Velasco," Kaylee said as she looked away, seeming shy all of a sudden.

Jisu of course looked straight in the direction of the statue. There was a group of boys erupting in laughter at something one of them had said.

"Which one is—"

"The one with longish black hair. Tan. How is he perfectly tan all the time? Maybe because he's Filipino? Also, I know he surfs a lot, but it's insane! Do you see him? Is he looking over here?" Kaylee looked up and, in an instant, switched back to her cheery, social-butterfly self. She waved over at the group of boys.

"Oh, my god, he's the only one who didn't wave back. Who does he think he is? At least Michael waved back. He's the one with the baseball cap."

How much farther was the Scribner Building? Jisu wanted to get to her first class already and get the day started.

"Oh, before I forget—tomorrow is the club fair. There'll be a bunch of tables set up on the lawn for each club and you can decide which ones you want to join," Kaylee said.

"How many clubs are people usually involved in?" Jisu asked.

"Oh, I'd say like seven or eight total, but I'm only super serious about like three or four clubs. I only give up my lunchtime and after-school time for things I'm actually interested in."

Jisu had been extensively involved in extracurricular activities in Seoul, and it seemed like Kaylee and other students at Wick-Helmering stayed busy, but not quite at the same level as Daewon. High school was tough as it was, so this was a bit of a relief. She let her shoulders drop and her step felt a bit lighter as she followed Kaylee to class. For the first time since landing in SFO, Jisu felt at ease. Maybe all of this wasn't such a bad idea; maybe this drastic change could be helpful. Maybe she could thrive.

"Everyone, we have a very special student who has come all the way from Asia." The English teacher, Ms. Hollis, drew the class's attention to the front of the room. There was something about the way she said the word *Asia* that was unsettling to Jisu, as if she were being described like a foreign zoo animal. Her fellow classmates craned their necks toward her, and their collective staring made Jisu want to curl up into a ball and disappear.

"Jisu! Why don't you come up to the front of the class and properly introduce yourself?" Ms. Hollis pronounced her name with the *J* and *S* enunciated too harshly, like a cacophonous clashing of letters. But she must have only good intentions—there was no way Ms. Hollis was aware of how odd her over-enunciating made Jisu's name sound. Still, Jisu tensed up and dug her nails into the fleshy parts of her palms.

"Hi, everyone, my name is Jisu Kim. I'm a senior and I just moved from Seoul, Korea. I'm looking forward to getting to know you all," Jisu stated simply.

"You know, I'm impressed," Ms. Hollis said. "Your English is quite good, and your sense of humor translates so well!"

Jisu smiled because Ms. Hollis was complimenting her, but the actual words themselves didn't feel so much like a compliment. Jisu had taken nine years of English at school, so of course her English was good. But Ms. Hollis may not necessarily know that. Still, why would she be placed in her class if she wasn't proficient enough?

Jisu returned to her seat and clamped her hands on her desk. She couldn't explain the uneasiness that was starting to take hold of her body. Ms. Hollis had tried earnestly to welcome her to the class, but the attempt somehow made Jisu feel out of place. It wasn't anger, no, but there was a nagging feeling. It was muted but very much present.

Jisu tried to shake it off and focus on the lesson, but her irritation was like a stubborn fog that wouldn't lift and disappear. Jisu was of course aware that she was the new girl at school and from a completely different country, but she had never actually felt like an outsider until now.

The "Need-A-Friend" table was exactly what it sounded like—an initiative with good intention. But it was simply where all the international students awkwardly huddled up in between and after classes. They were all from different cities around the world—Seoul, Perth, Copenhagen, Hong Kong, Karachi—but that was the only thing they had in common. *I'm here for one year. In and out. Good grades only. I don't need a friend, right?*

Jisu sent off another message to Euni, who was probably still sleeping.

Wick-Helmering sucks. Also, what kind of name is Wick-Helmering? Everyone here is way too cheerful and in love with their school. I'm miserable. Miss you, bestie.

"First day not going so great?"

Jisu looked up at the boy who had seated himself across from her. He had light brown eyes and bushy black eyebrows, the same color as his wavy, unruly, raven-colored hair. Jisu suddenly became aware that she was frowning. She had been hunched over her phone, too, which she realized when her spine automatically adjusted itself.

"Austin Velasco. Nice to meet you." He had a crooked smile that was somehow perfectly askew and emanated boyish charm.

So *this* was who Kaylee was swooning over earlier. He did look naturally sun-kissed, just as she had described.

"Nice to meet you, too…" Jisu said.

"So, you're the only senior international student, right?" Austin asked.

"Yup, that's me. I just moved from Seoul a few days ago." Was this normally how the Need-A-Friend table worked? Did you usually end up with a cute boy talking to you?

"How did you end up here?" Austin asked.

"It's a long story. But basically, I have to get perfect scores on everything to make uprooting my life worth it," Jisu explained.

"Yikes," he said. "I can't imagine doing that. It must be tough." Austin looked sympathetically at Jisu, and for the first time on her first day at school, she felt truly seen.

"It's not so bad. Kaylee is being helpful, and I'm only going to be here for one year." Jisu could feel Kaylee's gaze locked on her and Austin from across the cafeteria.

"So, what's South Korea like?" Austin asked. "You guys get any good waves there?"

"Waves? Uh, we have some good beaches. And islands, too! I go to Jeju Island with my family pretty often. They have these beautiful yellow canola fields that bloom every spring." Jisu took out her phone and scrolled through her photos.

"Actually, I have photos from the last time I went." She held out her phone to Austin.

"Wow, that's amazing." Austin took her phone and looked closely at the photos. "You took these?"

Jisu nodded. Austin looked up at her with that crooked smile again, and Jisu's stomach did a tiny flip. He started typing something into her phone. *What is he doing?* She panicked for a moment, remembering all the silly selfies he could see by simply swiping left and right. But before she could snatch back her phone, Austin handed it to her.

"There. Now I have this dope photo and you have my number." There it was on the screen. Austin Velasco had sent himself a text from Jisu's phone.

I guess this is one way to make friends? Jisu had never met someone so bold and so forward in their first interactions with her. She snatched her phone back, but made sure his number really had been saved. Jisu couldn't tell if she was more taken aback or intrigued.

"I work at the Tutoring Center, so if you need help dealing with class or anything really, just text me." Austin grinned as he got up from the table and rejoined his friends. Earlier that day, Kaylee had given Jisu her number in case she needed help, but Jisu had not felt nearly as flustered as she did now.

He's just being nice. Jisu remembered her mother's jansori about finding a good English tutor. *And I do need a tutor anyway.*

"Um, what was Austin Velasco talking to you about?" Kaylee had beelined across the cafeteria. The day wasn't even over yet, and Jisu was ready for a break from Kaylee.

"He told me that he's a tutor and can help me out if I need it."

"That's really nice of him. Austin is always so *nice* to the new kids," Kaylee said. But the way she said it sounded like she was assuring herself more than Jisu.

"Hey, Dave! Dave Kang!" Kaylee shouted. A guy standing a few tables down turned around. He was tall like Austin, though not quite as tan, and had dark eyes and jet-black hair with a sharp fade. He was wearing a Wick-Helmering Lacrosse hoodie.

"Dave, this is Jisu, the new international student in our year. She's also Korean!"

The strange uneasiness Jisu had felt in Ms. Hollis's class returned all over again. Anxiety? Embarrassment? Frustration? It was none of those things, but also a bit of all of those things. Jisu didn't know where to look, so she stared down at her hands.

"Kaylee, you're so embarrassing," said a student at the table next to them. "Just because they both happen to be Korean doesn't mean they have to be best friends."

Jisu looked over at him and felt relief. There was clarity in what he was saying.

"Landon! What do you mean?" Kaylee looked embarrassed, but not like she understood for what.

"This is like when you suggested that Jack and I date just because we happen to be the only two gay people you know."

Jisu covered her mouth with her hand and smiled, embarrassed for Kaylee and grateful for Landon. She looked up at Dave and saw he was also trying not to laugh. Landon was speaking the truth, and hearing it chipped away at the uneasiness Jisu had felt since English class.

"That's not true! Also, aren't you guys dating for real now?"

"That's beside the point." Landon waved Kaylee off and turned his attention back to his friends.

"Well, you're *welcome* for introducing you to your high school sweetheart!" Kaylee shouted.

Jisu and Dave exchanged a look, acknowledging the awkwardness, and both were unsure how to free themselves from it.

"So, should we do our secret, extra-complicated, very Korean handshake?" Dave sat down at the table. Jisu laughed, and the rest of the uneasiness disappeared instantly. *Thank god someone in this school has a sense of humor.*

"So, you're a fellow hanguk saram," Jisu said.

"Sorry, a what?" Dave looked confused.

Did he not know any Korean? She had wondered what it would be like to grow up Korean American. Which aspects of Koreanness did one hold on to and which aspects did one have less of a grasp on?

"Hanguk saram. Korean person! Dave, do you not speak any Korean?" Jisu asked.

"Oh! No, I know a little bit. I just got thrown off. I'm not used to hearing it a lot, especially not at school," he said.

"Do your parents speak Korean?" Jisu asked.

"Sometimes. It's mostly English. Sometimes Konglish," he said.

"Konglish?" Jisu asked, bewildered.

"Yeah, you know. Korean mixed with English."

Here was Dave Kang, one of just a handful of students that looked like Jisu, whose presence was enough to make her feel a bit more comfortable at Wick-Helmering, but he was wildly different from her.

The students started to get up and herded their way to the next class. It was the end of the lunch period.

"See you around, hanguk saram," Dave said as he walked away.

Jisu smiled. His pronunciation was clunky at best, but he still owned it. Had Dave's parents immigrated to the States, or had his grandparents made the move one generation before them? Did his family eat Korean food at home? All the time or only sometimes? Did they celebrate chuseok and eat seawood soup on birthdays?

Jisu's phone dinged. It was a text from Austin. A jolt of energy shot through her fingers as she swiped the notification open.

Hey, it's your new tutor. Want to watch a movie this Friday and go to Bo's Diner? The movie should be a good English lesson.

"Who are you texting with?" Kaylee asked, suddenly reappearing and in Jisu's face again. This girl was taking her job as class buddy a little too seriously. "Oh, my god, did Austin text you?" Kaylee peered at Jisu's phone.

"Yeah, I guess he wants to hang out this Friday and watch a movie." Jisu shrugged. She didn't want to alienate the one person who was helping her out at school. Kaylee had gushed about plenty of boys within the first ten minutes of their meeting, but she seemed to be crushing particularly hard on Austin.

"Well, that's nice of him, I guess," Kaylee said icily.

"Maybe he'll bring his friends—"

"Bo's Diner is everyone's hangout spot. There will definitely be other people there. I'll probably be there." Kaylee's initial warm and bubbly welcome was now unceremoniously snappy and cold. "Why...did you think he was asking you out on a date?"

The thought hadn't even occurred to Jisu.

"Honestly, I didn't even think it until you—"

"Austin Velasco does not just go on dates," Kaylee declared.

"All right, it's not a date." Jisu repeated Kaylee's words. That seemed to do the trick. Kaylee backed off and scurried away to her next class.

Not a date. Jisu had said it to get Kaylee off her back, but now she wondered if Austin *had* meant to ask her on a date. A real seon, set up naturally, without a matchmaker pulling the strings like a marionette master.

What made a date a *date* anyway? And if it was so *not* a date and Austin was so *not* the type to ask girls on dates, why was Kaylee so bothered by it?

DATE NO. 5

NAME: **Kim Jungho**

INTERESTS:
Electronics Design, Golf, '90s Rock

PARENT OCCUPATIONS:
Housewife and head of various charities;
Music manager

JUNGHO: All right, so you have to hear my start-up idea. I have, like, a million, but I'm really confident about this one.

JISU: Okay, shoot!

JUNGHO: So, you know how everyone is overworked and complaining about how tired they are?

JISU: Yeah, I follow.

JUNGHO: Have you heard of these super-progressive companies and tech start-ups with a lot of money who install fancy nap pods for their employees?

JISU: It sounds familiar. That actually sounds so nice.

JUNGHO: Right? Those nap pods are usually like a perk and a way for those companies to attract new employees.

JISU: Okay, so what's your point?

JUNGHO: Well, those nap pods are way fancier and more gimmicky than they need to be. So my idea is to introduce a portable and low-maintenance nap pod.

JISU: Okay. I don't think I even really know what a regular nap pod looks like, but what's the difference? It wouldn't be less comfortable?

JUNGHO: No, not at all. Same cushiony features, except you can bring this pod with you. Or companies can buy the portable versions en masse.

JISU: What's it made of?

JUNGHO: I'm thinking cotton, nylon, polyester. It's affordable.

JISU: And how big is it?

JUNGHO: Big enough for one person to fit in and recline comfortably.

JISU: Can I be honest with you?

JUNGHO: Yes, of course! I want to hear your thoughts—good or bad or both. I'm all ears.

JISU: It sounds like you're just describing a tent.

JUNGHO: I don't think you really get the full picture.

JISU: But doesn't it kind of sound like you're describing a tent?

JUNGHO: It would have certain features that would make it more than "just a tent." This is just the start of an idea. You don't have to go poking holes all over it. Besides, what would you know? I've interned for the top VCs in Korea, and next summer I'm going to intern at the Twitter campus in San Francisco.

JISU: You asked for my opinion—I'm just being honest!

JUNGHO: Whatever.

6

"**D**ressing up for your date?" Mandy asked as Jisu checked her reflection in the mirror.

"It's not a date. We discussed this," Jisu said. "We even consulted your magazines and their online quizzes."

"Right, but there is one rule that trumps it all," Mandy said.

"And what's that? I didn't realize you were the authority on dating, Mandy." Jisu took off her sweater and tried a different one. Did the peach-colored one look better with her skin tone, or was the bright blue better? Why did it even matter? Why did she care?

"If you're overthinking it, which you clearly are—this is your third outfit change now—then it's certainly a date, at least in your mind." Mandy smiled mischievously. Date or no date, having Mandy around only made Jisu more anxious about seeing Austin.

"Maybe I should cancel." Jisu sighed. "I have a lot of homework. I don't have time and I should be studying anyway."

"No!" Mandy put her hands on Jisu's shoulders. "You've been working all week and you deserve a break. Plus I want to hear everything that happens."

Jisu twiddled with the hem of her royal blue sweater. It was a striking color that made her feel confident and like her best self. She did want to see Austin, in the sense that she wanted to get to know her peers and make friends. At least she admitted that much to herself.

Jisu put her DSLR in her bag and walked out of her room. Mandy followed her downstairs and sat on the bottom step.

"Leaving already? Isn't your date not for another two hours?" she asked.

"I'm going to walk around the city with this." Jisu held up her camera. She snapped a candid photo of Mandy on the staircase.

"No pictures!" Mandy yelled, and dramatically covered her face as if she were a famous celebrity being chased by the paparazzi. Jisu turned on the flash and snapped some more, and the two of them fell over laughing.

Jisu didn't expect to work up a sweat from simply walking around the city, but the hills of San Francisco were steeper than she'd realized. Still, she loved the curvature of the streets. It reminded her of the winding streets of Itaewon, where she'd wander around to photograph impressive views of Seoul with the Namsan Tower looming not too far in the distance. Jisu weaved in and out of similarly narrow alleys and major streets, capturing the everyday pedestrians of San Francisco walking from point A to point B: an old bag lady pushing along her cart of belongings, a jogging father who was running with the stroller that held his cooing baby and several adorable dogs being walked by their respective owners.

She drank in the views from every angle and reached the top of Lombard Street just in time to capture the sun as the final golden rays of the day poured over the city.

She sent a photo of the view to Euni and Min.

Wish you guys were here with me. Miss you lots xox

Jisu checked her notifications. There was an unread text from Kaylee.

KAYLEE: Are you still seeing Austin today?

JISU: Yup! On my way to the theater now. Not a date. Lol.

KAYLEE: Of course it's not—who said it was?

Woof. Kaylee was still feeling some type of way about Jisu's solo time with Austin.

JISU: Omg, Kaylee. I was just joking! I'll ask him what he thinks about you.

KAYLEE: !!! Yes pls. But don't be too obvious. And let me know what he says.

JISU: Of course! Okay, on the tram now. Let's hope I don't miss my stop.

Kaylee sent Jisu three prayer hands emojis, and she knew they were all good.

This is not a date. This isn't like any of the seons I've been on. I'm just hanging out with a new friend, who just happens to be really cute and charming, who's also Kaylee's crush. It's not a big deal. It's not a date. Not. A. Date.

"Hey!" Austin walked over to Jisu just as she walked through the theater doors. "What's this?" He pointed to her camera bag.

"It's not a date," Jisu blurted without even thinking. She immediately covered her mouth, wanting to die. If lightning struck her dead right there, in that moment, she would be more than okay with it.

Austin looked stunned for a second, but immediately broke into laughter. "Ouch, Jisu. You sure you're okay being seen in public with me?" He was so gracious and charming. Jisu didn't know if that made her feel better or worse.

"Oh, my god, I'm so sorry." She could feel her face getting red. And the more she thought about how much she was blushing, the warmer her face got. It was mortifying.

"Girl, you need to chill." Austin put his hands on Jisu's shoulders as if to calm her down, but she only became hyperconscious about how close he was to her.

"I think some of Kaylee's neuroticism's rubbing off on you."

"Sorry," Jisu said. "I'm just so new to everything, I'm even nervous about making friends." Maybe he would buy this excuse.

"I get it. I get it." There wasn't a trace of worry on his face. He carried himself with an air of unbothered confidence.

Jisu followed Austin as he moved seamlessly from the ticket booth to the concessions to their seats. By the time they sat down, any trace of embarrassment she'd felt had all but disappeared. They were simply two new friends watching a movie together. Jisu visualized her nerves, all jittery and shaky, forming a tidal wave and slowly receding from her mind. The previews started playing, and she leaned back into her seat, finally at ease.

About halfway through the movie, the tidal wave of nerves appeared again. Every time Jisu laughed at a funny scene, she could sense Austin stealing glances and smiling at her.

What does it mean? Is that what normal friends do?

She'd never felt as hyperaware of every movement she made when she'd gone to the movies with Euni or Min. But she hadn't felt this way on any of her seons either.

You need to relax, Jisu thought. *New country, new city, new friends. Anyone would feel nervous. This isn't a date. Jisu Kim, you are not on a date!*

When the credits rolled, Jisu let out a deep breath. The rest of her body followed suit—the muscles in her neck, back and shoulders released. She didn't realize how tense she had been during the entire movie. Sitting next to a cute boy in the dark for two hours while tempering your thoughts was exhausting. All she wanted to do was go home, edit her photos and pass out.

"That was fun," Austin said. He stood close to Jisu. She could see the individual threads running through his shirt, and he could probably see the same in hers. Austin had the slightest tan line around his eyes that you could only notice if you were inches away from his face. What details did he notice? Jisu took a step back. Did he always stand so close to whomever he was talking to?

"You hungry?" he asked. "C'mon, let's grab a bite at Bo's."

He didn't even ask if she wanted to go or not, just if she was hungry. It was all so cavalier, so casual. But to her, every stop from the theater out to the parking lot felt significant— like it was all leading to something. Jisu imagined waves of energy undulating from her shoes and onto the concrete with every step she took.

And then she heard it. The collective jansori from her parents and Linda echoed in her mind. *What did you do all day? What progress have you made? Time is running out faster and faster.* She should say no, go home and chip away at all the homework she had. *You're already out. By the time you got home, you'd be so tired you'd go straight to bed anyway. It's rude to say no. How else are you supposed to make friends?* Her thoughts drowned out the jansori. Jisu let Austin take her hand and lead her away.

In the parking lot, other couples, both young and old, got into their respective cars and drove off into the night. Austin opened the passenger door of his car for Jisu and closed it gently when she got in. *He's being a gentleman, like any good person would,* Jisu told herself. But another wave of nerves came crashing back into the folds of her brain. Jisu let herself indulge in the nervous excitement. If this were a seon, it would be the first one she was genuinely thrilled about.

The tide of excitement pulled away just as quickly as it had come in when Austin and Jisu pulled up to the diner. Austin's crew of friends were already seated at a booth by the window and waved at them.

"This is my friend Jisu. She just transferred to Wick." Austin introduced her to the group. Kaylee was right about Bo's. The two of them were really just hanging out as friends after all. Jisu wondered if she had been imagining the tension from the last two hours.

It was true. They were simply two new friends spending time together, Jisu had said so herself. Still, she detected a small sinking feeling in the pit of her stomach. *I'm hungry,* she thought and focused on the menu.

"Jisu, right? You're the new girl!" Jisu had been staring so intently at the menu, she'd hardly noticed the two blond girls in matching cheerleader uniforms sitting across from her.

"I'm Jamie and this is Tiffany." Next to Jisu's petite frame, the two girls looked straight up Amazonian with their broad shoulders and toned arms. Jamie's hair was up in a high ponytail and Tiffany's was in braided pigtails. They weren't sisters, but they could be twins. Their movements were so synced that Jisu wondered how synchronized they looked when they were in cheer squad mode.

"We just came from practice, so we're ready to eat *every-*

thing," Jamie said just as the waitress showed up with an entire tray of food. There was a plate of pasta, two baked potatoes, an omelet, french fries, a plate of grilled vegetables and a cheesy quesadilla.

"This is all for just the two of you?" Jisu asked. "How do you stay so slim?"

"Nobody ever thinks this, but cheerleading is one of the most rigorous sports," Tiffany said as she heaped a serving of baked ziti onto her plate.

"Yeah, everyone thinks it's just cute girls in ponytails waving some pompoms—I mean, we *are* pretty cute—but people don't realize that we are literally throwing each other and hurling ourselves into the air." Jamie cut the quesadilla into thirds and offered Jisu some.

"I bet you could beat up every single guy at this booth," Jisu said as she bit into the quesadilla.

"That's 100 percent true!" Jamie and Tiffany said simultaneously and laughed.

"You remind me of those cheerleaders in *Bring It On*. They were so much better and cooler than the dumb football players in that movie."

"Oh, my god, that's our favorite old movie!" Jamie exclaimed. "Such a classic."

"How do you know *Bring It On*? Did they have that in Korea?" Tiffany asked.

"Tiffany, we get the internet in Korea, too. That movie defined my idea of American high schools, to be honest."

"Yeah, Tiffany." Jamie threw a fry at Tiffany. "The internet and technology there is so much faster than here. Duh."

"Well, that movie is hella old!" Tiffany defended herself. "I'm surprised any of us have seen it. That was like way before our time."

Jisu glanced at Austin on the other side of the booth. Each time she looked over, their eyes locked and he smiled. Was he being a flirt? Or just encouraging of her making new friends? Every question she asked herself resembled the stupid quizzes from Mandy's stack of magazines. But she had more questions for her questions and no answers. The ambiguity of it all was too distracting. Jisu started to miss the seons.

During the ride back home, Jisu replayed fragments of the night in her head: the way she'd introduced herself, how she'd spoken about Seoul, how she'd reacted to a funny comment. At least Austin was the one driving and not her. Since when was socializing so anxiety-inducing for her? Being in a new city in a new country definitely had something to do with it.

When Austin pulled up to the Murrays' residence, Jisu was ready to run up the stairs and head straight to her room to re-play those fragments a hundred more times before really de-compressing.

"Thanks for the ride," Jisu said as she loosened the seat belt.

"I'm glad you came out and met everyone. It's like you've already been going to Wick for the last three years." Austin smiled.

Jisu watched Austin drive off. By the time she made her way to room and plopped onto her bed, she decided that none of the events of the night meant anything beyond friendship. Austin, Tiffany and Jamie—all of them were her new friends. She was relieved just to have made friends within her first week in a new city.

And of course, Kaylee would be equally relieved to hear how the night went.

DATE NO. 6

NAME: **Lee Songsan**

INTERESTS:
International Studies, Communications, Sailing

PARENT OCCUPATIONS:
Politician; Retired oncologist,
now supporting husband's political career

JISU: Wow, I really did not know there were that many kinds of knots in sailing.

SONGSAN: Yup, and a real use for each one!

JISU: And you somehow have every single one of them all memorized.

SONGSAN: I've been sailing since I was a little kid, so it all comes naturally to me.

JISU: I think I need another cup of coffee. Do you want to order anything else?

SONGSAN: I'm all set. I try to avoid going near or over three cups a day. Too much caffeine can throw off the balance in your system and cause acid reflux if you're prone to that kind of stuff.

JISU: Sorry, what? Oh, acid reflux, sure. I've heard of that.

SONGSAN: Are you feeling all right, Jisu?

JISU: Hmm? Oh, yes. I'm good. Sorry, Songsan, I was just up a bit late trying to do some of the reading we got assigned over summer break.

SONGSAN: I've been there. Which subject?

JISU: World history.

SONGSAN: History is one of my favorite subjects! Which era is the summer reading on?

JISU: It's on revolutions: French, Bolshevik, American, Chinese, Korean—all of them.

SONGSAN: Revolutions are probably the most thrilling parts of history. The turning points, the pivot, they're like the real-life plot twists.

JISU: Songsan, I hate to sound rude, but can we talk about something else? I spent all night trying to do the boring reading and barely got a hundred pages in.

SONGSAN: Of course, of course. No problem. History can be dry, too. At least it is compared to everything that's happening in the world now.

JISU: What do you mean?

SONGSAN: Well, you have the Arab Spring and the repercussions in the years following, the ongoing Syrian civil war, all the chaos that's sprung upon the US since their last presidential election and of course the impeachment of our last president.

JISU: Mmm hmm.

SONGSAN: To be honest, in every discussion I see unfold online, in print or on TV about the current state of the world, there's a continuous thread that doesn't get highlighted or called out as often as I think it should.

SONGSAN: I don't think people realize how much climate change has a direct impact on all of these things happening. I can't imagine what it's like to be a scientist and having the leaders of the world ignore your advice or deny and claim your lifelong research as flawed or even worse—a hoax. Could you imagine?

SONGSAN: Jisu?

JISU: Hmm? Oh, yes, totally. I'm with you 100 percent.

SONGSAN: Did you just...fall asleep?

JISU: What! No, no. Fall asleep? I could never. This is my fourth cup today. I was just...admiring this latte art that they made. Look—it's shaped like a little leaf!

SONGSAN: Maybe you should head home. You seem tired.

JISU: I'm really sorry. I've just had a long day.

SONGSAN: Don't worry about it. We can always reschedule. Who knows what kind of crazy global developments can happen between now and next week, or whenever we meet.

JISU: I'm sure you can give me the full download.

SONGSAN: You bet. How's next Thursday for you?

JISU: Um, actually, I'm not too sure what my school schedule looks like. I'll figure it out and have Ms. Moon get in touch? I might not be free for another two or three weeks…

SONGSAN: Sounds good. Just let me know.

JISU: Sure. I'll do my best!

7

*A*nother girl might've been devastated by the nonchalant way Austin greeted her on Monday morning after spending all that precious face time with him the previous Friday. But when he gave Jisu a simple head nod as they passed each other in the hallway, she felt relief.

All that ambiguous tension of *Does he like me? Does he not?* was far more draining than any seon she had gone on. Sure, Austin was super cute and his charm was disarming, but Jisu had wasted a whole weekend distracted from her studies. She'd spent more time replaying every interaction with him than she had on homework.

How did her mother think she could date *and* stay focused? If Jisu managed to actually fall for any of the boring normies that Ms. Moon set her up with, everything would be over. If Jisu had learned anything about herself from her non-date with Austin, it was that a real romantic interest would throw her off the rails. Of course, according to Mrs. Kim, the boys on the seons were not a distraction but rather useful pawns to insure a brighter, better future. But it just wasn't that easy.

Jisu waved to Kaylee as they both approached their international studies class, but instead of greeting Jisu with her warm, bubbly self, Kaylee seemed to shoot darts with her eyes as she walked right past her.

Oh, Kaylee, Jisu thought. *If only you knew that Austin was always yours for the taking.*

The yearlong international studies course was one of the few classes that Jisu genuinely found interesting. As an international student, navigating her way through Wick-Helmering each day felt like an IS exercise. And unlike other teachers who constantly asked for her "unique perspective" as an international student or asked her to translate certain words into Korean, Mrs. French treated her the same way she treated all the other students.

"Settle down, everyone," Mrs. French said as she entered the classroom. The class eventually came to a hush as they watched her write on the chalkboard.

Head, Hands and Heart. It was the Wick-Helmering school motto and the core mission of the school curriculum.

"Today we are going to discuss your final senior project for IS: the infamous triple *H* project. I'm sure you've seen all the seniors before you work tirelessly on this. You and a classmate will have all year to develop a project that addresses one of the major issues of the international agenda listed on the class syllabus. The project must reflect the Wick-Helmering motto and combine matters of the three *H*'s. That includes your academic skills, your technical skills, your cultural understandings and, most important, your personal passions."

Mrs. French printed out a sheet of paper and taped it onto the chalkboard at the front of the classroom. "You have all been assigned a classmate. Link up and get going. You can come to me with any questions you have."

While half the class scattered to the front of the room to find out their partners, Jisu sat back and wondered how she was going to manage such a large project. The final grade in IS depended heavily on this one project, increasing the pressure to do well.

"Hey, partner. Why so serious?" Jisu looked up at Dave Kang, standing by her desk.

"Are we really partners?" Jisu asked.

"Well, if you say it like you've been given a prison sentence, you're gonna hurt my feelings." Dave pulled up a chair to Jisu's desk and eagerly flipped through the IS syllabus. Their assigned topic was "encouraging and increasing political involvement among the general public."

He was so enthusiastic about everything, like an overexcited golden retriever who didn't know how to calm down. Maybe that's how he was so popular with everyone? But his constant positivity had to take a break once in a while, too, didn't it? Jisu couldn't tell if this kind of upbeatness was something she envied or was purely confused by.

"Must be nice to reunite with your long-lost sister from the motherland," Bobby Leeman said. Bobby sat next to Jisu, but she hadn't noticed him much since class started. Until now.

"What?" Jisu gawked at Bobby, who was leaning back in his seat looking smug and satisfied with his dumb comment. Long-lost sister? Based on what? The fact that her and Dave were both Korean? Jisu didn't even know Bobby, and he didn't know her either. He hadn't said a word to her or even introduced himself since she had gotten to Wick. Who gave him the right? Kaylee had warned Jisu about Bobby. *He's a troll. An ignorant jerk who craves attention that he never got from his mom.* Jisu hadn't fully understood what Kaylee meant until now.

"How did you know?" Dave said to Bobby, sounding completely unbothered. "Must be because we look so alike. Is that it, Bobby? We all look the same to you?"

Bobby remained quiet. Jisu's heart started to race. She was just as taken aback by Dave's reaction as she was by Bobby's trolling.

"Say it, Bobby. You think all Asians look the same. Say it." Dave stood up and stared Bobby down. "Say it. I dare you." He was white-knuckled and ready to go. Jisu tugged at Dave's sleeve to calm him down, but she recognized the anger in his eyes. She saw it and realized she felt the same frustration, too, somewhere deep in her bones. And though Jisu was frightened that a fight might actually break out between Bobby and Dave, she was glad that Dave had shot back at him.

"Whatever, man." Bobby shrugged and slumped into his chair. Dave remained standing and didn't break eye contact.

"Coward," he said with disgust.

Jisu's heart was still racing. A crisis had been averted, but she could still feel the panic coursing through her veins.

"You know he only trolls people for attention," Jisu whispered to Dave. "You can't let him get to you like that."

"So you think it's okay to let him say racist stuff like that and get away with it?" Dave made a good point. Bobby *was* being blatantly racist. And Dave was so quick to hit back—how often was he subjected to comments like that by the likes of Bobby? Jisu felt like throwing up.

"That's not what I'm saying," Jisu protested. She wanted to fully explain that she was capable of standing up for herself, but she wasn't going to fan the flames. She wasn't in the mood to defend herself against someone who was already on her side. "Just don't let him get to you that much. He's not worth it."

Jisu sighed. The whole encounter had thrown them off entirely. She could barely focus on the assignment sheet in front of her, and Dave was still seething, she could tell. Stupid Bobby Leeman. He caused a scene and got a reaction. He got exactly what he wanted.

"You know what?" Jisu said. "I think we should find another time to meet up and brainstorm. When we're in a better headspace."

"Sure, that works." Dave took out his phone and pulled up his calendar. He took a deep breath then exhaled.

"Can you meet this Wednesday?" Jisu asked, trying to sound as chipper as she could, desperate to lift the mood.

"No, I have swim practice after school."

"Okay, how about Thursday after school?"

"I have a fencing match."

Are you serious? What sport doesn't this guy play? How does he find time to get actual schoolwork done?

"At lunch, then?" Jisu asked, a bit more impatient. Dave was getting on her last nerve.

"Debate club meeting—hey, didn't you say you were going to that?"

"Class takes priority over clubs. Are you free at all anytime this weekend?"

"Ah, no. I'm going mountain climbing. I'm usually free though."

Mountain climbing? Is he training to be in the army?

"Well, then, when *can* you meet?" Jisu knew she sounded exasperated. "You're not being helpful. At all."

"I know, I know. I'm sorry, Jees."

Jees? That was a new nickname. Jisu wasn't sure she liked the way it sounded coming out of his mouth. *Jees.* It sounded abrupt and ultra-Americanized.

"Give me your number. I'll text you when I figure out a time." Dave handed Jisu his phone. She thought briefly of Austin. It was the same, harmless gesture.

★ ★ ★

Jisu had taken two steps out of the classroom when Kaylee appeared next to her.

"Second week at school and you're already passing out your number left and right, hmm?"

"Kaylee, I've never met anyone who loves stirring the pot more than you do," Jisu said. Why wouldn't this girl leave her alone?

"I'm not stirring any pot. I'm just making observations," she quipped. "You know Dave has a girlfriend, right?"

Girlfriend. Girl. Friend. The G word. It only made sense that he had a girlfriend. Dave had a bright smile that lit up the room, and the upbeat energy everyone liked about him was genuine. He was Mr. Congeniality. So of course he had a girlfriend.

"What does that have to do with anything?" Jisu asked.

Who is she? What does she look like? More questions lined up against the back of her teeth. All Jisu had to do was open her mouth and ask. But she kept it shut.

Kaylee shrugged and gave Jisu an innocuous look. *And I thought Min was fickle. Min is like a monk compared to Kaylee.*

Despite trying to downplay her reaction, part of Jisu was taken aback, and as the day wore on, she grew more and more curious about Dave's girlfriend. Kaylee had all the answers, but Jisu let her questions pile up in her mind and pretended not to care.

DATE NO. 7

NAME: **Yoon Bumsoo**

INTERESTS:
Gymnastics, Physics, Veganism

PARENT OCCUPATIONS:
Korean Astronomy and Space Institute
researcher; Museum curator

BUMSOO: Sorry, I usually don't do this but I have to send this back.

JISU: Oh, no! What's wrong with your mac and cheese? Did they not substitute with vegan cheese?

BUMSOO: No, they managed to do that. It's just my food is cold.

JISU: At least that's an easy fix. They can reheat it!

BUMSOO: You know what they do when you just ask them to reheat it, right? They stick it in the microwave for thirty seconds and wait a bit so you think they properly popped it in the oven or something.

BUMSOO: Excuse me. Sir. No, everything's great. The cashew nut cheese looks like it'd taste great, but my food is cold. Do you see how the cheese has congealed here? And there? I can't eat this, man. Can I get fresh new plate, please? Hot out of the oven? I don't want this same plate reheated.

JISU: So...how long have you been vegan?

BUMSOO: Veganism is just something I've been trying for the last six months. I consider myself more of a food purist than a vegan.

JISU: A what?

BUMSOO: A food purist.

JISU: What's the difference? Veganism seems pretty altruistic in and of itself. I mean, I could never do it, but—

BUMSOO: I know vegans who abide by all the rules and don't eat meat or dairy, but they're constantly snacking on all this fake sugar, sour candy nonsense.

JISU: That sounds amazing. Maybe I should become a bad vegan!

BUMSOO: It's not something to joke about. Those vegans are better off reintroducing meat into their system—at least then they'd get some proper protein.

JISU: Wow, so you're really into health and diet.

BUMSOO: Ever since I started gymnastics as a kid. They go hand in hand.

JISU: I played softball and volleyball all the way through middle school, but those sports feel like child's play compared to gymnastics.

BUMSOO: I mean, all sports require a certain drive and focus that, let's be honest, most kids just don't have or care about.

JISU: True! It's a miracle my parents came to all of my games. I can't imagine how boring it must be.

BUMSOO: Which positions did you play?

JISU: Outfielder in softball, which meant I was never paying any attention to the game. And in volleyball, I was the setter, because what I lack in height, I made up for by getting the ball way up for the strikers. And you? I don't think I even know the basic terminology for gymnastics.

BUMSOO: I still participate, actually. And I do a bit of everything. There's the floor, the rings, the vault, which is my favorite, the pommel horse—I'm boring you with all my gymnastics talk, aren't I?

JISU: Hmm? What, no! Please continue.

BUMSOO: Nah, I could see your eyes glaze over. I don't blame you though. Unless you're actually competing or tuning in to the Olympics every four years, it's not that interesting unless you're actually doing it.

JISU: To be honest, sports in general aren't really my thing.

BUMSOO: Says the girl who's participated in not one, but two sports!

JISU: I know, I know. But it's not like I was ever any good or super passionate about them. I feel like half the sports or extracurricular activities we all do aren't even genuine interests. We're all just forcing ourselves to do everything in the hopes that we can seem a little bit interesting on our college applications.

BUMSOO: Finally! Here comes my food. Thank you, sir. Can you hang back while I try a bite? Hmm. Yeah, no, that's way too salty. Did the chef get upset because I wanted a new batch? Because it's just too salty now. It tastes deliberately oversalted.

JISU: Bumsoo, I'm sure it's fine. It can't be that bad, right?

BUMSOO: Have a bite and tell me yourself. You can't expect anyone to actually eat this heap of sodium.

JISU: It's really not bad! Also, it's nice and warm like you asked.

BUMSOO: No, I'd like to send this back please. And can you just bring over a cup of green tea? That should be simple enough.

JISU: Bumsoo! I think they really tried their best.

BUMSOO: I'm sorry I brought us here. The service used to be so much better—

JISU: Dude, it's just mac and cheese.

BUMSOO: What?

JISU: It's just noodles and cheese—and they had the fancy fake cheese you wanted. It tasted great, which I know because I literally tried it. I don't see why you had to make such a big deal.

BUMSOO: Let me guess. You think I'm super picky and obnoxious because I'm vegan.

JISU: Not at all. I have friends who are vegan and would love this place. I think you're just rude.

BUMSOO: Excuse me? I think you're the one being rude.

JISU: No, I'm being honest.

BUMSOO: You know, I've been on a bunch of these seons and I've never met anyone as disrespectful as you.

JISU: Disrespectful! You're one to talk about disrespect.

BUMSOO: I'm not going to stand for this. I'm leaving.

JISU: Go ahead. I'm going to wait for the check and make sure to tip generously.

BUMSOO: I can't believe this.

JISU: What are you still doing here? Bye!

8

Jisu was helping Linda set the dining room table for lunch when she heard Jeff Murray come in through the front door.

"Daaaaad!" Mandy yelled as she ran down the steps and into her father's arms. Mr. Murray was home from his business trip, and Jisu and the Murrays were going to finally have a proper family meal.

"We've been cooking all morning just for you, Dad," Mandy said. Linda and Jisu exchanged a look. Of course, the two of them had been the ones to toil away in the kitchen while Mandy was upstairs, FaceTiming with her friends.

Mr. Murray made his way into the kitchen and embraced his wife. He was at least a foot taller than her, but they were both the same shade of blond. And while Linda's eyes were a simple brown, his shared the same green color as Mandy's. He looked like he could sunburn easily. "Whatever you're making, it smells amazing." He turned to Jisu. "And you must be our new guest. It's so nice to meet you, Jisu. I'm sorry to have missed your first couple weeks here, but welcome."

"Thank you, Mr. Murray!" Jisu said. "It's nice to finally meet you, too."

"Please, call me Jeff." He waved off the formality just as Linda had done when Jisu first landed in San Francisco.

Jisu went in for a handshake, but he went for a full-on bear hug. On the surface, the Murrays looked like an almost too-perfect, pristine Stepford-like family. But they truly were warm, friendly people.

Seeing all three of them together made Jisu's heart ache. She yearned for Sunday mornings in Seoul. She wanted to be back in her parents' dining room. Jisu closed her eyes and could see her dad sitting across from her, taking sips from his coffee while reading the morning paper, giving her a breakdown of current events. She could see her mom piling steamed vegetables and sweet black beans onto her dish to make sure her daughter got her nutrients. Jisu would give anything to eat her mother's banchan again. The steamed tofu, mini anchovies, scallion pancakes, cucumber kimchi—she missed all of it.

Jisu opened her eyes. The Murrays were sitting where she had imagined her own parents. *Just two and a half months until you're back in Seoul.* The countdown clock in Jisu's brain could not move any slower.

"So, tell me, Jisu. How do you like Wick-Helmering so far?" Jeff asked as he passed the plate of grilled vegetables to his wife. The weather in the Bay Area had been unseasonably warmer than usual, and Linda had said it was an excuse to use the grill one more time.

"I actually really like it," Jisu said. And it was true. Transitioning to a whole new country was not without its difficulties, but Wick—as great of a reputation as it had for academic excellence—was much more relaxed than Daewon. Jisu was easing into her classes without much struggle and she had time to actually attend her photography club meetings and make new friends like Jamie and Tiffany. Even Kaylee was warming up to her again. "I just really miss home, is all."

"Trust me, I know a thing or two about homesickness," Jeff said. "These two here will tell you how often I'm on the road."

"What do you do when you miss home?" Jisu asked.

"Well, for one, I'll FaceTime with Linda, and also Mandy, if she's not too busy hanging out with her friends."

"Dad, that was just one time." Mandy rolled her eyes.

"Otherwise, I keep myself as busy as I can," Jeff said. "Have you joined any clubs or any teams?"

"Jisu is an excellent photographer," Linda said. Jisu had probably shown her no more than four or five of her stills, but Linda spoke as if she had studied Jisu's whole portfolio and carefully curated a selection of the best pictures. It was the kind of confidence that only a proud, supportive parent could learn to exude.

"I'm an amateur, but yes. I went to the first club meeting the other day and I think I'm going to participate in some of the contests this year."

Jisu never had time to actually join the photography club at Daewon. She probably was better off spending whatever free time she had to start looking into and preparing for college admissions, but she was no longer in Seoul and no longer a Daewon student. She was miles and miles away and she was going to do what she wanted.

"That's great! You should join more clubs—it'll get your mind off home," Jeff said. "And when you do catch up with your parents and your friends, you'll have so much to fill them in on."

"Jisu, honey, you've barely touched your plate. Are you feeling all right?" Linda asked. Jisu looked down. They had spent the morning cooking together and Jisu had been excited to eat, but thoughts of home had eliminated her appetite. Still… she didn't want to be rude.

"No, this is great!" she said as she lifted a forkful of food to her mouth. "So, did you go anywhere exciting for this trip?"

"I went to the glamorous Midwest—outside Chicago, not even in the actual city. So no, nothing exciting." Jeff laughed.

"There was that one time we all got to go to Hawaii," Mandy said. "We made a family trip out of it. Have you been, Jisu?"

"I actually haven't. My parents like to travel around Asia mostly, and sometimes Europe. I have been to New York once though, and I loved it." Jisu wished her parents could be here to explore San Francisco with her as they had all the other cities they'd traveled to.

"Have you guys ever been to Seoul?" she asked.

"We haven't! But now we have no excuse not to," Linda said. "I've actually never been to Asia. The long flights are just so daunting."

"We should visit Jisu in the summer!" Mandy suggested.

"You should. Seoul is the best," Jisu said. "And I could be your tour guide!"

In her mind, Jisu conjured up lists of places to eat and shop. She mentally visited all the hangout spots that she'd frequented with Euni and Min. Had they discovered any new ones since she'd been gone?

She started to feel physically ill and excused herself from the table at the earliest moment she could without being rude. After trudging upstairs, she plopped herself onto her bed and tried to call her parents. Voice mail. The sun probably hadn't even risen over Seoul yet, so a part of her was quietly relieved that they hadn't answered all grumpy in a half-awake stupor.

Earlier in the week, Jisu had learned the hard way that spending countless hours scrolling through her friends' Instagram pages made the homesickness worse. Distance makes the heart grow fonder, but distance plus social media makes the heart crumble from intense, unbearable waves of FOMO and homesickness.

She'd promised herself not to check social media so often, but in a moment of weakness, Jisu peeked at Euni's and Min's photos. Seeing their selfies, aerial shots of their smoothies and concert photos made her briefly feel that she was there with them. But the ache returned immediately. Jisu wanted so badly to be there next to her friends. She wanted them here, too, in her room. She wanted to tell them about everything: the Murrays, all the crazy different non-uniformed outfits people wore at school, the amazing burritos and pho she'd been eating nonstop since arriving in the Bay Area, her new giant blonde goddess friends Jamie and Tiffany, her annoying classmates, the faux Korean Dave, even about Austin…

Jisu's phone buzzed. She grabbed it to check her notifications. Maybe Euni was up early and down to video chat?

REMINDER: Text Dave Kang about IS project.

Ughhh. Jisu yelled into her pillow. Stupid Dave had promised to text Jisu his schedule, but he still hadn't reached out. He was probably busy scaling a mountain somewhere, so that he could use the experience as a long-winded metaphor in his college application essays. They still had a lot of time, but Jisu needed to get her work done, too.

JISU: Hello? When are we meeting up for the IS project? Time is ticking.

DAVE: Yes, Master Kim! Whenever you want.

JISU: This isn't a joke. We really need to start. And I can meet whenever! You're the one with the impossible schedule!

DAVE: I know, I know. Sorry I'm being flaky. How about Weds after school? Practice got canceled.

JISU: Works. See you at the library.

Finally. Figuring out a time to meet Dave was like pulling teeth. Just how difficult was it going to be to put together an entire project with this guy?

DATE NO. 8

NAME: **Lee Dongjoo**

INTERESTS:
Son Heungmin, Steve Jobs, LeBron James

ACCOMPLISHMENTS:
Perfect SAT Score, Youngest Intern at Microsoft,
2nd Place in National Robotics Competition

JISU: So, you grew up splitting your time between Seoul and New York? What was that like?

DONGJOO: The jet lag is just awful. There's no easy way around it. I still haven't figured it out! And I had two Black-Berrys—remember those?

JISU: I never really had a need for one, but yeah, I remember my dad used one before switching over to the Android.

DONGJOO: I have my last two BlackBerrys mounted and framed in my study.

JISU: No way, that's so silly!

DONGJOO: I know, but I was really attached to them! I've good memories. When I got the email notifying me that I got the internship at Microsoft, I read it on my New York Black-Berry. And then when I found out that I made runner-up for the National Robotics Competition, I found it through my Seoul BlackBerry.

JISU: Sentimental value. I get it. It's kind of like this old, broken watch that I—

DONGJOO: Hang on, sorry. I just got an email I've been waiting on all day. Do you mind if I—

JISU: No, not at all. You do your thing. I have to use the restroom anyway, so I'll be right back.

Ten minutes later

JISU: Everything go okay? Put out some fires?

DONGJOO: What? Oh, the email. Yeah, everything's handled. My buddy and I have a few meetings set up with some VCs who are interested in our start-up idea and we're just dealing with some scheduling snafus.

JISU: It happens. All good! So, what's the start-up idea? Must be good if you've already got people lined up to hear your pitch.

DONGJOO: Shoot, sorry. I just need to reply to this text real quick.

JISU: Sure. Go ahead.

DONGJOO: Sorry, I know I'm being so rude. It's never like this.

DONGJOO: Um, where were we?

JISU: We were barely thirty minutes into the date when you checked your phone for the second time. That's where we're at.

DONGJOO: You're mad. And you have every right to be. It's just that—

JISU: Your phone's ringing. Are you going to at least mute it? People are starting to stare…

DONGJOO: It's kind of an emergency, so I'm—

JISU: Go. Take the call. I'm leaving.

DONGJOO: No! Don't leave.

JISU: Look, we tried, right? We can at least report that back to Ms. Moon. I'm not even mad, really. Let's just not waste each other's time. Because then I *will* get mad.

DONGJOO: Okay, but if we leave right now, both our parents will know that this was super short and if your parents are anything like mine, they'll nag you about how they're trying sooo hard and you're only putting in the minimum effort.

JISU: You're not wrong. So what are you proposing?

DONGJOO: Clearly you already hate me—which you have every right to—and this isn't going anywhere. I'm sure you have your matters of business to attend to. Why don't we just stay here and do our thing for another half hour or so and then we can part ways?

JISU: Fine.

DONGJOO: Great! And I'm so sorry, Jisu. It's just that my work is everything to me right now. But my parents... You get it. Right?

JISU: Oh, I get it. But I'm still going to sit here and text all my friends about what a jerk you are.

DONGJOO: As you should! I'm a total jerk.

JISU: At least you're straightforward. I'm setting an alarm for thirty minutes from now. When it rings, we can be free from each other.

DONGJOO: Deal. And again, sorry.

9

"Today's assignment is on the board. Everyone pair up with the person on your left and get to work," Mrs. French said as everyone entered the classroom and took their seats. "I need to take a very important phone call, so I'll be in the hallway if you need me."

Jisu looked to her left. Her class partner for today was none other than Bobby the Troll. Ugh. Pairing up with chatty Kaylee, everything's-peachy Dave or any one of his bros would've been less torturous. Anyone but Bobby! He was wearing that stupid red hoodie he always wore. It was like a bright warning sign—you would spot him walking down the hallway and either avoid him or brace for whatever ignorant comment he was going to make as he walked past you.

Just be cool. Jisu remembered the fight that nearly broke out last time she and Bobby had spoken. *Don't give him the atten-*

tion he wants. Just get the work done. Jisu opened her notebook to a new page and turned to Bobby.

"Jisu Kim." He was already smirking at her, eager to start off on the wrong foot. "Guess I don't have to worry about getting a perfect score now. Or doing any of the work."

Was he trying to compliment her intellect? But he was talking like he was trying to annoy her. And what a weird way to announce that you would be slacking.

Bobby looked around the class for a reaction from someone, anyone. But no one was paying attention.

"Let's just get the assignment done, okay?" Jisu felt irritable. Everything Bobby said to her made her feel uneasy. He was always pointing out things she already knew about herself, but singling them out like it was a bad thing. Jisu was a hardworking, smart student. He didn't have to make her feel weird about it. Jisu opened her textbook to chapter nine. They were assigned to read it together and answer the given questions.

"You people are always way too serious about getting good grades," Bobby said. "Besides, what are you so pressed about? You're probably gonna get into Harvard or Cornell or whatever anyway."

"You people?" The way Bobby said it made Jisu feel the most uncomfortable she'd felt at Wick. Bobby was doing his best to make her feel like an outsider, and it was actually working. Jisu clenched her fist. She wanted to get as far away from Bobby as possible.

None of her classmates had heard, or if they had, they didn't react. Trolls should be ignored, but Jisu wished someone, maybe even Dave, would say something and put Bobby in his place. Again. She could ignore a lot of his dumb comments, but she couldn't let him get away with this one.

"What do you mean, *you people?*" she asked again.

"I meant like you guys...you know," he said, sounding a bit set back, as if he hadn't expected Jisu to stand up for herself.

"No, Bobby. I don't know." But it was clear now to Jisu what he meant. He meant people who looked like her. Like Dave. Like all the other students at Wick who were Korean, Chinese, Vietnamese, Japanese. Asians. Jisu was lucky to have never encountered jerks like Bobby back at home. But she was quickly learning that the best way to deal with them was to confront them head-on. Jisu grilled him harder. "What did you mean when you said *you people*?"

Some of her classmates, probably sensing real tension, started to turn toward them. Bobby squirmed in his chair.

Not so fond of the attention all of a sudden, huh, Bobby?

After a moment, Bobby pushed the hoodie off his head, acting as if he'd gained some twisted sense of confidence from everyone watching.

"Good for you, Jisu. I didn't know Asian girls ever talked back." He smirked. "Isn't that why everyone wants an Asian girlfriend though? Because they never talk back?"

Bobby's words hit Jisu hard like a punch to the gut. Were people really dumb enough to believe that about girls who looked like her? Where did he even get off on saying such ridiculous things?

Jisu was shaking with anger, and she tried to hold herself together. She knew every word that came out of Bobby's mouth was empty and meaningless, but it didn't change the fact that it was still hurtful and ostracizing. The students around her gasped. But none of them said anything.

Where was Mrs. French when you needed a grown-up to step in? Of course she was still taking her "very important phone call" in the hallway, away from this mess. What would Jisu's parents make of the fact that their tuition money was going toward her learning to fend for herself against racist classmates instead of focusing on international studies? Although, to be fair, those two things probably shared more than a few parallels.

Stupid Bobby Leeman. Even at his most confident, full troll self, he was hunched over in his chair with the posture of a decrepit eighty-year-old man. Kaylee was right—he probably hadn't ever gotten enough attention from his parents. Whatever his issues were, Jisu didn't care enough to try to understand him. That wasn't her job. The only person who could unpack the loneliness that drove Bobby's sad, desperate ploys for attention was Bobby himself.

Jisu was floundering through all the new layers of her anger and frustration when Hiba Khoury, a classmate she knew in passing, stepped in.

"What would you know about girlfriends, Bobby?" she said. "Not even dead girls would go out with you."

The whole class jeered at this and cheered Hiba on. Hiba nudged her assigned partner, Jordan Rodriguez.

"Jordan, take one for the team and switch with Jisu." Jordan shrugged and Hiba stood up.

"Get up, Bobby. Go sit with Jordan," she ordered. Jisu watched in awe as Bobby sidestepped away from her with his head down.

Hiba sat down next to Jisu, who marveled at her new friend. She had met Hiba during the first days of school, but they hadn't really chatted outside of that initial interaction.

Jisu had always admired Hiba's fashion sense—she wore bright, vibrant colors and her outfits were always perfectly coordinated, from her hijab down to her shoes. Today she looked impeccably chic in an all-black outfit. Her sweater had gold roses embroidered on the shoulders and her Mary Janes looked a lot like a pair Jisu had seen and coveted the last time she had gone to Neiman Marcus with Linda and Mandy.

When class ended, Bobby sneaked off quietly and disappeared into the crowded hallway.

"Looks like the troll is going back under the bridge for

lunchtime," Hiba said. She turned to Jisu. "Are you okay though?" she asked with a serious look.

"Oh, I'm fine. Idiots like Bobby can't get to me." Jisu smiled. It felt good to be seen the way Hiba looked at her.

"You've learned that a lot faster than I did," Hiba said. "Bobby has always been a bully. He's never been nice to me since my first day at Wick."

"Kaylee says it's because his mom never gave him enough attention, which makes me feel more sad for him than mad," Jisu said.

"Yeah, some people try to be too nice and say that he's just awkward and doesn't fit in. But being a jerk is not the same as being awkward. And people will go so far as to say he's 'kinda biased' when really he's kinda racist!" Hiba said. "No one ever wants to use the R word and offend anyone, when really the idiotic things he says are more offensive."

Jisu nodded her head as she walked down the hallway with Hiba. All of this was so new to her, but it made complete sense. Jisu let her shoulders drop and felt some relief. Listening to Hiba talk was like finding a new word in the dictionary to match a feeling you constantly felt but couldn't name before.

"Do you want to eat lunch together?" Jisu asked.

"Yes, of course!" Hiba exclaimed, much to Jisu's delight.

The two of them walked to the main lawn. They threw their books and backpacks onto the grass and pulled out their lunches. Hiba took a bite out of her sandwich. Jisu opened her lunchbox. The plastic container was divided into sections. In each one, she packed servings of bulgogi, white rice, a packet of roasted seaweed and steamed vegetables.

"Oh, my god, that looks so good!" Hiba said. "And it smells amazing."

"Thanks! I even made the bulgogi myself," Jisu said, feeling proud of her amateur culinary accomplishments. She hadn't cooked at all in Korea, but ever since she moved in with the

Murrays, she had mastered a number of dishes. Emulating her mother's cooking was the best way to cope with homesickness. Jisu ripped open the seaweed strips.

"Do you want one?" she offered. Hiba took one and ate it immediately.

"I love these. They're so crispy and salty. Honestly, they're even better than popcorn. I would eat this at the movies," she said as she licked her lips and the salt off her fingers.

Jisu remembered when she'd first eaten lunch with Jamie and Tiffany. They weren't dismissive in any way, but the way they had said, *What's that? And that? I think I ate this at that Korean restaurant last week. Oh, my god, I actually love kimchi so much*, hadn't felt quite as genuine and natural as the way Hiba reacted.

"So, you moved here when?" Jisu asked.

"My parents and I emigrated from Lebanon when I was nine. I actually skipped a grade and started fifth grade early," Hiba said.

"Okay, so that definitely has to be the main thing written all over your college applications," Jisu said.

"How did you know?" Hiba laughed.

"But seriously, the whole college application process is freaking me out." Early applications were due in November, giving her only two months to get everything together. And then the rest of the applications would be due in January, which wasn't that long after. Everything was hurtling forward. Jisu pushed the rice around her lunchbox. Her appetite had disappeared. "I know I'm not behind, but I feel like if I stop to breathe even for one second, I'll fall to the end of the class."

"First of all, everyone overdoes it with the whole early-college-prep thing," Hiba said. "Also, if I can be honest, it seems like you're fitting in really easily here, at a completely new school in a completely new country. If you can do that, you can do anything."

"Do you know which schools you're applying to?"

"Princeton," Hiba said firmly. "I want to go there for undergrad and then for law school."

"What kind of law do you want to study?"

"Probably international law. It's why I love Mrs. French's class so much."

"See? That's what I'm talking about. You know exactly what you want and what you're going to do with your life." Jisu sighed. "It took me like a week to figure out a time to meet Dave for the IS project."

"Well, Dave is always doing a million extracurricular activities, so that's not on you."

"That makes me feel even more guilty," Jisu said. "He's out there, racking up all these accomplishments and awards to tack onto his résumé. I don't know what I'm doing."

"Hey." Hiba placed her hand on Jisu's arm. "Nobody in this school really knows what they're doing. I'm just following my older sister's footsteps. Dave is just doing what his parents are telling him to do. You're doing great. There are plenty of people in our grade who aren't even half as prepared as you are."

Jisu knew all of this was true, but it was reassuring to hear Hiba say it. For the first time in weeks, she felt her anxiety go down.

"Jisu! We've been looking for you!" Jamie and Tiffany ran across the courtyard and plopped themselves down on the grass.

"We just had the most boring US history class," Jamie said. "I'm so over high school. I can't wait to go to college and just party."

Hiba glanced at Jisu. *See? You're way ahead of these girls*, she seemed to say with a look. Jisu stifled her laughter.

"Will you guys tell me if you see Jordan Rodriguez? I'm trying to avoid him," Tiffany said.

"Jisu and I were just in class with him. What happened?" Hiba asked.

"He asked me out on a date and caught me off guard. And I said yes because I like him, but I was so awkward about it. I wanted to die. And now I never want to see him again." Tiffany nervously pulled at the fringed hem of her skirt.

"Maybe your matchmaker from Seoul can set Tiffany up on some dates," Jamie said to Jisu.

"Matchmaker?" Hiba turned to Jisu with wide eyes.

"It's not that crazy," Jisu said. "It's more like a glorified version of my mom trying to set me up on dates with her friends' sons."

"Oh, my parents do that to me, too," Hiba said. "Every time we go to mosque, they point out another boy my age and talk about what a nice man he's grown to be, or how he's so good to his parents."

"Don't they know you're busy trying to get into Princeton first?" Jisu said.

"I know!" Hiba threw her hands up. "If I bring home a good grade, they ask me why I'm not dating so-and-so from mosque. If I spend too much time socializing, they scold me for not studying enough."

"You just can't win," Jisu said.

"But I've never been on a real blind date. I grew up with all the boys that my parents are trying to set me up with. What are the blind dates like?" Hiba asked. Jamie and Tiffany also seemed eager to hear.

"Honestly, they're really not that glamorous," Jisu said. "One time, I was on such a boring date that I actually fell asleep."

The girls collectively gasped.

"You did not!" Tiffany screamed.

"I'm not proud," Jisu said, trying not to laugh. "I dozed off for like just one second while he was blabbing on about something—I can't even remember what—but he definitely noticed. And he called me out on it!"

"Oh, my god! Why would he do that?" Jamie looked bewildered.

"Yeah, seriously. Just take the L and move on," Hiba said. "Boys are so dumb."

Jisu checked her phone as the girls got up to go to class. There was a text from Austin.

Wyd Weds? Supposed to be the last warm day of the year. Wanna go surfing?

Jisu looked at Jamie and Tiffany. They were adjusting each other's hair—Jamie making sure Tiffany's braids were intact and Tiffany adjusting Jamie's bangs. They didn't seem to have gotten any texts from Austin, so maybe it wasn't just another friend hang.

Jisu's stomach did a tiny flip. Was he asking her out on a real date?

I don't know how to surf :(

Jisu checked next Wednesday in her calendar. *IS project with Dave K.* Of course, the one time Dave could manage to find a time to squeeze her into his busy schedule was when Austin wanted to hang.

I can teach you :) c'monnnn

Jisu wanted to say yes. Why did she have to bend over backward to make it work for Dave? She had a life, too. She started a new message, this one to Dave.

Sorry, can't do Weds anymore. But we'll find another time!

Jisu had no idea when exactly that might be. She didn't know what her schedule looked like the following week or for the next. But she had plans with Austin, and for now she was happy just to have that in her calendar.

DATE NO. 9

NAME: **Park Changmin**

INTERESTS:
Seoul SK Knights, Marvel Comics, Comedy

ACCOMPLISHMENTS:
Skipped two grades; Early admittance to
Cambridge University; Currently a Physics major
at Cambridge

JISU: You know, I've been to the UK but I've never been to Cambridge.

CHANGMIN: Oh, word.

JISU: I've been to London and Oxford. Is Cambridge a lot like Oxford? I know you guys are major rivals, right?

CHANGMIN: Yeah, but I don't really pay attention to that school rivalry stuff.

JISU: Oh…got it. So, what are you studying at Cambridge?

CHANGMIN: Physics.

JISU: Do you like it?

CHANGMIN: Enough to major in it, yeah.

JISU: I see.

JISU: I heard you skipped a few grades and even got into Cambridge early. Is that true?

CHANGMIN: Yeah, it's true.

JISU: That's amazing! So wait, does that mean we're actually the same age?

CHANGMIN: How old are you?

JISU: Seventeen. I turn eighteen in October. How old are you?

CHANGMIN: I turn nineteen next month. Do you go on these seons often?

JISU: Hmm? I've just been on a few. Not that many. Some were boring. Most of them were perfectly nice, but that's about it. On paper though, I think you've got the most interesting résumé.

CHANGMIN: Really? If I'm the most interesting dude, then you need to fire your matchmaker. Or she should quit her job.

JISU: What! Don't say that. Getting into college two years early and then going to Cambridge is pretty interesting. Although, I have to be honest, I don't really care much for physics. I'm actually very bad at it and barely passed last year.

134

CHANGMIN: A physics nerd at Cambridge couldn't really interest a lot of people. Or anyone for that matter.

JISU: Well, that isn't the only thing that defines you!

CHANGMIN: True, I suppose.

JISU: What do you do at Cambridge outside of class? Is it true that you guys always have fancy dinners where everyone gets dressed up?

CHANGMIN: You're probably thinking about the Formal Halls.

JISU: Do you dress up? I bet you look great in a suit.

CHANGMIN: I do get dressed up. And you go with your friends, bring a bottle of wine, sit down to eat in a big hall that was built centuries ago and socialize with your fellow classmates.

JISU: That sounds *so* nice.

CHANGMIN: Do you want to go to Cambridge? Or any school in the UK?

JISU: I'd be lucky if I got into any university at this point. Korean universities are super selective, so I'm looking at more options in America. But who knows if anyone will take me.

CHANGMIN: You're being too hard on yourself.

JISU: How would you know?

CHANGMIN: You seem smart and snappy. Like book smart but also sensible.

JISU: Really? You think so? If I applied to Cambridge, would you write me a letter of recommendation?

CHANGMIN: I'm flattered you'd ask, but I have a feeling a recommendation letter from one of their own students wouldn't really help.

JISU: It might if that student is a physics genius who got into college at the age of sixteen.

CHANGMIN: I hate to tell you, but I don't even make the list of top ten smartest people at Cambridge. You'll get to campus and become completely unimpressed.

JISU: Damn, then I definitely can't get into Cambridge. I don't think I've met anyone who's skipped a grade, no less two. So that probably makes you the smartest person I've met. When do you go back to the UK?

CHANGMIN: I'm actually going back a little early, in a few weeks. I want to spend some of the summer there, and it's also my girlfriend's birthday in August.

JISU: Girlfriend?

CHANGMIN: Yeah...wait, did you not see my text before we met up?

JISU: I haven't checked my phone...

CHANGMIN: I'm just out here to see my family and the seons are to keep my mom happy. She'd be mortified if she knew I had an English girlfriend. Shoot. I'm sorry, Jisu, I thought you got my text—

JISU: No, it's cool! I'm really only doing this for my parents anyway, too, so...

CHANGMIN: Good! I'm so relieved. Also because I think you're actually kinda cool. The first two seons I went on were kind of a mess. Especially after I told both of the girls that I already had a girlfriend.

JISU: Yeah...I can imagine how they felt.

CHANGMIN: But you're so chill. I bet if you did come to Cambridge, we'd be friends. And I bet you and Margaret would get along.

JISU: Margaret?

CHANGMIN: My girlfriend.

JISU: Riiight. Oh, look at that. I just got an urgent text from my friend. I think she needs me.

CHANGMIN: I drove here. Want me to give you a ride?

JISU: That's not necessary! I'm just gonna go right now.

CHANGMIN: Okay. Well, if you ever end up in Cambridge, feel free to hit me up!

10

"What are you so nervous about?" Mandy asked.

Jisu had plenty to be nervous about. It was Wednesday, 4:26 p.m. It was balmy outside—a perfect 77°F September day. Austin was going to drive down the street any minute now to take Jisu surfing, something she had never done before.

Jisu had two swimsuits—a simple black one-piece and a cute pink gingham bikini—but she had changed in and out of them multiple times before opting for the sensible one-piece. They were going to the beach to surf and not to lounge idly and tan after all.

She had been sitting at the top of the staircase, tapping her foot and watching the grandfather clock inch slowly toward 4:30 p.m., when Mandy emerged from her room and inserted her nosy self.

"I'm not nervous. What are you talking about?" Jisu tucked

her hair behind her ears and cupped her hands around her shins, as if to calm her restless legs.

"You're shaking like Mom does when she has too much coffee in the morning." Mandy stared at Jisu suspiciously. "You're going to see a boy, aren't you?"

Jisu rolled her eyes. Mandy was incredibly skilled in the art of taking something you were avoiding and forcing you to confront it head-on.

"I'm hanging out with Austin. We're going to the beach to surf," Jisu said. "But that's not why I'm nervous. I'm nervous because I don't know how to surf."

Jisu's phone dinged and a car honked outside. Her heart jumped, but not because she was startled. It felt like she had just sprinted up and down the stairs. He was right on time. She placed a hand on her chest to signal her heart to calm down.

"Oookay. If you say so. Have fun on your second date!" Mandy retreated to her room before Jisu could reiterate that it wasn't a date. And that the first time they had hung out, it wasn't a date either. They were just hanging out. That was it.

Silly Mandy. What does she know?

Jisu made her way down the stairs and checked her reflection in the hallway mirror. She practiced a few different smiles, each one feeling more fake and manic than the last. Why were her nerves acting up all of a sudden? Jisu pinched her cheeks so she could both snap out of it and also attain a natural rosy complexion. *Jisu Kim, why do you care what your hair looks like? It's going to get wet anyway. Does my hair look okay when it's wet? What if I look like a scary gwisin? Should I tie it in a bun?* She twisted her hair into a topknot and stepped into the bright afternoon sunshine.

"Jisu!" Austin shouted out the car window. She caught his eye and waved at him. He was blasting some hip-hop track that she didn't recognize. But the beat was catchy and she couldn't help smiling and bopping her head. Thank god for music. It filled in the spaces in between and made Jisu feel a little less like a bundle of nerves. She opened the passenger door and slid into the car.

"What song is this?" Jisu put her seat belt on.

"It's Migos. You don't recognize it?" Austin turned up the volume and hit the gas. The combination of the music blasting, the wind blowing through the windows and Austin at the wheel, driving them at high speed toward the beach, left Jisu feeling giddy and lightheaded.

"So, where exactly are we going?" she asked, not recognizing any of the streets they were whizzing past.

"Pacifica. No one's taken you there yet, right?"

"No, I haven't been." Jisu had yet to explore this part of the city.

"Good." Austin's excitement to show her a new part of town excited Jisu.

She thought of the quizzes she had read in magazines.

Non-date: You both hang out and do the same boring things.

Date: You both go exploring and try something new.

None of this was new to Austin, but he knew it was new for her and had taken it upon himself to take her out. The tide of nervous energy returned, but Jisu didn't mind and let it wash over her.

"I didn't realize people in the Bay Area went surfing. I always thought of it as a more LA thing."

"All of California goes surfing. But there are probably more people who go in LA. The few who surf here all year-round are the real ones though. I've been surfing since I was a kid. You know I'm from Torrance, right?"

"Where?"

"It's outside LA. I used to surf all the time, and then my mom moved us up here to be with her sisters, after my dad died." Austin kept both hands on the wheel and stared intently at the road ahead. On the radio, there was a heavy layer of silence in between tracks.

"Austin, I'm so sorry. I didn't know." It was hard for Jisu to be away from her dad, but she messaged him on Kakao every day and had her weekly video chats with her parents. She couldn't imagine what it would be like to lose one of her parents.

"It was a long time ago. It sounds super cheesy, but ever since he died, I've learned to live life to the fullest and do what I want." Austin parked the car. He switched back and smiled at Jisu. "Like going surfing at Pacifica in September. But first we're going to make one stop."

They were practically under the Golden Gate Bridge. Jisu stared in awe at the iconic red bridge.

"You didn't tell me we'd be stopping by the bridge!" she exclaimed. Jisu hopped out of the car and immediately started snapping away with her digital camera.

"Do you always have a camera on you?" Austin asked.

"You never know when the perfect photo opportunity will present itself." Jisu pointed her DSLR at him and snapped a few more photos.

"There's a good photo op over there. Do you recognize that corner?" Austin pointed to an old military building perched underneath the bridge. "There's a scene from an old movie… a famous movie…"

"I know some American shows and movies, but I don't really know the old stuff. Except *Titanic* or *Gone with the Wind*. But *Titanic* was in the Atlantic Ocean and *Gone with the Wind* was in the South, right?"

"Jimmy Stewart... Kim Novak... Hitchcock?" Austin looked at Jisu expectantly.

"Sounds familiar..." Jisu lied. "Austin, I'm not a film buff."

"Okay, you don't need me to be your English tutor. What you need is a pop-culture tutor. Today when you go home, you're going to watch this movie called *Vertigo*. I think it's on Netflix." Austin's attentiveness made Jisu's stomach do another tiny flip. Whatever remaining guilt she felt for canceling on Dave disappeared entirely. *Yes, this is a real date*, Jisu decided. And it was already better than any seon she had ever been on.

Once Austin convinced Jisu that she had taken more than enough photos, they got back into his car to drive down to Pacifica State Beach. Jisu eased right into the passenger seat. She no longer felt as hyperaware of every movement—she could easily reach over Austin's arm to grab the aux cord and play music without overthinking it. She leaned back and marveled at the ocean view to the right as they drove down Cabrillo Highway.

"You didn't bring a wet suit by any chance, did you?" Austin asked as he grabbed his out of the trunk. Jisu didn't have to answer because the look of confusion on her face indicated enough to him.

"Lucky for you, I conjured one up." Austin grabbed another. "Here, this should fit."

"Thanks!" Jisu said, but she immediately wondered where the suit came from. Did the last girl he took to the beach to surf use this suit? How many girls did he take surfing? Maybe he just bought one and this was his thing—showing girls his surfing spots before he made a move.

Was he going to make a move?

Jisu quickly put the wet suit on and was quietly relieved it didn't take too much effort or require an embarrassing amount of help from Austin. The two of them ran into the water. Jisu shivered with excitement but also because the water was freezing. Austin somehow seemed unfazed. She couldn't get over the sensation of being covered in water but not entirely wet. Was this how it felt to be a dolphin? Jisu had not surfed a day in her life, but the simple act of putting the wet suit on made her feel like she could get up on the board and do anything.

Austin showed her how to paddle and hop up onto the board, repeating the motions over and over again. Jisu watched intently. She did want to get it down. Austin repeated the motions for Jisu once more, but she couldn't concentrate.

Can't. Stop. Shivering. At least I put my hair up and I don't look like a gwisin.

The cold water, the incessant wind, the wet suits outlining their entire bodies like a second layer of skin—it was all too distracting. How did she look? What was he thinking about her?

The ocean swayed them out and Jisu could see a wave forming on the horizon.

Okay, I'm going to get it right this time.

She plunged her arms into the water and paddled forward. She let the wave carry her up, and at the right moment she hopped onto her board.

"I did it!" she yelled. "I'm doing it!"

The exhilaration lasted for only a few seconds before Jisu lost her balance and fell into the water. But it didn't matter. She had done it! She'd gotten herself on that board and skimmed the surface of the water like she was Jesus.

Jisu resurfaced and Austin pulled her out of the ocean and onto her board. Her body was completely drained of energy and her limbs felt like rubber, but adrenaline was gushing through her veins and her heart was racing so fast she could hear it beating in her ears.

"Are you okay?" Austin asked. Jisu was still freezing, but a warmth radiated inside her when she saw the look of concern in his face.

"Yeah," Jisu huffed. She was still trying to catch her breath. "I feel amazing. I can't believe I did that!"

Austin and Jisu swam back to shore. They walked around the beach to dry themselves off. Jisu marveled at the palm trees. She could never get sick of looking at them. The high from her small but still totally major accomplishment still hadn't worn off, and she couldn't stop smiling. Euni and Min would never believe her. *Surfing? You? No way.* Jisu even wanted to tell them about Austin. Her new friend, who happened to be a boy. A really cute boy.

The sun was starting to set and a warm glow washed over everything. Jisu and Austin stood silently side by side and drank in the view. Today really was a perfect day.

Jisu stared beyond the ocean. Somewhere far across the Pacific, past several time zones, was home. Her chest tightened and she felt a twinge of pain.

"You all right?" Austin asked, seeming to have detected the shift in her mood.

"How long do you think it would take for me to swim all the way back to Seoul?"

"There's probably an easier way to get back. Like a plane." Austin put his arm around her and drew her into him.

Jisu tensed. All of a sudden, she was aware of every cell and atom in her body. She tried to calm her nerves by directing her sensory awareness away from the placement of Austin's arm on her shoulder to the ocean in front of them. Jisu took a deep breath and gazed at the waves. But her nerves didn't relent. So she let them flutter about in her stomach. She leaned her head on his shoulder.

"I remember being homesick for LA when I first got here," Austin said. "But it'll go away. This place will grow on you."

"No, it already has," Jisu said. "I just feel guilty."

"Guilty about what?"

"I actually feel happy, and I didn't think I would. And I

shouldn't. Going to Wick for one year was supposed to be all cramming. No fun. But I have independence here. I'm working on my photography more. I'm making new, real friends. I learned how to surf today. And I'm somehow not flunking any of my classes."

"So what are you guilty of? Living your life?"

"Things are too good. And I could always study harder. You know, I flaked on a group project to come out here with you."

"Can I be honest?" Austin asked. Jisu motioned him to continue. "I think you need to loosen up. Why are you always stressing yourself out so much?" The question hung in the space in between them. She had no answer. The pressure to do well, to sacrifice her present for her future—whatever that looked like—had always been a part of her life.

"I'm not saying it's the same, but I think I know what you mean. My mom's a single mom, and I'm the oldest of four kids. Everyone's looking to me to be the 'man of the family,' whatever that means. My uncles want me to take over the family restaurant, but I want to go to college and do my own thing. I decided a long time ago that I could please my family as best as I can, but I still need to be happy."

Jisu let his words sink in. He was brave to put himself first. It felt against nature and against her inherent self to do such a thing. But she wanted to be more like him.

Austin stared far across the Pacific, looking deep in thought. She wanted to take a photo of him. Of his strong profile against the soft pink sky. She wanted to show him how she saw him in this moment. But Jisu held her gaze and recorded it in her memory. This wasn't something she'd forget.

"Are you hungry?" Austin checked the time. "'Cuz I'm starving."

"I could eat anything right now." Jisu's stomach growled at the thought of food. She clutched her belly, embarrassed at how loud it was. They walked to the parking lot.

"You go to El Farolito yet?"

All these names, movies and places she didn't know. Everything felt new around Austin. "No, but I don't care. I'm so hungry, I'll eat literally anything."

"It's going to be the best burrito you've ever had," he said.

"Ooh, burritos! I had one at a Mexican restaurant in Seoul—"

"No, no. This is a real proper California-Mexican burrito." Austin pulled out of the parking spot and maneuvered onto the road. "I'm gonna give you a whole list of spots you need to try. For your pop-culture homework."

"Pop-culture homework? Really?"

"It's what a good tutor does." Austin smiled. "You'll thank me for it later."

El Farolito was different from some of the Mexican spots Jisu had gone to in Seoul. A handful of them were in Itaewon, where most of the expats in Seoul lived. Jisu had her fair share of tacos and burritos with Min and Euni, but they all had some Korean fusion aspect to them, whether the carnitas was replaced with bulgogi or the rice in the burrito was kimchi-fried rice. Now she could have a proper California-Mexican burrito, whatever that meant. El Farolito was simple, casual and crowded. Hungry patrons lined up along the counter to place their orders and then seated themselves in the booths.

Austin and Jisu picked up their orders: carne asada for her, al pastor for him. They grabbed a booth and devoured their burritos. Maybe it was because she was so tired and hungry from all the surfing and walking. And simply staying alert and being on her toes around Austin was exhausting, too. But the steak burrito was unlike anything she'd ever eaten. It was so good, it felt like healing. How water must taste in the middle of the desert. How real food must taste after recovering from a weeklong stomach bug. Nothing was as simple and as good

as rice, beans and meat. Austin was right—it was the best burrito she'd ever had.

And just as Jisu took the last bite of the perfect meal to cap
off the perfect day, she spotted him from the corner of her eye.

Was…? Was that…Dave Kang?

Crap. It *was* him. He was placing his order at the counter.
He was with a girl. His girlfriend? She wrapped an arm around
Dave and laughed at something he said. She had brown hair,
brown eyes and freckles scattered across her pale face. She
was wearing the female Bay Area uniform: an oatmeal-col-
ored fleece, blue jeans and worn-out tan boots. Honestly, she
was…kinda basic.

Austin turned around to see what Jisu was staring so intently at.

"Yo! Dave Kang!" Austin shouted before Jisu could stop
him. She ducked, hoping they would simply wave back, not
see her and move along. But no. Austin, being the nice guy
that he was, beckoned them over.

"We were just finishing up. You guys should take our
table." Austin slid out of the booth and gave Dave a fist bump.

"Thanks, man," Dave said. He turned to Jisu, but she
couldn't bear to look at him. She was caught red-handed.

"Sophie! What's up, girl? You know Jisu, right?" Austin
said, pseudo-introducing them.

"Hey, I'm Sophie." Sophie stuck out her hand and smiled.
She did seem like someone Jisu could be friends with. It only
made sense that Dave's girlfriend was equally as warm and inviting as he was. Jisu shook Sophie's hand.

"I'm Jisu. It's nice to meet you… I love that necklace!" Sophie was wearing a simple chain, nothing really remarkable.
And it certainly wasn't a necklace Jisu would get for herself,
but in the last few weeks of constantly meeting new people,
Jisu found that throwing someone a simple compliment helped
to break the ice.

Austin's phone started to ring. "Sorry, guys. It's my uncle calling from the restaurant. I gotta take this."

Don't leave me with them. Take me with you! Jisu looked up slowly and met Dave's gaze. Her insides curdled and she wanted to hide under the table and never come back out.

"Jisu and I are partnered up for that big IS project and were supposed to meet up today actually." Dave looked straight into Jisu's eyes. "But she told me she had something urgent come up."

Jisu's face warmed. Stupid Dave was enjoying every second of this. Sure, it wasn't okay for her to flake on him, but he didn't have to rub it in.

"Austin's fun to hang out with," Sophie said with a knowing smile. "I totally get it."

"What? What do you mean you totally get it?" Dave asked, just as the cashier called out their order number. Sophie left the table to get their food, leaving Jisu and Dave alone. Where the hell was Austin? Would it be cool if she just got up and left?

"Listen, Dave. I'm sorry for flaking. But I did have plans with Austin that I forgot about. I felt bad and didn't want to cancel on him," Jisu explained.

"But you were cool canceling on me. Got it."

God, he was so sensitive. "Oh, come on. You get to have a nice night out with your girlfriend. It kinda works out, right?"

"And you? Are you and Austin dating?"

"No…" Jisu hesitated. Were they dating? It still wasn't clear to her. "We aren't dating. We're just hanging out."

"Just be careful around him." Austin was outside, still on the phone, pacing back and forth. "Austin's charming and nice and all, but you know he messes around with different girls all the time, right?"

"Uh…no…?" Jisu said. What the hell was Dave talking about? What did he know? Also, she'd made it clear. They. Were. Not. Dating.

"That's his thing. He'll get really friendly with one girl, hang out with her, get close, do the whole boyfriend experience and then drop her out of nowhere when he's ready to move on to the next one."

Jisu couldn't believe what Dave was saying. She refused to believe it. He was just trying to ruin her day. All because she'd flaked on him.

"Austin and I are friends," Jisu said. "Besides, it's none of your business."

"Just looking out for you, Jees," Dave said. That annoying nickname again.

"Whatever. I don't need you or anyone to look out for me." Jisu glared at him. "I'm good."

Sophie returned with two large burritos, clearly unaware of the heated exchange that had just occurred. Outside, Austin hung up the phone and waved Jisu over.

"Just let me know when you're free to work on the project next week," Dave said. "I'll make whatever time work."

Jisu ignored him. "It was nice meeting you, Sophie. Enjoy your food."

"Thanks, girlie!" Sophie smiled widely. *Dave should stick to looking out for her. This girl's completely oblivious.*

DATE NO. 10

NAME: **Hwang Taejin**

INTERESTS:
Painting, Italian, Metalwork

PARENT OCCUPATIONS:
Chief Financial Offer at Geum Nara;
Criminal prosecutor

5:58 p.m.

TAEJIN: Hey, Jisu, I'm sitting at the table at the far right. I just got myself a cappuccino and I'm reading a book.

6:07 p.m.

TAEJIN: How far away are you? ETA?

6:14 p.m.

JISU: OMG, Taejin! I'm so sorry. I completely forgot about today. For some reason, I had it in my calendar for Thursday and not Tuesday. I'm so sorry.

6:15 p.m.

TAEJIN: Am I being stood up right now?

6:15 p.m.

JISU: No! Absolutely not. I'm just a dummy and got the day wrong. Omg. Please don't hate me!

6:16 p.m.

TAEJIN: Thank god I brought a book. Otherwise I would've looked like an idiot.

6:17 p.m.

JISU: I'm so, so sorry. Let's definitely reschedule. Does this Thursday work for you?

11:34 a.m.

JISU: Hey, Taejin. I still feel really bad about yesterday, but I truly just blanked. You have every right to be annoyed at me, but I would still love to meet up. Let me know if you have time this week.

1:00 p.m.

TAEJIN: Don't worry about it. I believe you. It's all good.

1:04 p.m.

JISU: Let me buy you coffee! Please :)

1:05 p.m.

TAEJIN: I can't. My family and I are going to Italy.

1:06 p.m.

TAEJIN: My parents just bought a house in Tuscany, so they want to take full advantage. And we're also going to explore more of the South and do Capri for a week, too.

1:15 p.m.

JISU: I bet you all will last two weeks tops before homesickness and cravings for kimchi bring you back here.

1:17 p.m.

TAEJIN: I bet I could find kimchi in Tuscany. Korean food is trendy and acceptable almost every in the world now, Jisu.

1:18 p.m.

JISU: Yeah, and I guess all that yummy pasta won't hurt either.

1:20 p.m.

TAEJIN: I'll just hit you up when I'm back?

1:25 p.m.

JISU: Okay! I really am sorry about yesterday. Hope you have a great trip. Can't wait to hear about it!

11

Jisu rang the doorbell to Dave's house and tried to bleach the awful encounter at El Farolito from her memory. When she had gotten home and replayed the events of the day, she'd had to be honest with herself. Dave had meant well. He might have been a little salty in his delivery, but he was only saying an iteration of what Kaylee had said, too. Austin didn't date anyone.

None of it mattered though. Because she wasn't trying to date Austin. They were both simply living their lives, going where the wind carried them.

Through the opaque glass, Jisu could see a tall figure approaching the door. She braced herself. If he was going to be cold to her, she deserved it, partially, maybe.

"Suuuup, Jees?" Dave welcomed her in, his usual friendly self. "Just a warning. I told my mom I was having a friend come over and when she found out you were Korean, she kinda went nuts in the kitchen. You're gonna leave ten pounds heavier."

Jisu broke into a smile. Maybe it was all good and they were back to normal.

The living room was not what she expected. There was no slick coffee table made of birch or a rigid, midcentury-style couch like the Murrays'. Instead there was a plush white leather sofa (still chic in its own way) and a rich chestnut-colored sang, a Korean-style low-level table. Four bang-seok, floor cushions surrounded it. Jisu and her parents didn't even eat every meal at a sang, but sitting on the cushion with her legs folded and feet tucked under made her feel immediately at home.

"Omo, omo! Bul suh wassuh? She's already here?" a woman Jisu assumed was Mrs. Kang shouted as she hurried into the living room with a plate filled with sliced persimmon and Korean pear.

Jisu sprang to her feet and bowed her head. A respectable person always stood up and greeted their elders properly. "Anyoung ha say yo," she said politely.

"Wah, so polite. Dave, do you see this? Jisu, please teach Dave how to be a good Korean." Mrs. Kang clasped her hands together and smiled. "Eat as much as you want. And you can bring home the leftovers." Jisu resisted every urge to give Mrs. Kang a bear hug. She smiled and thanked her profusely. It felt nice to have a Korean mom overwhelm her with care.

"Where in Seoul do you live?" Mrs. Kang spoke to Jisu in Korean. Music to Jisu's ears. The only Korean Jisu got to speak now was through a poor connection over the phone or via video chat with her parents. It was so nice to speak the language with someone in person. *It's too bad Dave doesn't speak much.*

"My parents live in Daechi-dong, near the Han River."

"Gangnam! I hear it's such a nice area now. Everyone tells

me that Seoul changes entirely every three years because of all the rapid developments."

"That's kinda true. Do you not visit Seoul often?" Jisu asked Mrs. Kang, and also looked to Dave in case he understood any part of their conversation. He shrugged and ate another piece of persimmon.

"No, it's been almost fifteen years now," Mrs. Kang said. "The last time we went, this guy was only three. He probably doesn't remember." She pinched her son's cheek.

"Ow, Mom!" Dave put his fork down. "The fruit is delicious. And I'm glad you like Jisu, but we actually have some schoolwork to do."

"Okay, okay." Mrs. Kang relented, switching back to English. "But it's dinnertime. You guys need to eat," she said, as if she hadn't just stuffed heaps of fruit down their throats. "Jisu, you like namul bap?"

"I love everything. I'll eat whatever you give me." Jisu beamed at Mrs. Kang.

"Aigoo, even her English is so good! Dave, you need to take Korean lessons again. She speaks both so fluently." Mrs. Kang went back into the kitchen and reemerged with a tray full of food. "Jisu-ya, why don't you teach my son Korean? I'll feed you and pay you."

"Mom," Dave said, sounding exasperated. He covered his face with his hand. Jisu couldn't help but laugh. "By the way, I ordered myself a pizza."

"Aigoo, Dave!" Mrs. Kang smacked her son on the shoulder. "Sometimes I wonder if I really gave birth to a Korean or not."

Jisu ate a warm spoonful of the namul bap. It was the perfect bite with the right amount of rice, spinach, nameul and sesame oil. "This is so delicious," Jisu said in Korean, much to Mrs. Kang's delight.

The bell rang and Dave went to get the door.

"It's so nice to have a Korean girl around the house. You

know, Sophie only recently came around to trying kimchi," Mrs. Kang said. "I don't think she even likes it."

Dave returned to the living room, the pizza box open in one hand and a slice already half eaten in the other.

"Dave, have some manners! We have a guest," Mrs. Kang scolded her son. "I'm going to leave a plate of namul bap on the kitchen counter in case you're still hungry, okay?"

"Thank you, Mom." Dave gave his mother a hug, with pizza slice still in his hand. He towered over her tiny frame. She hugged him back and then hurried out of the room.

"She can be a lot, I know," Dave said to Jisu as he sat back down at the table.

"No, I love your mom! She's so sweet," Jisu said and she meant it. It was so nice to be taken care of by an overly caring ajumma. It was a different kind of care from what Linda showed her family. Jisu knew Linda loved Jeff and Mandy, but it was different from the overflowing warmth that Mrs. Kang had.

Dave grabbed his notebook from his backpack and placed the assignment sheet on the table.

"Before we get into this, I just want to apologize for the other day at El Farolito—"

"Dave, don't worry about it. Really. It's all good," Jisu said, hoping they could quickly move on to the actual task at hand.

"No, I want you to know that I didn't mean what I said in a mean way. I consider you a friend, and I was just looking out. Not that you need looking out for, but—"

"Dave." Jisu pointed her spoon at him. "Your mom is feeding me the best Korean food I've had in weeks. We're cool."

"All right, Jees. All right." Dave laughed, and Jisu didn't mind the nickname this time. No wonder everyone in their class liked him. He was actually a really nice dude. He didn't *have* to apologize—if anything, Jisu should've been the one to say sorry for overreacting.

One large pizza and two bowls of namul bap later, Jisu and Dave were still at square one with zero good ideas. Their assigned topic was "encouraging and increasing political involvement among the general public." And it had to be somehow tied to their motto: Head, Hands and Heart. It could be anything, and it could be nothing. They were stumped.

"Maybe we should go for a walk," Dave suggested. "I've heard that walking helps clear your mind."

"Okay, good, because I'm *so* full. I need to move around."

They walked from Dave's house to Bernal Heights Park, where they wandered around the fields. They stopped to pet every other dog that was being taken for its evening stroll. They followed a trail up a large hill. By the time they got to the top, the sun was starting to go down, and they still hadn't come up with a good plan for the project.

"You haven't been to this park yet, have you?" Dave asked. "This is supposed to be the main attraction." He led her to a tree at the top of the hill. A wooden swing hung off a large branch.

"A swing!" Jisu ran over and hopped on.

"I knew you'd like it."

Jisu kicked her legs into the air. "Okay, so our ideas so far are—"

"They're terrible, Jees. Our ideas so far are terrible." Dave leaned against the tree and sighed. Jisu kicked a little harder and pushed herself higher each time.

"What about following around a local politician? Making a guerrilla-style documentary?" she asked, pumping her feet and swinging farther out. It felt like she could jump off the swing, flap her arms and fly over the city like a bird.

"No, that narrows it down to one aspect of local politics. And our focus is grassroots, not necessarily the local political scene. That takes the international part out of it. It needs to be broader."

Jisu could tell that Dave was deep in thought. He slightly tilted his head when he concentrated, she'd noticed. He narrowed his eyes like he was trying to get a lens to focus.

The sun disappeared into the horizon and the blue of the sky deepened. Jisu let the swing slow down. They hadn't cracked the project, but they had made an earnest effort. A few bad ideas would inevitably lead to a good one.

"Dave, I don't think I can do any more brainstorming." She hopped off the swing and leaned on the tree next to him. She felt light-headed—it was probably from swaying back and forth on the swing so much.

"Let me walk you home."

He didn't have to. Jisu knew her way back, and the Murrays weren't that far from the park. But she didn't protest. It was nice to have someone walk next to you. The streetlights turned on one by one as they made their way toward the Murrays' house. Jisu wondered how they looked together walking down the street as the day slowly turned to night.

When they got to the Murrays', Jisu and Dave hugged each other goodbye.

"Thanks a lot for today," Jisu said.

"It was nothing! And my mom can be a bit much—she loves having people over and can overwhelm them—so thanks for being a good sport about that." Dave rubbed the back of his neck and looked down at his feet, seeming a bit embarrassed.

"Not at all! I'm so happy I met her. Really. And all that food. I've been so homesick and I think she helped ease some of that."

"Well, that's good! I should probably head back. My mom's probably going to start worrying and blow up my phone."

"Today was fun." Jisu smiled at Dave. "And productive."

"It was fun. Have a good night, Jees." Dave walked down the driveway onto the street and waved. "See you at school!"

Jisu sat at her desk to keep brainstorming. Her journal was open where she'd left it last, when she was scribbling down her scattered thoughts after spending the day surfing with Austin.

Picks you up and drops you off without asking

Introduces you to new things

Looks out for you

Introduces you to his friends and family

These were bullet points from that silly magazine quiz that Mandy had left in her room. Jisu remembered Austin basking in that afternoon sunlight, his long black hair still wet from the ocean. The more time they spent together, alone, the more she liked him. But did he like her?

And then there was Dave. Her schoolmate, class partner and friend. In that order. But a lot of the bullet points she'd checked off for Austin also applied to Dave.

Jisu stopped herself. Why was she comparing Austin to Dave? She was actually into Austin. He was carefree and living his best life. Dave was more serious. Jisu wanted to see Austin again and again. She would be fine if she never saw Dave outside of Wick. No, if anything, this was a sign that she should be more forward with Austin, *especially* if things between them were on the same level as her whatever friendship with Dave.

Why am I thinking about a stupid dating quiz? Why am I so caught up about any of this? Why was her mind so much clearer when she was knocking out several seons per week, but now that she had a break from Ms. Moon, all she could think about were boys? No, just one boy. Singular. Austin was the one who preoccupied her thoughts.

Jisu could hear the faint noise of a TV show through the wall. Mandy was probably catching up on *Riverdale* on her iPad. On her way up to her room, she had seen Jeff in his study, talking into his Bluetooth and gesticulating wildly. He was probably on a conference call. And when she'd walked past the living room, Linda had been reading a book and chomping away at a handful of celery and carrot sticks—she was on a new diet. Jisu had been to Dave's for the first time today and met Mrs. Kang merely hours ago, but the Kang household felt more like home than the Murrays' did.

Jisu Kim, she said to herself. *Focus. Stop thinking about Austin. Stop thinking about Dave.* She was homesick, and some parts of Dave's life reminded her of home. That was why she liked him, why today had been so nice, even if they hadn't gotten far with their project. Plus, she couldn't actually *like* him. He had a girlfriend. Sophie. Simple Sophie. *A really boring girlfriend who doesn't even like kimchi. Oh, Dave. How could you bring a girl home to your mom if she doesn't like kimchi?*

DATE NO. 11

NAME: **Oh Minho**

INTERESTS:
Broadway Shows, Baseball, Sneakers

DISLIKES:
Chemistry Class, Flakes, Heights

JISU: What's the best thing that happened to you this year?

MINHO: I saw *Hamilton*! I have cousins who live in New York and I went to visit them during spring break. It was around my birthday, so they surprised me with tickets.

JISU: That's amazing. I've been listening to the soundtrack. I haven't seen it yet, but I'm obsessed.

MINHO: I mean, how could you not? The story is so good, the cast is amazing, everyone has such an amazing voice.

JISU: Which one is your favorite?

MINHO: Wow, that's hard. That's like asking a mother to choose her favorite child. I love them all equally.

JISU: Okay, but if you had to narrow it down.

MINHO: Hmm. I like "My Shot" and "The Schuyler Sisters." I also really like "It's Quiet Uptown." God. I cried my eyes out when they did that one.

JISU: I know! Poor Philip.

MINHO: "Philip, you would like it uptown, it's quiet uptown."

JISU: Oh, my god, you're going to make me cry. That song is so sad.

MINHO: I absolutely bawled my eyes out when they sang it.

JISU: I know! Just listening to the soundtrack is a whole roller coaster of emotions for me. I can't imagine what it was like seeing the actual thing.

MINHO: Jisu, you *have* to go. It will change your life.

JISU: Do you like any other Broadway shows?

MINHO: Like them? I'm kind of obsessed with theater. Not that I want to act in any way. I just love musicals.

JISU: Do you want to work in the theater otherwise?

MINHO: I actually really like set design. And costumes.

JISU: Why?

MINHO: You know why…

JISU: Why?

MINHO: Jisu, I'm gay. Can you really not tell?

JISU: Well, I never want to assume and wouldn't in this case just because you like theater. Anyone can like theater.

MINHO: Well, I do play up the "I love theater soo much," because I sort of do want people to know right away. And what could be more stereotypical than that? But guess what else I like? Baseball! But apparently that doesn't fit the part.

JISU: What do you mean?

MINHO: One time, I went on a seon with a girl who was born in Philadelphia and moved to Seoul later, so naturally I brought up Kim Hyunsoo and how great I thought he was. And at the end of the date, when I really had to spell it out for her, she didn't believe me and cited my interest in baseball.

JISU: Yikes.

MINHO: Yikes is right. It's honestly shocking how small someone's brain can be.

JISU: So, I assume we're on this seon because your parents don't know?

MINHO: Yeah…but you know what, I've met and made some really good friends through the seons.

JISU: Are there any girls who didn't realize?

MINHO: Oh, yeah, there are some truly clueless ones. One girl kept following up with me weeks after we met. She put me in a tough spot! I had to figure out how to let her down nicely without embarrassing her. It made me wonder if I was really giving off a masc vibe.

JISU: Would coming out to your parents be difficult for you?

MINHO: It wouldn't be difficult for me at all. But it might be for them. I'm their first kid. I'm the only boy in the family. They do everything for me—they're even supportive of my dreams to work in set design. Honestly, they must know.

JISU: But you can't be happy if you don't tell them and live honestly as who you really are.

MINHO: I know, I know. It just almost feels selfish. Selfish for me to do that at the expense of shattering the illusion of their nice, straight son, who goes on dates with girls.

JISU: Who says they won't like you the way you are? You're still the same person you always were.

MINHO: It's so much more complicated. Because I'm not really in the closet among my friends or anything. It's a self-preservation thing.

JISU: Minho. I think you're a great person. And I think your parents will love you no matter what and, deep down, they'd want their son to be happy. Isn't that what all our parents want? Even if they send us out to these crazy seons, hoping some of us will hit it off with an eligible, wealthy, Ivy-bound kid. In the end, it's not really about that shallow stuff—they just want peace of mind and to know that when they're no longer around, their kids will be okay and happy.

MINHO: Damn, Jisu. Way to drop that on my head. You must be really close with your parents.

JISU: What do you mean?

MINHO: From what you're saying, it sounds like you guys are really tight.

JISU: Close enough. Everyone has one issue or another with their parents. Mine are just always on me about schoolwork and making sure I get into a good college. I don't think they really care what I study once I actually get to college.

MINHO: So tell them that!

JISU: Tell them what?

MINHO: That you feel like they're suffocating you!

JISU: Nah. Then they'll just say, "Well, what exactly is it that you want to do?" And I don't even have an answer for that, because I'm seventeen and what teenager knows what the rest of her life should be like at age seventeen?

MINHO: I think that is exactly what you should tell them. It's what you would tell me to do, right?

JISU: That's fair, I guess.

MINHO: I hope one day we'll run into each other on the street.

Me, a proud gay man, completely out of the closet, and you, a confident professional in whatever field you are actually passionate about.

JISU: That does sound nice. I want that, too.

12

*H*iba walked just as fast as she talked, if not faster. This was the second time today already that Jisu had nearly lost sight of her friend. At Pier 39, two kids were giggling and pointing at the famous sea lions that lazed in the sun on docks just below the piers. Jisu crouched low at the right angle to frame the image, mimicking the seasoned street photographers she watched on YouTube and Instagram. She wanted to get the perfect shot of the children's unadulterated amusement. Jisu snapped away until she realized Hiba was no longer standing next to her.

They were both members of Wick's photography club. The actual club itself didn't meet more than once every three weeks. It was mostly about the different photography challenges assigned at each meeting and the final art show and contest at the end of each year. Hiba and Jisu had decided to spend the day walking around North Beach, capturing whatever stood out and sparked inspiration. They had made a deal: Hiba would show Jisu around the city, and Jisu would teach her how to do more than simply point and shoot. Hiba rapidly learned the basics of photography, but Jisu didn't catch on to the street names as quickly.

Jisu scanned the crowds, growing slightly more frantic with each passing second. If she ended up missing and her dead body washed up a week later somewhere next to a confused sea lion, it would all be Hiba's fault. She was close to giving up and redirecting her attention to figuring out how to take the BART home when she spotted Hiba's pale blue hijab. She was back by the Pier entrance. Thank goodness Hiba had a penchant for bright, pretty colors. It made her easy to spot.

"Hiba!" Jisu yelled. "You totally abandoned me!"

"Oh, sorry!" Hiba said, but didn't look at all worried. She smiled apologetically, but also as if to say, *Calm down, I've been here the whole time.* "I'll buy you the best tiramisu you've ever had to make up for it?"

"Hmm." Jisu took her time pretending she was still upset. "Okay, I guess that would do it."

Stella Bakery was only a ten-minute walk from the Pier, but between wandering into the City Lights Bookstore, where Jisu listened intently to every bit of literary history about Kerouac that Hiba dropped, and stopping every few feet to take more photos of the sky, the buildings and the pedestrians, the two of them wound up at the bakery nearly an hour later.

Jisu took a bite of the tiramisu. The rich coffee and cocoa flavors seeped from the sponge straight into her taste buds. It was heavenly. Hiba sat across from her, a knowing smile stretching across her face.

"I'm so glad we did this," Hiba said. "I couldn't spend another Saturday on college apps."

"I know," Jisu groaned. The thought capping off a perfect day by going back home to incomplete college applications made Jisu want to scream. Even though she knew Hiba had to be so much more prepared than she was. For Hiba, the remaining work was probably just a matter of filling out forms. Aside from Mrs. Kim's top Ivy League choices—Harvard because it was number one and then Princeton simply because it was just as good, and also because both their mascot and the national animal of South Korea was a tiger—Jisu hadn't even narrowed down her college selections. And this was just for the American colleges. She was also working on her Korean applications simultaneously. She knew deep down her parents ideally wanted her to stay in the country and go to Seoul National University, where they met as two young, bright scholars. The incomplete applications nagged at Jisu, but for once she didn't regret setting herself free from the shackles of school. She would not feel guilty for putting herself first.

"Oh, my god," Hiba gasped.

"What?"

"How did your post already get more than a hundred likes?" Hiba held her phone to Jisu's face. It was her post of the kids marveling at the sea lions. Jisu had uploaded it to Instagram no more than fifteen minutes ago.

"Wait, you have over two thousand followers. How?" Hiba asked.

"I think half of them are bots?" Jisu said. "Also, it's not that big a deal unless you have at least ten thousand followers, I think."

She thought briefly about her seon with Sejun the narcissist. The only good thing that had come out of that date was the boost in her followers. She wondered if those headshots she had taken of him served him well.

"Okay, I can see why you have so many followers." Hiba scrolled down Jisu's feed. "Everything looks so...polished. And professional. What app do you use to edit?"

"I just use VSCO and play around with their editing tools.

If I'm really serious about it, I'll actually use Lightroom on my laptop, save the photo, email it to myself, download it onto my phone and then post it onto Instagram."

"Okay, you need to teach me all that." Hiba looked up at Jisu. "Are you applying to any art schools?"

Maybe it was because her parents were always adamant about Jisu not spending too much time with her cameras, but the thought hadn't even occurred to her. All her knowledge was gained through trial and error and YouTube tutorials. Photography was a hobby, like watching makeup vlogs, playing intramural volleyball or catching up on *Riverdale* with friends and a big bowl of popcorn.

Art school was for kids who sketched all the time in class. The painters, sculptors, even the graphic designers who spent their whole day in the computer lab. But Jisu and photography? She flipped through the photos she had spent all day taking. She knew she had a good eye and a knack for this, but just because you were good at something and enjoyed it didn't mean you had to dedicate your whole life to it.

"But just because you're good at something doesn't mean you have to major in it," Hiba backtracked, sensing an identity crisis about to unfold before her.

"I'm afraid I'll start disliking photography if I take it seriously." Jisu stirred her iced coffee with a straw. "But whenever someone asks me what I want to major in in college, I have no idea what to tell them."

"My sister changed her major three times before she declared one in her sophomore year in college. Just start with what you like. What are you good at?"

It was such a simple question. Jisu looked around the café. An elderly couple gingerly walked up to the counter. They held hands as they perused the pastry case. In front of them, a woman signed a receipt and accepted a large box of cookies. Her toddler son held her hand and gnawed away at a sugar cookie the size of his face. The lady behind the counter expertly boxed up a large cake with quick precision, while taking an order on the phone.

"I like people," Jisu said. "I like watching them, capturing them on camera."

"You're also kind of a social butterfly."

"A what?" Jisu was fluent in English, but the idioms always caught her off guard.

"Social butterfly. You know, you like to socialize and be around people. You pretty much befriended half the class in your first week at Wick." Hiba thought for a moment. "Maybe you could work in hospitality or open a restaurant. Or a gallery! A gallery that displays works of the coolest photographers, you included."

They were all real viable jobs and careers—Jisu had just never thought of them in relation to herself. She could imagine herself walking around a gallery, checking in on the staff and the guests, ensuring everything was working well, like a puppet master pulling each string with precision. Curating select pieces and coordinating their placement in a space.

Suddenly the openness of college no longer seemed as daunting and vast as it always had.

"I bet you could even run a nice café like Stella," Hiba said. "But I bet it would be more polished than this. Ooh, and you would have your photographs and other artwork hanging on the walls. But it wouldn't be like the cheesy art that they put up at Starbucks. Basically, you're a visual learner."

"Hibaaaa." Jisu gave her friend a hug and squeezed her tightly. "You really think I'm too good for Starbucks?" The girls laughed.

Good friends gave good pep talks. Jisu was pretty sure nobody their age (not even Hiba) actually knew what the hell they were doing. But it was nice to support and cheer each other along, even though deep down inside she was pretty sure everyone was terrified about how to approach the future.

Despite being tired from walking around all day, as soon as she got back to the Murrays', Jisu uploaded all her photos onto her laptop and started to edit them. Hiba had been like her personal life coach today and sparked something in her. Now, each edit and change she made to enhance the photos felt so much more significant. She *did* have a knack for this. It *was* more than just a hobby. Jisu looked at her Instagram page with new eyes. Maybe there was a way to incorporate her feed into her college applications. But would they care about any of this? Did Ivy League schools actually want visual learners?

Jisu opened Kakao and sent a sampling of her photos from the day to her grandfather.

Hi, Haraboji! As promised, here are some more photos. I walked around San Francisco with my friend Hiba and took these.

Jisu went back to Instagram to check her notifications. The sea lions post was still gaining a steady amount of likes. There were a lot on a photo of a hostess standing outside an Italian restaurant, frantically—and somewhat desperately—waving around menus to attract diners. But the post of two men posing for their engagement photos had gotten three times more likes than the other photos. She checked the Pier 39 geotag and the hashtag #loveislove, and her photo showed up as the top image for both.

Jisu's phone vibrated—there was a Kakao notification. Haraboji had already seen the photos and replied back.

Wow, Jisu! Who knew my granddaughter had such a great eye! Haraboji is very proud!

The message was accompanied by five thumbs-up emojis. For an old man well into his eighties, Haraboji's style of texting was akin to a teenager's: more is more. Jisu smiled. Every bit of affirmation from her grandfather left her feeling a little bigger, a little stronger. Like a spring bud being encouraged to bloom. When she first expressed interest in photography, her parents simply nodded their heads. Haraboji was the one who gave Jisu her first camera.

Visiting Haraboji had been as easy as hopping on a bus and riding it for three stops. Who was making sure he was watering his houseplants now? Surely Mr. Kim was still visiting his father regularly, but Jisu wished for a bus that would take her from the Bay Area to her grandfather's apartment. At least she could stay in contact with him through Kakao. Surviving here would be difficult without his encouragement. How did anyone survive without their phones?

Jisu checked Instagram again. In the comments section, Min had added several emojis. Euni had also chimed in.

Amazing shot, Jisu!

Hiba had also commented five minutes ago.

Luv this and u so much!

Aside from the occasional bigot and troll, people—both friends and random internet strangers—were gushing about the soon-to-be wed couple in both Korean and English. It was bizarre and oddly uplifting to see strangers from two different continents converge in Jisu's corner of the internet.

And then it hit her. Jisu scrolled through her photos to find the one. There it was. It was a candid of Hiba looking up at the Japanese Consulate building. All the consulate buildings of various countries were within walking distance from the

North Beach neighborhood. Whenever they'd walked past one, Hiba had pointed out the flag waving outside the building: Switzerland, Japan, Mexico, Sweden, France, Indonesia, Brazil. Jisu closed Instagram and called Dave.

"'Sup, Jees?"

That stupid nickname was starting to grow on her.

"I figured it out."

"Figured what out?"

"Our IS project."

"Oh, word? What's your idea?"

"Go on my Instagram page. The latest post. It's blowing up."

"Did you just call me to impress me with your professional IG feed?"

"No, Dave," Jisu said sternly. "Just let me get to my point."

"Okay, okay. I'm listening, Jees."

"I've never gotten this many likes on a post. I've also never posted anything as overtly political."

"All right. I still don't see where this is going—"

"I looked up the geotags for all the different consulates around North Beach. Sweden, Switzerland, Brazil. Some of them have tagged photos from different cultural holidays, others from parades. Then I thought, what if we mine all this data from Instagram to track how social media—"

"How social media can impact political efforts?" Dave finished her thought. Normally this would annoy Jisu, but today she was relieved that he understood the concept. After weeks, they finally had a good idea. And it seemed like it was going to stick.

"That's a really good idea," Dave said. He sat quiet for a minute. Jisu could sense him thinking the concept through. She imagined him sitting in his room, deep in thought, tilting his head to the side. "And we can use it for any location. Polling booths, courthouses, city hall. This is really smart."

"Some of the art galleries on Mission Street are showing political art. I'm sure they do events there that could get tagged."

"That, too! I think you just saved our project. Mrs. French is gonna love this," Dave said. "I'm glad I got paired up with you."

"Thanks, Dave." Jisu smiled. A little too hard. She pulled at her cheek to stop herself from smiling. *Why do I care what Dave thinks?* She was just glad she hadn't told Dave about the idea in person. Then he would've seen how his compliments had her smiling like an idiot.

DATE NO. 12

NAME: **Lee Eunsong**

ACCOMPLISHMENTS:
Solo Violin Performance at Carnegie Hall

DISLIKES:
Crowds, Skiing, Lizards

JISU: Did you really have a solo performance at Carnegie Hall?

EUNSONG: Yeah, it was a few years ago. Ms. Moon really likes to flash that fact around when she sets me up on these seons.

JISU: What do you play?

EUNSONG: The violin. Been playing since I was five. Most five-year-olds can't even hold a fork the right way at five. But me? I was just starting to perfect my bow grip.

JISU: That's impressive! What did you perform?

EUNSONG: *Scottish Fantasy* by Max Bruch and Mendelssohn's *Violin Concerto.*

JISU: I'm going to be honest, I don't know either of those pieces. Although I do recognize the composers' names.

EUNSONG: That's fine. No one really knows the solo stuff unless it's super famous. Everyone just sort of recognizes one of the Beethoven symphonies.

JISU: Carnegie Hall though. That must have been like a real dream come true.

EUNSONG: For the first time, it really was! You know I've performed there close to five times now, right? Not all solo performances, but I've gotten pretty well acquainted with it.

EUNSONG: Did you know that people used to live in Carnegie Hall? They ousted the final tenants, but there were these artists that used to live there. It's incredible. I wish I was born earlier so I could do that.

JISU: That sounds amazing. I've never been to Carnegie Hall. I visited NYC once when I was a child, and I think we even walked past the hall, but I've never been inside.

EUNSONG: They have a man-operated elevator that takes you to the balcony seats. There are so few of those kinds of elevators left. It's kinda neat.

JISU: Is that your favorite performance hall?

EUNSONG: I don't know actually. It's so hard to choose. Maybe because it's older, but something about Carnegie feels more intimate compared to a place like Avery Fisher.

JISU: Which one's that?

EUNSONG: It's where the New York Philharmonic plays in Lincoln Center. It's actually called David Geffen Hall now, but it was Avery Fisher for like years before they sold the name to some other billionaire. Honestly, it'll always be Avery Fisher to me.

JISU: Have you performed there?

EUNSONG: No, but I will one day, I'm sure.

JISU: You seem very confident.

EUNSONG: Usually, if I put my head into it, I'll get it done.

JISU: Just like that.

EUNSONG: Google Science Fair. I'm not even a huge science nerd. I just had this one good idea and I thought—how can I make good use out of this? It was a proposal on more effective ways to recycle. I submitted it and then boom—first place. First place in the world.

JISU: That's great! Good for you.

EUNSONG: One time, my little sister entered me into a really competitive painting contest. I think she just wanted to see me lose for once.

JISU: Let me guess. You won that, too?

EUNSONG: No, I came in runner-up. But there was no way

I should've done well. There were a bunch of art school kids that didn't even place in the top three. Anyway, my sister was annoyed. But it really wasn't bad!

JISU: What did your piece look like?

EUNSONG: Well, I've only ever taken a few basic art classes. So I decided to throw a swath of colors onto a canvas and call it abstract. The judges praised my use of color and said I had a great eye. You can't teach an artist to have a good instinct with colors. So I don't feel like a complete fraud.

JISU: Is there ever a time when you do feel like a fraud?

EUNSONG: Hmm. Actually, you know what, probably not.

JISU: Yeah, that's what I thought.

13

Jisu's only plans for the day were to sleep in and continue chipping away at her college applications, but she woke up early, still buzzing with excitement after her call with Dave.

I'm glad I got paired up with you.

No, it was the fact that she finally figured out their IS project. The excitement had nothing to do with Dave.

But the words lingered in Jisu's mind.

She splashed cold water onto her face to shake off her slumber. Of course he should be glad to be paired up with her— she had just saved them from getting an incomplete in the class! They did make a good pair. Dave would sit back and let Jisu freely think things out loud. But he was resourceful, too. Right after they'd hung up, he'd sent an email dividing up the workload so they could get right to it. They were a good duo. A good *working* duo.

Jisu's phone rang. *Call from: Umma.* They had just spoken

the day before yesterday. Her mother had to know it was early Saturday morning in San Francisco. What did she want?

"Hello?"

"Jisu! Good morning. My daughter is up already. I didn't wake you, did I?" Mrs. Kim sounded awfully chipper.

"No, Umma. I'm actually doing some work."

"Not editing photos, I hope?"

Jisu rolled her eyes. "I'm working on a school project."

"Are you behind? Do you need another tutor?"

Jisu briefly muted her phone to let out a groan. She kicked her legs underneath her duvet cover and eventually rolled herself up. Jisu was still half asleep, but fully annoyed.

"Hello? Jisu? Are you there?"

She had woken up in a great mood, ready to spring into action. Why hadn't she just let the call go to voice mail?

"No, Umma, I'm actually on track. It's a class that I really like, international studies. The teacher, Mrs. French, is—"

"That all sounds nice and well, Jisu. Oh, your Haraboji showed me your photos of the Golden Gate. Why didn't you send those to me and Appa also?"

Lately, Jisu had been sending more photos to her grandfather than to her parents. The more photos she sent to her parents, the more likely they'd criticize her for spending too much time wandering the streets of San Francisco. But her grandfather would never. Haraboji's eyesight hadn't been good in ages, but he always demanded to see more. In the last few email exchanges, he even offered his own critique and made suggestions on lighting and composition where he could. Regardless of how well Haraboji could look at her photos, he saw Jisu's vision and inspiration in each one better than her parents could.

"Your father and I are dying to see photos of our Jisu! Make sure you send them to us also, okay?" Mrs. Kim sounded a little too at ease. It was late in Seoul. She was probably getting ready for bed and feeling relaxed after book club. Ajummas only ever drank wine and gossiped at those biweekly meetings. "Jisu, I really do think they look great. I'm glad you're getting to see the city, too."

"Okay, next time I'll send you some photos, too." The tenderness in her mother's voice was comforting, albeit slightly suspicious. As long as they weren't talking about academics and college applications, Jisu and her mother got along just fine. And distance did make the heart grow fonder.

Distance had also granted Jisu an independence she'd never dreamed of.

The pressure to get into an Ivy League school would always be there, but her parents were no longer breathing down her back. It was like her wings had been tied her whole life and she was just getting to use them. None of this was at the expense of any academic merit either. The workload at Wick was more manageable. And being able to make time for photography, new friends and even Austin—doing what she liked in between fulfilling her academic duties—in a sense helped her do better at school. Appa was right, a school that gave her a bit of breathing room made all the difference.

"It seems like you're settling well into school, which is great," Mrs. Kim said. Jisu held on to these words and etched them into her memory.

"Thanks, Umma. I think I'm actually happy at Wick. Sometimes I get really homesick, but I'm making new friends, the Murrays are nice—"

"Well, now that you are settled in and have a good grasp on schoolwork, I think we can resume the seons."

Of course. Of course the initial pleasantries were leading up to this. Jisu clenched her fist.

"Umma, I can't. I'm focusing on schoolwork. You can't expect me to go on dates if you want me to get into Harvard. At least, not until I get all my college applications out," Jisu said. She thought about how she had spent a whole afternoon at Pacifica with Austin. She hadn't heard from him since. It had been almost two weeks. Why hadn't he at least texted her?

"We have to always be prepared, Jisu." Mrs. Kim spoke with that condescending tone that drove Jisu mad. "In case you aren't accepted to a reputable—"

"I am not a terrible student. It's not like I won't get into any college. You're acting like no one will accept me." A fiery ball of anger rolled up her throat. "But I won't fail. I can't, because I *am* actually a good student. And no matter what happens, I'm doing my best and will go wherever that takes me, Ivy or not."

Hot tears dripped down her face. Jisu cleared her throat. She didn't want her mother to know she was crying. "If you're going to spend so much time and energy investing in my future, shouldn't you at least have a little faith in your own daughter?"

This anger always lived inside Jisu, but she had made sure to keep it dormant. Each time the frustration and resentment threatened to crawl out of her throat, she swallowed it back down. She had always been obedient. Maybe it was the time difference or the actual physical distance, but the anger managed to push through this time.

Mrs. Kim was silent. Jisu wondered if her mother, baffled by her audacity, had hung up on her.

They stood at either end of the line, waiting for the other to break the silence first.

"One month." Her mother finally spoke. "You've only been there a month and you're already acting like an American. All this talk of trying your best and settling for wherever that takes you." Mrs. Kim let out a deep sigh. Jisu could see her sitting in their dining room, frowning and rubbing her temples. "I know I didn't raise a daughter who would be so naive to think that her parents are making all these sacrifices for anyone but her."

"I never said that, Umma. I'm simply saying that all this pressure you're putting on me can backfire—"

"I heard what you said. The seons can resume after you've gotten all your applications in. Rest assured, they will continue."

Jisu hung up the phone and accepted her fate. It was a compromise, something that rarely happened with her mother, but she still felt like she'd lost.

Her morning—no, the entire day—was soured. It was like the universe had given her a break and a small streak of happiness only to stab her in the back. Again.

The call had knocked the wind out of her. Jisu looked at Dave's email. The project outline, which was inspiring in all its organized glory just this morning, now felt daunting and burdensome. What was the point in trying, in going the extra mile, if no one—especially not her mother—was going to recognize it?

At the end of the day, Jisu was her parents' puppet. She would give them a 4.0 GPA, she would faithfully attend all the seons and settle for the least offensive date, and she would live the life that they picked out for her. If this was her destiny no matter what, what was the point in being the good girl when she was thousands of miles from home?

Jisu opened the last text message from Austin. They had exchanged photos they'd taken of each other at Pacifica. They'd had zero communication since. Didn't he want to see her again?

That day was a little over a week ago, but the freedom and happiness she'd felt then seemed years away. What would happen between them once the seons resumed? Was there even anything there? It didn't matter if there was something. Because the moment Jisu submitted her last college application,

Ms. Moon would reenter her life. Jisu's fate was sealed. So until she was forced to reckon with it, she was going to do whatever she wanted and live for the one person she never prioritized: herself.

Austin! When are we going to hang out again?

She hit Send and waited. A few seconds later, her phone dinged, and Jisu smiled.

AUGUST 16, SUMMER BREAK

DATE NO. 13

NAME: **Cho Sungbaek**

INTERESTS:
Genetics, German Club, Bicycling

DISLIKES:
Conformity, Jell-O, Cold Tofu

SUNGBAEK: You'll never guess where I was just twenty-four hours ago.

JISU: Where?

SUNGBAEK: Berlin.

JISU: Oh, wow! And now you're here. What were you doing in Berlin?

SUNGBAEK: Well, I've been learning German since I was in elementary school and I'm pretty much fluent and I've always wanted to go.

JISU: Nice. Was it a solo trip?

SUNGBAEK: Oh, no. I went with one of my best friends, Stella.

JISU: Just the two of you?

SUNGBAEK: Yeah, we've known each other since we were kids. Our families used to go on vacations together. But now that everyone's busy—and who wants to vacation with their parents anyway—we try to do a trip every now and then.

JISU: Oh…okay. My best friend Eunice and I still go on trips with our parents. I'm not gonna lie, it's really nice that we don't have to worry about booking anything or setting up an itinerary.

SUNGBAEK: Oh, Stella and I never actually do that on our own. We use a travel agency that does everything. Do your parents really book and organize everything on their own? They must be very particular.

JISU: No, they just don't mind doing it. My mom is generally a very organized person, so she would do it better than a travel agent, honestly.

SUNGBAEK: Yeah, it's awful when they mess things up. Because it's either perfect and the trip goes without a hitch, or there's one disastrous mistake that ruins everything.

JISU: Everything?

SUNGBAEK: Yes, everything. One time they somehow put me and Stella on two different connecting flights, even though we had the same outbound flight. This was on our trip to Spain. So poor Stella lands in Barcelona and has to wait an extra two hours for me to show up. Meanwhile, I was still waiting for my layover in Amsterdam to take off.

JISU: Couldn't she just go straight to the hotel?

SUNGBAEK: They booked the hotel under my name. Not hers. And of course we landed at dawn, so it's not like a quick phone call from the agency could fix it.

JISU: That's really nice of her to wait. I probably would've ditched you and found a different hotel and some new friends.

SUNGBAEK: It was nice of her! She's a dear friend. And I would've done the same thing if she were the one getting in late.

JISU: So, what do you do aside from traveling?

SUNGBAEK: Well, I like to bike. I'm actually quite serious about it. Not just an easy ride through the park on Sunday afternoons.

JISU: Are you a competitive biker?

SUNGBAEK: No, but actually, Stella has been pushing me to get into it. She's been nagging about it for months, talking about how it would make me happier, give me a sense of purpose and whatnot.

JISU: Wow, sounds like you and Stella are inseparable.

SUNGBAEK: I mean, when it comes to these things, she really is one of just a few people who know me better than myself.

JISU: And who would those other people be?

SUNGBAEK: My mom, my dad, my two younger brothers, my dog…and yeah, that's it. And Stella.

JISU: She sounds like a lovely girl.

SUNGBAEK: She is! Smart, funny, good with the elders. You should meet her. You probably will meet her if this goes anywhere, to be honest. She'll be my best man at my wedding, and at her wedding, I'll be her maid of honor.

JISU: Reaaaallly?

SUNGBAEK: Yeah. We also joke that if we hit thirty-five and still haven't gotten married, we're going to—

JISU: Marry each other? Like a good old-fashioned rom-com?

SUNGBAEK: What? No, we joke that we're going to kill each other to end our sad single misery. A joke, of course. Everyone's so obsessed, not just with getting married, but marrying the right person.

JISU: Hmm.

SUNGBAEK: Sorry, it's probably a bad move to even bring up the topic of marriage on a first date.

JISU: No, that's totally fine. Although, to be honest, I don't think Stella would be so thrilled to meet me, or to meet any of your dates for that matter.

SUNGBAEK: Why wouldn't she? You know, she's also a client of Ms. Moon's and goes on seons, too. She signed up right after I did.

JISU: Okay, that's it.

SUNGBAEK: What? What's wrong?

JISU: Nothing's wrong. It's just probably totally not my place to be saying this, but—

SUNGBAEK: But?

JISU: Stella's in love with you. And you're in love with her.

SUNGBAEK: I'm sorry, what?

JISU: Childhood best friends, trips to Europe, "she knows me better than I do"—do I really have to spell it out for you?

SUNGBAEK: Oh, no, you don't understand. And you haven't even met Stella yet! If something were to happen, it would've happened ages ago. We're best friends, but that's all.

JISU: Exactly! The fact that you two are still somehow secretly in love with each other, even though it's within plain view of a stranger like me, is mind-boggling.

SUNGBAEK: Oh…

JISU: Have none of your friends brought this up before?

SUNGBAEK: No…not that I remember…

JISU: Hey, congrats to you, Sungbaek. You and Stella can get out of the seon scene and run off into the sunset.

SUNGBAEK: Oh…my god. I think…I think you're right.

JISU: Of course I'm right!

SUNGBAEK: I…need to go. Jisu, I'm sorry to cut this so short—

JISU: No need to apologize. Go, go! And invite me to the wedding!

14

Austin had instructed her to wear something comfortable. His specific words were, "Something loose, baggy and warm. The more you look like a hobo, the better."

Whatever he was planning, it was definitely nothing refined or romantic. Not that she wanted either of those things. Jisu had spent a whole summer trying to stay awake through "refined" and "romantic" first dates. But at least those things were clear indicators that you were actually on a date.

How was she supposed to look like a comfortable hobo and still look cute? Sweatpants and a cropped sweater? Leggings and a sweaterdress? She didn't want to look like she was trying too hard, but she cared what he thought. Jisu liked Austin, but she didn't know if he liked her the same. She couldn't show up in an outfit that screamed *Look at me—and only me!* Or maybe she could. Knowing that she would be put back on Ms. Moon's roster only made Jisu a lot more willing to shoot her shot with Austin. Still, she thought hanging out with him more would make everything easier, just as it would when hanging out with any other friend. But no, the more time Jisu spent alone with Austin, the more significant it felt. And her nerves multiplied each time. The clock was going to strike midnight no matter what—why not have fun at the ball while you were there?

Jisu checked Kakao. She had sent a mirror selfie of two potential outfits to Euni and Min, but the group chat was silent. The time difference had taken a toll on the girls' catch-up sessions. Everyone at Daewon was already sending out applications, so time was scarce for them all. Jisu wanted to tell them more about Wick-Helmering and Austin. But she didn't want to burden them with her stories if they were stressed.

Here. It was a text from Austin. For such a self-professed "spiritual" guy who liked to wax poetic at lunchtime, he was concise when he texted.

Jisu was now in outfit number three: black leggings and an oversize cable-knit sweater. *Whatever. This will have to do.* She grabbed her bag and quickly made her way to the door before Mandy could emerge from her room and interrogate her about her plans for the day.

"Okay, you have to tell me where we're going," Jisu said as she got into Austin's car.

"You'll find out when we get there." Austin grinned. Was she really not going to find out until they arrived? He was always keeping her on her toes.

They didn't talk much on the way to wherever it was they were going. But it didn't feel awkward. On the radio, contestants called in and answered random trivia questions to win a trip to Hawaii. Jisu and Austin laughed at the same funny moments. Neither of them felt the need to make conversation just to fill up the space between them. They were comfortable with each other's presence.

Austin pulled up to an ice rink, and Jisu felt a shot of confidence. All those amateur ice-skating lessons her mom had put her through were not for naught. If they couldn't catch the eye of a college admissions director, at the very least she could put them to use here and impress Austin.

"In the summertime, I give surfing lessons. And in the fall and winter, I teach kids how to skate," Austin explained as he handed Jisu a pair of rental skates. "You know how to skate? Or do you need me to teach you along with the rest of these kids?"

A table next to the rink was covered with a pink tablecloth and had an arrangement of purple paper plates, cups and napkins. Clusters of large, pastel-colored balloons were tied at both ends of the table. A banner that read HAPPY 8TH BIRTHDAY, GINA! hung above the table. The birthday cake hadn't been served yet, but candy had been put out and the eight-year-olds were already amped up on sugar. They were screaming and running around like tiny little demons while the parents stood in a corner, looking exhausted.

"Hi, I'm Gina's mom." One of the mothers approached Jisu and Austin. "You can teach them anything you want—leaps, twirls, whatever. You can even just have them skate around the rink. Just make sure they get so exhausted they all pass out when they get home. All the parents would be indebted to you."

"Not a problem." Austin smiled. "My friend Jisu is here to help me, so the kids will really get their energy out."

Friend. The word echoed in Jisu's mind. It *would* be weird for him to introduce Jisu as his date to this mom they'd just met. At her kid's party. Which was also his job.

"Great!" Gina's mother handed them two glittery party hats and promptly retreated to the parents' corner.

Austin stepped onto the rink and glided to the center. "Can everybody gather around?" he said and the children quickly skated toward him. Despite their intense sugar high, even the kids couldn't resist Austin's energy.

The two of them managed to maintain the children's attention long enough to teach them how to skate sideways, backward and even spin. Austin handled all of them with ease, even the ones who at first were too scared to let go of the rink walls. It was easy for him to gain a kid's trust. Jisu held hands with the kids, skated in circles and laughed with them. She felt like a little kid again. These hyperactive kids were lucky to have zero menacing thoughts about college hovering over them like a dark cloud.

"All right, everyone," Austin yelled over the giggling and shrieking. "Now let's see who can do the most laps around the rink."

The kids took off like a pack of wolves. Or more like a pack of wolf puppies that were still learning how to run properly, some of them toppling over each other. Jisu leaned against the ice-rink boards. She was exhausted. Austin skated up to her.

"This is the last and easiest part of the job," he said. "Where you just watch and let them tire themselves out."

Austin made silly faces at the kids and gave them an encouraging thumbs-up as they skated by. Something inside of Jisu melted. How did he even end up with these random odd jobs, teaching kids how to surf and skate? It was probably just another off-the-cuff decision. A classic Austin move, going wherever life led him, doing whatever he wanted.

She was nothing like him. Hitting up Austin to get together had been an impulsive move that was out of character for Jisu, but she was happy to be here with him. Even if they were kicking it with a dozen kids and their parents.

"Wanna get some real food?" Austin tossed his plate of cake into the trash bin. They had both consumed sweets all afternoon, and Jisu's head had started to ache.

"Yes." Jisu threw away her half-eaten slice of cake, too. "All this sugar is making my head throb."

"What are you in the mood for? Have anywhere in mind?"

"You pick. I'll go wherever," Jisu said. And she meant it. She liked it when Austin took the lead. She liked being in the passenger seat when he drove. It was nice to let someone like him take the wheel and just go along for the ride.

They ended up at Tito's Kitchen. Tito's was tucked between a sushi restaurant and a UPS shipping store. All of the best restaurants Jisu had been to since she'd arrived were located in the most inconspicuous spots. This was a good sign. The awning was simple, with TITO'S KITCHEN written in all caps in bright blue and red against a white backdrop. A golden yellow sun was painted between the words *Tito's* and *Kitchen*. A green neon light that spelled OPEN glowed in the window. Both sides of a long, verbose menu were taped below the neon sign.

"You ever hear about this place?" Austin asked.

"I haven't. Is that bad?" One of these days, Austin was going to ask her about a local restaurant, the latest indie movie or a B-list American pop star, and she was going to know what he was talking about. But today was not that day. She hadn't caught up on any of Austin's pop-culture assignments.

"I mean, it's only the first restaurant on the list I gave you of places to eat," he teased. Austin could list every restaurant in the Bay Area and ramble on about each one. Jisu would listen to all of it.

"If you ever hear anyone talk shit about Tito's, you need to tell me so I can set them straight," he said as he opened the restaurant door for her. Like a real gentleman. "My uncles run this restaurant. It's *literally* their kitchen."

The smell of garlic and pork hit Jisu as soon as she stepped in. They had arrived just as the dinner rush was ending. Only a handful of patrons were scattered throughout the room, most of them lingering over their last bites and asking for the check. A stout middle-aged man dressed in a button-down shirt, jacket and slacks leaned against the kitchen counter in the back and chatted away with the chef. The chef was taller and his long hair was tied back into a ponytail. They looked alike. You could tell by the way the chef moved around the kitchen that he was younger. The bell tied to the entrance door rang as Austin stepped inside behind Jisu. It was like a Pavlovian effect, the way the older man immediately straightened up and turned around to greet them. A look of recognition flashed in his eyes and he threw his hands up.

"Look who it is!"

"Hey, Tito Ron." Austin gave the man a hug. He looked to the chef in the kitchen. "Hi, Tito Jhun!"

"And who is this young lady?" Tito Ron asked.

"This is my friend Jisu. We just got back from teaching kids how to skate at the rink for a birthday party," Austin said.

Friend.

"Jhun!" Ron yelled. "You can whip something up for these two, yeah?"

"You got it, kuya!" Jhun shouted back.

"You guys came at the right time." Ron seated Jisu and Austin at a table by the kitchen. He pulled up a chair and sat next to Austin. "Tito Jhun and I were thinking about doing some karaoke in the back room after closing."

"Just the two of you?"

"We invited some of our buddies who are getting off work soon. But what's wrong with karaoke with two people anyway?"

"Nothing!" Austin laughed. "I think our family does karaoke more than the customers. Do people even know there's a room in the back?"

"Of course! They go crazy about it all over Yelp!" Ron turned to Jisu. "You ever do karaoke?"

"I actually used to go a lot with my family and friends back in Korea."

"Oh, you're Korean. You guys can give us a run for our money when it comes to karaoke. But nobody beats Filipinos." Tito Ron grinned. He and Austin shared the same playful, crooked smile. "After you eat, you two are joining us," he said definitively, as if they had no choice.

Of course they didn't have a choice.

Jhun soon appeared with heaps of food. Ron described each plate in detail—pancit, lumpias, pork adobo and spam fries—but Jisu was too busy taking bites of everything to pay full attention to the ingredient breakdown of each dish. Chasing hyperactive children around an ice rink all afternoon had left her famished.

This was her first time eating Filipino food, but there was a familiarity and close comfort in each spoonful of steamy garlic rice and each salty bite of pork.

Jisu and Austin nearly finished every plate of food, and she was ready to go home and pass out. There was no way she could participate, no less sit through, a round of karaoke. But Ron and Jhun were in the back room and already on their third song. Through the door, she could hear them belting the lyrics to "My Way" with a fervent passion.

"We can just ditch them," Austin said. He looked tired, too. "They won't care."

Even though Jisu was beat, a part of her did want to stay. They'd been generous to feed her enough to keep her full through the rest of the weekend. Jisu was also low-key curious to know if Austin could hold a note. She didn't want today to end just yet.

"Let's stay," she said. "I'm going to record you singing, and it'll go viral."

"That." Austin took Jisu's hand and led her to the back. "That is not going to happen."

The room was lit in a deep shade of pink. A mini disco ball hung from the ceiling and flashed brightly as it spun around. A huge TV displayed the lyrics against an old Filipino music video.

"I've lived a life that's full," they sang, as Ron loosened up his tie and Jhun crumpled up his white apron and tossed it aside. The two brothers each held a mic and swayed back and forth with the music. Ron pulled Austin to his side and wrapped his arm tightly around him. He was singing with such fervent passion that it looked like he had his nephew in a headlock. Ron handed Austin the mic as the song swelled into the chorus. Austin turned back to Jisu, looking slightly embarrassed.

"Go, Austin!" Jisu smiled and cheered him on.

He was always so confident that he commanded the attention of any room he walked into. But this reserved version of him was new.

"I did it my way," Austin crooned. He wasn't a bad singer, but his uncles overpowered and outperformed him. He kept turning around between verses and looking at Jisu as if to say, *These guys are so crazy!* And then he'd turn back, harmonize with his uncles and sing all the backup singer parts. He was being a good sport. Who else got to see this side of him? Jisu cheered them all on. She wanted Austin to know that she was happy to be here with him. It was rare to spend a whole day with someone and not grow sick of that person. Even with Euni, Min or Hiba, Jisu needed her space after spending an entire afternoon with them, working at the library or getting lunch and watching a movie.

But she had been with Austin from the morning well into the evening, and she could've stayed in that karaoke room for several more hours. Jisu wondered if he felt the same way. If he didn't, they would've parted ways and gone home a long time ago, right?

Ron and Jhun kept them in the karaoke room for four more songs, until their friends finally showed up. It was nearly midnight, and Jisu's eyelids felt heavy as they finally got into the car.

"Thanks for hanging out with me today," Austin said as he turned the engine on. "You're the chillest girl I've ever met. I feel like everyone at Wick is way too uptight and freaked out about senior year and college, but you..." Austin ran his hand through Jisu's hair. The tiny hairs on her neck stood up.

Relax, Jisu thought to herself. *Relax*.

The heat from his hand warmed the back of her neck. His brown eyes stared into hers. She could pass out from the mix of nerves, excitement and anxiety that bubbled inside her.

"You just go with the flow, like you've got things figured out," he said. But Jisu felt paralyzed. The more cavalier and smooth Austin was, the more Jisu felt tense with nervous excitement.

Be cool. Be the cool girl he thinks you are. You are a cool girl. You've gone on how many seons with how many dudes? And turned them all down? Shoot. The seons. Was that something she should tell him about? *No. Why ruin the moment? Live in it.* She was just going with the flow.

"Austin," Jisu said. He interlocked his fingers with hers. His hand was warm and reassuring. Jisu wondered if he could sense how quick her pulse was. She didn't want him to know that she was essentially a tangled bundle of nerves about to fall apart at any moment. "I really like you," she whispered just loud enough for him to hear.

Austin pulled her in. He let go of her hand and held her face. He kissed her. The million nervous thoughts that were racing through her mind disappeared. She kissed him back. Jisu had kissed boys before. Those were sweet, shy, vanilla, one-note. But it had never felt like this. This was different. This was a shot through her heart. A megawatt jolt of energy. A million adrenaline explosions. A taste of something she wanted more of.

Austin ran his hand down her back and held Jisu by the waist. He pulled her over to his side of the car. Jisu was hyperaware of every moving joint, muscle and limb in her body. She was quickly approaching a place she hadn't gone before, and she was nervous and enthralled to approach the line in the sand. But she was here, in a new place, with a new person, and she was ready to do what she wanted. She felt light as a feather, the way he so easily moved her over to him. He kept kissing her, and she didn't want him to stop. It was wonderful to be there on top of him in the driver's seat and make out with him until her lips went numb. She wrapped her arms around his neck and ran her fingers through his hair, because that's what she noticed girls did in movies. And because Austin had beautiful, shiny black locks. How could she not touch them?

Austin sat up and pulled her closer to him. There was no space between them now. Jisu worried she might be pinning him down, but he kept kissing her all over, on her neck and down to her chest, reassuring her again and again. She put a hand on his chest. He pulled it down and guided her under his shirt. He touched her neck with his other hand, and she led him down to her chest, following the trail of kisses he had left moments ago.

The loose, baggy sweater Jisu had worn came off easily. She had forgotten which bra she was wearing and was relieved it was the frilly blue one and not the ratty nude one. Austin's shirt came off just as easily. They had already seen each other like this at the beach. But Austin looked different seated underneath her legs, knowing that the heat of her lips still lingered on his. It was frustrating how she couldn't keep looking at all of him and kiss him at the same time.

Jisu felt Austin's fingers climb up her spine and slide under the back of her bra. They were long past where she had been before and she let him lead the way. Everything felt right with him.

The light pole they were parked next to flickered, as if to apologize for the abrupt intrusion.

Austin checked the time on the dashboard. "Shoot. My uncles are going to come out any second." He leaned back and grabbed his shirt from the back seat, where it had been tossed aside.

"Okay," Jisu said. She slid back into the passenger seat and wiggled back into her sweater.

He turned the key in the ignition. Before he drove out of the parking spot, he leaned over. Jisu felt like a newer, bolder version of herself. She met him halfway and kissed him. They could've quickly resumed where they had left off, but somewhere outside they heard a door open and shut. Before either of them could check to see if it was Tito Ron or Jhun closing down the restaurant, Austin sped away.

When Austin pulled up to the Murrays', it took every bit of effort for Jisu to peel herself out of the passenger seat. All things, even a perfect day, had to end at some point. She quietly crept into the house. Hours ago, she had texted Linda, saying she was binge-watching *Riverdale* with Hiba at her house and would be home late. All the lights were out. The Murrays were all fast asleep. Even if Linda were to appear in the hallway with her arms crossed and unleash a lecture about breaking curfew, it couldn't break Jisu's good mood. Her legs carried her through the door, up the stairs and into her room, but the rest of her was floating higher, somewhere outside, beyond the roof and up in the sky.

One question lingered in the back of her mind. *What happens now?* If her supposed go-with-the-flow attitude was what he liked so much about her, would he get scared off if she wanted something more? *Did* she want something more?

Austin could be the end to all the seons. God, she was not looking forward to more of them. Everyone she'd met was either boring, full of himself or friend material. The thoughts of seons swarmed in her mind like an annoying flock of mosquitos. She swatted them away. She would deal with the seons when they started again.

If they started again.

DATE NO. 14

NAME: **Park Hongki**

OCCUPATION:
Student, Soccer Team Captain

INTERESTS:
Stock Market, World Cup, Poetry

HONGKI: Jisu! It's nice to meet you.

JISU: Yeah, sorry I'm late. The subway was super delayed.

HONGKI: Don't be. Really. We're here now!

HONGKI: So what's Daewon like? I almost went there. But my high school has a better soccer team, so I ended up there instead.

JISU: Daewon's great. I mean, it's super competitive like any other major high school. But I really like all my teachers and everyone in my class.

HONGKI: Everyone thinks American universities are hardest to get into. They should try getting into Seoul National University, or even just surviving a Seoul private high school.

JISU: Seriously! So, what do you want to study in college?

HONGKI: I wanna study business, then get an MBA in Finance, probably be an analyst for a few years and then see what happens.

JISU: Live your whole life...and then see what happens?

HONGKI: I know, I know. It's like a fifteen-year plan, not a five-year plan.

JISU: So, what else do you like, outside of school and work stuff?

HONGKI: Well, I really like keeping track of the stock market. I like to stay on top of stuff like that. Always good information to know.

JISU: Sure! What about soccer? I think you mentioned that you played?

HONGKI: Oh, that. I've been playing since fifth grade just kind of out of necessity.

JISU: Necessity?

HONGKI: Yeah, gotta have at least one sport on your résumé if you wanna get into a good college.

JISU: Right, right.

HONGKI: Do you play any sports?

JISU: I played on the school volleyball team my freshman and sophomore year. And then it just got too intense for me, so I play intramural. For fun.

HONGKI: Nice! Yeah, soccer's not that fun for me anymore. Hasn't been in years. Honestly, I can't wait to get into college and stop playing.

JISU: If you don't like it, you shouldn't do it!

HONGKI: I mean, I've come so far already, haven't I? And it's for school, so…

JISU: Hongki, you're allowed to have a life outside of school. You're allowed to have interests outside of your fifteen-year plan. You know that, right?

HONGKI: I know, but what if I don't want to?

JISU: Why wouldn't you want to?

HONGKI: I don't know. I think I'm just the type who likes school way too much.

JISU: Yeah…you might be.

HONGKI: Honestly, I'm so happy summer's over and we're back in school. Just means we're all that much closer to getting into the college we're going to attend.

JISU: I don't think I've ever heard someone say that they're happy summer is over in earnest.

HONGKI: I mean, it's kinda boring, right? There's like nothing to do.

JISU: I'm sure you could find something you enjoy that's not related to school.

HONGKI: Yeah, maybe. But hey, you were the one that missed our date last week because you were cooped up in hagwon.

JISU: Oh, yeah…right…

HONGKI: You can't tell me to live my life if you're not living yours!

15

Click. Jisu hit the Submit button. She exhaled deeply. The first of ten college applications was done. The thought of having to do this nine more times grew more daunting the more she thought about it. That pesky number nine. Jisu wanted to quickly get another application out of the way so the number would be eight. But she let herself take a breath and rest easy. She'd gotten one out of the way. Completed. Checked off the list.

"Did you do it?" Hiba whispered. Jamie and Tiffany also peeked at Jisu from behind their laptops. The four of them were spending all of study hall at the library.

Jisu nodded enthusiastically. They high-fived each other lightly and did a quiet little celebratory dance in their seats. They were trying their best to be as silent as possible so the librarian wouldn't shush them again and threaten to kick them out.

Jisu relaxed back into her seat. She felt a tiny sliver of relief. Her grades were solid, and she had good recommendations lined up from both Daewon and Wick. But there were still nine more applications to go—six non-Ivies and three Ivies, the last of them being Harvard. Jisu took a deep breath and exhaled slowly, like she had reached the peak of a steep hill. But it was a tiny hill and she still had the rest of Mount Everest to climb. And the more college applications she completed and crossed off her list, the closer and more eager her mother was to set up her Korean-American seons.

Jisu checked her phone again. No new notifications. Nothing from Euni or Min. And nothing from Austin. Ugh. Since she made out with Austin in his car, Jisu had been weightless and without a single worry, but two weeks had passed now, and she hadn't heard from him.

They didn't share any classes, and she hadn't run into him in the cafeteria or in the parking lot like she usually would. Jisu had never gone from feeling confident and unstoppable to jittery and anxious in such a short amount of time. *He's probably just busy. Maybe his uncles needed him at the restaurant. Or one of his siblings is sick and he needs to take care of them. Or he's sick. I hope he's not sick.*

Jisu opened and closed her messages. The last exchange was at 12:38 a.m., shortly after Austin had dropped her off at the Murrays' that night. That perfect night.

I didn't want today to end!

It was the kind of text that had made sense to send when she'd sent it, her head all the way up in the clouds. He had replied with a simple smiley face, and she'd buried her smiling face under the covers, all of a sudden coy in front of no one, before falling asleep.

But the more time passed without another exchange, the

more she felt shortchanged by his wordless response. Should she have played it cool and not texted him until the next day? What did Mandy's magazines have to say about that? A few silent days later, Jisu tried to pry the conversation open and texted Austin a photo she took of him at the beach. But there was no response.

"Don't tell me you're constantly refreshing your emails now. You literally just hit submit!" Hiba must've noticed how often Jisu was checking her phone. She quietly closed out of her messages and placed her phone facedown on the table.

"It's not that." She hesitated, wondering if she should tell them about Austin. But why shouldn't she? They were her friends. This was the exact kind of stuff you confided in them about.

"So, I've been spending a lot of time with Austin," Jisu said. "Like a good amount."

Hiba slammed her laptop shut. Jamie and Tiffany put down their books. Jisu had their full attention now.

"Austin Velasco?" Jamie asked.

"Yes. We've been hanging out…as friends. Or so I thought. Until he kissed me the last time I saw him." Jisu wasn't sure how much to tell them. She wished Euni and Min were sitting with her instead.

Jamie clasped her hands. "Which was when?" she asked.

"About two weeks ago," Jisu answered, unsure if this was a normal amount of time to go without being in touch with someone you were on top of and making out with late at night in an empty parking lot.

"Kaylee is going to be pissed when she hears." Tiffany broke into a fit of giggles.

"No! Please don't tell anyone," Jisu said. The last thing she wanted was for people to find out what was happening between her and Austin before she even managed to define it herself.

"I don't know, Jisu," Hiba said. "Have you guys been *dating*-dating? Or you're going to start dating? I didn't think Austin was the dating type."

"Yeah, are you trying to *date* him?" Jamie asked.

"I don't know," Jisu said. "But I've been getting to know him pretty well. I think I might like him."

Tiffany looked at Jisu with more concern. "Austin's a friend, and he's fun to be around," she said. "But he does have a tendency to go from one person to another."

"Didn't he ditch Amy Saunders right after they hooked up?" Hiba asked.

"Yeah, but she was acting possessive," Tiffany said. "She was going to Europe the whole summer and wanted him to be her long-distance boyfriend."

"Okay, but I heard that summer he hooked up with like half the lifeguards he worked with," Hiba said.

"That sounds like an exaggeration," Jamie said. "But it's probably true."

Jisu groaned and buried her face in her hands. It was a mistake bringing this up. All this backstory—whether any of it was true—was the last thing she wanted to know.

"He *is* really cute," Tiffany said, head down as she scrolled through her phone. "I mean, look at that side profile." She held up her phone for all of them to see.

It was Austin's Instagram page. And the latest photo...the one Jisu had sent him weeks ago only to get no response... was posted two days ago. There he was on Tiffany's screen at Pacifica State Beach, sitting on the sand and looking into the sunset. His surfboard was perched upright by him. The sunlight hit his hair and wet suit in a way that revealed that he was only partially dry. Jisu had taken this photo to remember how he had shared a passion of his with her and taught her something new.

Never not surfing. Always a good, easy surf at Pacifica.
#surfing #pacifica #sunset #pacificasunset #beach #bayarea
#surfsup

Jisu grabbed Tiffany's phone with one hand and clutched
her stomach with the other as if someone had kicked her right
in the gut. So he *had* gotten her photo. His phone wasn't broken, and her text message wasn't lost in transit. If he liked it so
much, why couldn't he tell her so? And he couldn't even give
her a proper photo credit in the caption? Jisu's cheeks grew hot.

Tiffany took her phone back, completely unaware of the
revelation Jisu was having. "Cute as he is, he's got a bit of
a reputation," she said. "You should have fun if you want
to though! As long as you also play the game, you can't get
burned, right?"

Jisu forced a smile, like she imagined a willing participant
of the game would, but it didn't help the sinking feeling she
felt inside, the feeling of a slowly wilting plant being deprived
of sunlight. Everyone's comments only confirmed what she
feared: the time they spent together was more significant to
her than it was to him.

Jisu reached back into her mind and played back all the
times they had spent together. They *did* pass a lot of time *not*
hooking up. There was all the walking around the city. They'd
successfully led a skating class filled with hyper children. For
god's sake, he'd introduced her to his uncles and they'd even
sung karaoke together! You didn't do all of that just to hook
up with a girl and then go MIA for two weeks.

But then Jisu remembered the other parts. The hazy, un-
clear, foggy parts. The stretches of time in between their hang-
outs. Hangout. They never called it a date. They never called
it anything. They were always just…hanging out.

Jisu flopped over onto the table like a deflated balloon. For the sake of her pride, she was glad she hadn't revealed the full timeline of events to her friends.

"I need to stop by my locker before my next class." Jisu shoved everything into her bag and hurried out of the library.

And then she saw him. Standing by his locker, chatting away with his friends. Smiling. Laughing.

Austin met her gaze and walked up to her. "Hey!" he greeted her cheerfully, picking up right where they left off. As if the line of communication between them hadn't been dead for the last two weeks. Was this how he'd made Amy Saunders feel?

Maybe Jisu was overreacting. It would've been one thing if Austin was cold and indifferent. It would confirm what she was starting to suspect, what her friends had observed—that her time was up and he was done. She could deal with rejection.

"How's it going?" His casual greeting made her question for a moment if her feeling upset was even really valid. Maybe she had been overthinking it?

"Good," Jisu lied. "It's been a minute."

"Has it? I feel like I just saw you," Austin said. "But I mean, it's good to see you now."

No, she hadn't been overthinking it. Jisu had every right to be annoyed at Austin. Especially now.

"But yeah..." he continued. "My uncle Ron had to fly down to LA last minute because of a family thing." Austin sighed and looked serious all of a sudden. "And I had to help out at the restaurant, so it's been kinda crazy for me."

"Oh... I hope everything's okay," Jisu said. Austin looked and sounded sincere.

"He's coming back this weekend. It's whatever." He shrugged, reverting right back to his casual self. That's how he was. Nonchalant about everything. But some things in life were more than just "whatever."

"Are you free on Saturday?" he asked. "We can binge-watch all those TV shows on Netflix I told you about. I bet you haven't checked any of them out yet." Austin nudged her elbow and smiled. Was he orbiting back toward her direction now?

Jisu wanted to say yes, but she didn't want to cave so easily. And she was supposed to dedicate the coming weekend to finishing her college applications. She wanted to sit down and get them all out and over with. And of course there was the IS project. Jisu reminded herself to track down Dave and find a time that might work for his ever-shifting, busy schedule.

"I actually can't meet up," Jisu said, despite what she wanted. She had to be responsible. And she wouldn't give in so easily.

"Oh, all right!" Austin said and started to turn away.

Was this it? Would it be another two weeks before she had another tepid hallway interaction with Austin?

"But maybe the week after?" Jisu blurted out.

"Yeah, sure!" Austin said without breaking his stride. He was walking down the hall in the opposite direction now. "I'll text you."

She wanted to believe him. That sinking feeling reemerged in the pit of her stomach. Austin wasn't actually doing anything wrong. He wasn't ignoring her, but still. He seemed a million miles away. It felt like she was trying to grab on to a handful of sand. The more she tried to hold on, the more it slipped through her fingers.

DATE NO. 15

NAME: **Kang William**

INTERESTS:
Acting, Political Studies

DISLIKES:
Pork, Superhero Movies, Dentist Appointments

WILLIAM: So wait, you're like *from* Korea?

JISU: Yup! I moved from Seoul a few months ago. I transferred over to Wick-Helmering.

WILLIAM: Oh, word. I know a few people who go to Wick. Do you like it there?

JISU: I do, actually! I mean, I miss home like crazy. But I also really like San Francisco. Were you born and raised here?

WILLIAM: Yeah, my grandparents were the ones who immigrated here. So I'm second generation.

JISU: And they somehow have you going on seons?

WILLIAM: Ah well, my grandmother is very traditional and stubborn. No one can cross Halmoni.

JISU: This place is really cool. I don't think I've ever been to a skate park.

WILLIAM: There's gotta be a few cool spots around Seoul. I bet there's a whole underground group of Korean skaters. Have you never skateboarded?

JISU: No, I'm scared I'd just fall and break an arm or something.

WILLIAM: I've broken my left arm. Twice. Also have some not-so-pretty scars.

JISU: Hmm, you're really selling me on this whole skateboarding thing.

WILLIAM: As long as you're not trying difficult tricks, there's usually no broken limbs. Here, just try standing on my board.

JISU: Like this? Ah, I'm going to fall. Both legs?

WILLIAM: Yeah, both legs. You got it. Half of skateboarding is just standing and balancing on the board.

JISU: So, how soon until I can skate on that ramp?

WILLIAM: Listen, I've been skating since I was ten and I'm still intimidated by that ramp.

JISU: I'm really glad we didn't meet at a boring coffee shop like Ms. Moon would've wanted.

WILLIAM: I didn't realize I could take things into my own hands until this one girl I met decided we should go to Alcatraz for our first date.

JISU: That's…an interesting choice. How did that go?

WILLIAM: It wasn't that bad actually. The worst part was that there were a bunch of tourists. She lived in the Bay Area her whole life and never did any of the tourist stuff, so I guess she wanted to cross it off her list.

JISU: Prison. How romantic.

WILLIAM: Yeahhhh. That was the first and only date we had.

JISU: So, how are college apps going for you? Do you know what you wanna do?

WILLIAM: Oh, I'm not going to college. I know. Shocking, right? Technically, I am—there's no way Ms. Moon would keep me on as a client if I wasn't. But the plan is to get into college, wherever my parents want me to go, and then move down to LA.

JISU: What's in LA?

WILLIAM: Hollywood. I want to be an actor.

JISU: That's cool! One of my best friends in Korea wants to be a pop star and she's basically been training since she was nine. I think it's really cool that you're going for it.

WILLIAM: Yeah, it's not going to be easy, for sure. But it's what I want to do. I just need to make sure everything is figured out. What do you want to do?

JISU: Well... I really like photography but not enough to dive headfirst and go to an art school. But the plan is to figure it out once I get into college.

WILLIAM: Photography. Interesting! But like career-wise, you don't know what you want to do?

JISU: I mean, those two things aren't mutually exclusive.

WILLIAM: Yeah, but that's gotta be a hard way to make a living. Freelancing and all that.

JISU: Said the actor. With zero credits to his name.

WILLIAM: Hey, I've done a bunch of plays.

JISU: It doesn't count if they were high school productions.

WILLIAM: Okay, fine. Fair. I've just always seen myself as the artsy half of a couple. You know? I'm sure that's what you see for yourself, too.

JISU: No, not really.

WILLIAM: Come on. No one can be a truly happy, successful artist if they can't work on their craft full-time.

JISU: No artist can be truly happy unless they have a partner to bankroll their creative pursuits? Is that what you're saying?

WILLIAM: No! Well, not really. Obviously the basis of a relationship should be that two people like each other—

JISU: But it doesn't hurt if the person you're seeing can pay your rent.

WILLIAM: You're assuming that I'll never make it big.

JISU: You're very optimistic!

WILLIAM: Not too optimistic though—I'm also practical and realistic. Isn't that what everyone else does when they go on these seons?

JISU: I…guess.

WILLIAM: I've upset you.

JISU: No, it's fine. We're both just too artsy to be compatible or something, I guess.

WILLIAM: You think I could act in Korea? If it doesn't work out for me here? Or maybe I'm not Korean enough.

JISU: No, I think you'd be just fine! You're a good-looking dude and that'll work in whatever country you try to act in.

16

"You all right, Jees?" Dave asked. "You seem a little out of it."

They were in the Mission District, walking down 16th Street, toward The Lab. It was the opening night for their latest exhibit: *Feminism in the Digital Age*. In the past few weeks, Jisu and Dave had spent their free time scoping out any local event with a political bent that was open to the public: a rally for union workers at the courthouse, a literary event about politics at City Lights and today an opening for a feminist art show.

Dave had no idea, but Jisu was coming straight from her first American seon. Did Dave know about the business of seons, or even what the word *seon* meant? Jisu let Dave's question hang in the air. Part of her wanted to tell him how her date had gone, how it was just fine and ended with no real connection, how futile it all felt, how she dreaded seons for this reason in general. She could blab all about it to Hiba or text away in the group chat with Euni and Min. But she felt weird talking about it with him. Plus, they were only a block from the gallery.

"I'm fine." Jisu forced a smile. "Just tired is all."

The gallery was one giant open space. It was dimly lit and painted in stark white from ceiling to floor. Projectors played video clips on the walls. Mini TVs playing other works of art were spread throughout the floor. It was only about a half hour into the event, and the space was filling up quickly.

They had a system: Dave worked the floor and chatted with attendees. Eventually he tracked down whoever was in charge of social media and publicity. While he interviewed them about outreach and turnout, Jisu hung back and captured everything with her camera. At the end of each event, they combined notes and tracked the event's imprint across all online platforms.

The people at this event had the most interesting outfits, by far. The main curator, a woman with shocking white-blond hair, was dressed in a sleek black dress with an asymmetrical hem. She stood in front of a video installment and explained the piece to a small crowd. One woman was covered in chunky, colorful costume jewelry. Another stood out just as much in a simple dark denim jumpsuit. Several women had brought their young daughters. They held their hands and walked around the gallery space, explaining whatever they could understand. Some people wore sunglasses—oversize tortoise shell, bright cobalt blue and classic black cat eye. Jisu snapped photos of them all.

"How are things going?" Dave asked Jisu.

"I think this is my favorite one so far. I didn't even think I was going to be into it. *Feminism in the Digital Age* sounds like the name of a boring lecture."

Jisu had noticed that many women (and men!) of San Francisco were often vocal and active about their feminism. It felt louder, bolder and a lot more normalized than it was in Seoul. The conversations everyone was having at the show were never ones she had had so explicitly in Seoul. They felt like more freely expressed versions of the thoughts she'd always had in her brain.

"Me, too. I nearly fell asleep at that reading yesterday," Dave said.

"I know! It was so boring. I felt bad. I really wanted to be more into it. Did you get some good soundbites?"

Dave held up his notepad, which was covered with scribbles. She had no idea how he could decipher his own handwriting.

"You get good photos?" he asked.

Jisu proudly showed him some of the stills she captured.

"How's everything else going?" Dave asked. "Like with Austin?"

Her hand stilled. Why would he want to know?

"It's good!" she lied.

"Are you guys dating now?"

"Oh…no. I don't really believe in labels. We're just hanging out, having fun, you know." Jisu pulled her camera up to her face. She looked at Dave through the lens, standing tall among the crowd. He looked serious. He pushed Jisu's camera away.

"I don't want to be nosy, but before, when we were on our way here, you seemed upset. And I know how Austin can be with girls…and it might not even be that. And I know it's none of my business…"

It had been annoying the first time he'd said something about Austin, but Jisu knew now that Dave was coming from a good place. It felt nice to know he was looking out for her.

She let her camera hang around her neck. "You sound a lot like my mother with all your jansori," she said. Dave laughed. "Wait—you know what jansori means?"

"Ooookay. I may not be fluent, but I am still the son of two

Korean immigrants. I know a few things. Especially jansori. I only get an earful every time I come home."

"But your mom is so nice! And you're like the perfect son," Jisu said.

"*Only* son. And you know how much pressure Koreans put on their sons."

"Not as much as they do with their only kids!"

"All right, all right. You win." Dave laughed again. Jisu liked the way his eyes creased into half-moons. His laugh was hearty and warm. Genuine. Her boring seon really had sucked the life out of her, but Jisu was glad she'd trudged over to the gallery with Dave and hadn't gone home, plopped onto her bed and sulked until she fell asleep.

A bad date could throw everything off, but at the end of the day, that's all it was: one bad date. It was easy to forget all the good things Jisu had going for her. Aside from the confusing state of things with Austin, she had found good friends at Wick, and they were helping each other make sense of the most stressful year of their lives. She was making good headway with her college applications, with her early applications all completed. The more she got out of the way, the more confident she felt. It was hard to be kind to yourself when your parents kept second-guessing every move you made, but Jisu was doing her best and that was enough. All that was left was waiting for everything to fall into place.

The event was starting to wrap up. Jisu reached into her bag to search for the lens cover and noticed that her phone was vibrating. She'd put it on silent and was alarmed to see six missed calls and a slew of Kakao messages from Min. Her phone vibrated again. Min was calling for the seventh time.

"Hey, Min, sorry. I was at an event for class." Jisu covered her other ear with her hand. She could barely hear Min as she squeezed her way out of the crowd.

"Hello? Jisu? Can you hear me?"

Jisu walked toward the door and motioned at Dave to come outside.

"Min, I'm here. I can hear you now. Is everything okay?"

She stepped out into the quiet street. She could hear now that Min was crying.

"Jisu… Euni… She…"

Jisu could barely make out what Min was saying, but she started to tremble. "Min. Please…just tell me what's going on."

"Eunice fainted at hagwon yesterday. She's been a little sick, but I didn't know how bad it was…which is why I didn't tell you. And Euni wouldn't want you to worry about her like that. But I guess it was worse than I thought. She's in the hospital now. Jisu-ya, I really wish you were here," Min sobbed. Jisu felt her knees go weak.

"What happened?" Jisu couldn't help the tears that ran down her face. She didn't care if anyone saw her crying on the street.

"You know Euni is not the strongest girl. It's just been so hard for everyone right now, with exams and getting ready for college. I guess the stress was too much…" Min could barely keep it together.

Jisu's head was throbbing and she couldn't see straight. She felt consumed with guilt. Senior year at Wick wasn't a walk in the park, but she knew how tough and arduous things got at Daewon. One of her best friends was sick, and Jisu was on the other side of the world, worrying about whether a boy liked her or not and taking silly photos. She'd never felt so small and powerless.

"I miss you guys so much." Jisu squatted down and sat on the curb. From the corner of her eye, she could see Dave making his way outside. "And I'm so sorry I'm not there."

"No, Jisu. Don't be sorry. We'll all be together soon," Min said. "And Euni will recover and be fine. She's being discharged tomorrow, and I'm going to the hospital now to visit her."

"Tell her I love her and to get better." Jisu tried to subtly wipe her tears away, but they wouldn't stop. "I love you, Min."

"I love you, too, Jisu." Min's voice cracked, and something in Jisu cracked also.

"We'll all be together in just a few weeks," Jisu said, trying to sound hopeful.

"Yeah, for Christmas!" Min was trying, too. "Okay I have to go. I'll text you when I see Euni."

Jisu hung up and buried her face in her lap. She wished the world would stop moving, stop spinning for just one second, so that she could have a good cry, let it all out and move on. But that wasn't how the world worked. She could hear Dave walking toward her, his sneakers shuffling on the sidewalk. Maybe if she kept her head down, he would think she was someone else and walk away.

"Tired, Jees?" Dave crouched next to her. There was no point trying to hide it. Jisu lifted her head and revealed her snotty, tearstained face. Dave didn't recoil like she'd thought he might.

"Hey, hey." He put a hand on her shoulder. "What happened?"

"My friend back in Seoul is in the hospital." Jisu sniffed. "And I'm stuck here…taking photos. I can't be there for her. I feel…I feel terrible."

"I'm sorry to hear that." Dave looked at her earnestly. "But, Jisu, you can't blame yourself for any of this."

"I know, but I should be there. Right now. Next to her."

"But you can't, and none of it is your fault. You're in a whole new country, at a new school. You're working hard in all your classes. And you're a good friend to the people around you here. I know you're doing your best, Jisu. Don't be so hard on yourself."

Jisu felt even more tears falling down her face. Dave pulled her in for a side hug, and she leaned her head on his shoulder and buried her face in her hands. Jisu tried so hard to stop crying, but she couldn't. At least Dave didn't seem to mind.

Jisu wanted to tell him that he was a good friend, too. That she was grateful that Kaylee had called him over in the cafeteria on her first day. That he was always looking out for her. That he gave her jansori. That he was kind.

The words sat heavy at the tip of her tongue.

The last of the night's tears trickled down her face. She wiped them away and stared out into the street.

"Dave," she said. "I'm glad I got paired up with you."

DATE NO. 16

NAME: **Shim Jimoon**

INTERESTS:
Piano, Russian Literature, Art History

PARENT OCCUPATIONS:
Art collector; Fashion industry editorial director

JIMOON: What did you do this weekend?

JISU: I actually did something really cool! Usually I only have boring answers to that question, like studying or shopping or watching movies on Netflix.

JIMOON: So, what'd you do?

JISU: I went to this gallery in the Mission District.

JIMOON: Oh, I spend a bunch of time there. My mom's an art collector. Which gallery?

JISU: It was this place called The Lab.

JIMOON: The Lab's great! Super experimental. And it's not just a gallery, right? They have people perform there and stuff.

JISU: Yeah…I think so? It was my first time there.

JIMOON: What show do they have up there now?

JISU: It's called *Feminism in the Digital Age*. I honestly had no idea what to expect, but I ended up really liking it!

JIMOON: Is that the one that Sally McPherson curated? The one that showed at that gallery in New York… What's it called? I always forget the name.

JISU: Umm. New York? Like the MoMA?

JIMOON: No, no. Much smaller. Could you imagine? Taking your show from MoMA to the humble little Lab. Although the MoMA could benefit from being a little more self-aware about the current state of things. Feminism is probably something they could've done a show on *years* ago.

JISU: Right…yeah, totally.

JIMOON: God, what is the name of that place. Anyway, I'll probably remember the moment we've parted ways.

JISU: Yeah, I hate it when that happens.

JIMOON: So, how was the show—at The Lab?

JISU: It was good! Though I couldn't see too much of the works—it was the opening night.

JIMOON: Yeah, no one actually looks at the art on opening night. Too crowded. Everyone goes back the next day.

JISU: Exactly! And I was taking photos, so I couldn't take the time to really look.

JIMOON: You're into photography?

JISU: Self-taught. Nothing fancy.

JIMOON: I don't know if you've been, but the Ansel Adams show that's on at the SF MOMA is really good.

JISU: Sorry, which show?

JIMOON: Ansel Adams… You do know who he is, right?

JISU: Hmm? Yeah, totally. The…photographer.

JIMOON: Yeah exactly! He's *the* photographer.

JISU: So, who else are your favorite photographers?

JIMOON: The obvious ones like Ansel, Diane Arbus, Lewis Wickes Hine. My mom actually has a few Arbus pieces. Who do you like?

JISU: Oh…uh the same. Arbus, Hine, all of them. Yup. What do you like about their photos?

JIMOON: I love nature, so Adams's black-and-white photographs are probably among my favorite. With Arbus—this probably sounds too obvious, but she just captures people in a way no one else really can. Ordinary people, dwarfs, gangsters, children, singers, body contortionists. She treats them all the same.

JISU: That's what I like best about photography. When you can capture the honesty of the person in front of you.

JIMOON: What's your favorite work?

JISU: Like work of photography?

JIMOON: Yeah, just like your favorite one.

JISU: Hmm… I don't think I have a favorite one. And I really don't know all that much about it, to be honest. I just recently picked up a camera and played around with it.

JIMOON: Gotcha. Well, if you're a real photographer, you gotta know the works of the masters.

JISU: I guess. I'm still learning, taking it one photo at a time.

17

"Aigoo, why does our daughter sound so sad?" Jisu's father asked.

"No reason, Appa. I'm just tired." There was only one week left before winter vacation. One week before she submitted the last of her college applications. Just a week before she would hop on a plane back to Seoul. Back home.

"Make sure you get lots of sleep. And drink water!" Her father's voice trailed off. Mrs. Kim was taking the phone from him, Jisu could tell.

"Jisu-ya, are you sick? Why are you feeling tired? Everything okay?"

Jisu sighed. "Yes, Umma, I was just up a little later than usual studying." She knew exactly which lines to use and when to use them.

"Aigoo, working so hard. But it'll be Christmas soon."

"I know! I can't wait to be back. I miss everyone so much."

Jisu thought about all the proper catching up she had to do with Euni and Min. Euni had texted a little with Jisu on Kakao, but the conversations were sparse and she wasn't quite well enough yet to video chat with her.

"Actually, your dad and I have a surprise," Mrs. Kim said.

Surprise? Were they going to fly her out early? Or transferring her back to Daewon?

"Your father and I—*and* your grandfather—are going to come to you for Christmas! We just booked the tickets the other day."

Jisu's heart dropped. *No. No, no, no.* Ever since she had gotten that devastating phone call from Min, the promise of returning home but for a short week and half was the only thing that had kept Jisu going.

"Umma...that sounds great and all but—"

"So great, right? You can show us all your favorite places. And we'll take pictures by the Golden Gate Bridge..."

"You can't come here," Jisu blurted out.

Silence.

"Why? What's wrong? Did something happen?" Her mother sounded genuinely worried.

"I need to go to back to Seoul."

"Jisu-ya, I know you are homesick. But we are bringing the home to you! And then you don't have to deal with the terrible jet lag when you go back to school."

Of course. Of course her mother's reasoning was tied with Jisu and her academics. It always was. It was always this way.

"No, you don't understand," Jisu said, her voice shaking. "Euni is sick. She was just in the hospital. I need to see her."

"Oh... I heard about Eunice," Mrs. Kim said.

Then why hadn't she told Jisu about it?

She'd probably thought that she shouldn't distract her daughter with such news. Such news regarding *her best friend.* That was exactly what had happened.

"Jisu-ya, I'm really sorry. Eunice is a lovely, smart girl. But you know how weak she is. Even all the mothers joke that gym class is the only class where she's not in first place."

"This isn't a joke, Umma." Jisu was seething. How could she dare to talk about Euni like this?

"I know it's not a joke. I didn't mean it like that. I'm sorry," Mrs. Kim said. "But we've already booked the flights, Jisu. You can video chat with Euni when she's fully recovered. Min can keep you updated. But the plan is set, my dear."

Jisu wanted to scream. She wanted to scream so loudly that everyone in the Bay Area, across the Pacific Ocean and in Seoul would hear her. But she was tired of fighting, tired of resisting. And so she quietly hung up the phone.

She collapsed onto the bed, feeling helpless. Like a tiny, anchorless boat lost at sea. She wanted to call Dave and vent. *You won't believe what my mother just did.* But he was probably busy with Sophie, and she didn't want to burden him. Hiba? Jamie and Tiffany? Everyone was busy right now.

Jisu hovered a finger over her phone above Austin's name and number. All she had to do was press the screen.

She tossed her phone aside and wandered into Mandy's room.

"Oh, my god, I love the green dress. Wear the green dress!" Mandy was busy FaceTiming with a friend. "Oh, hey, Jisu. What's up?" Mandy pointed her phone at Jisu. "That's Jisu. I told you about her. She's an exchange student from Korea. She's in high school."

Jisu waved to the phone awkwardly.

"I'm helping Dana pick out a dress to wear to Eliza's bat mitzvah next weekend. Wanna help?"

"I'll leave you guys alone," Jisu said. She closed Mandy's door shut and walked back to her room.

I shouldn't text him. I shouldn't be the first one to text. Jisu's hand lingered over her phone. *Ugh, I don't care.* She did, but not enough to stop her from texting Austin. Hey.

Her finger hovered over the Send button. Jisu closed her eyes and pressed down. Then she threw her phone onto the carpeted floor and hid underneath her covers. Why did texting boys have to be so excruciating?

She was prepared to fall asleep underneath those covers, wake up the next morning and see no text from Austin. But only a moment later, her phone dinged. Her ears perked up and she sat straight up in bed.

Yooooo.

It was her turn to write back. Part of her wished she hadn't texted him at all.

What are you doing?

Right now? At Tito's. On a smoke break.

You smoke?

Nah. But the other guys do. Smoking is gross, btw.

Jisu didn't know how to continue the conversation. She knew what she wanted—to see Austin—but she didn't know how to do that anymore at the expense of her pride. She'd texted him first. It was his move next!

What are you doing?

Just in my room. Bored.

Wanna hang out? I can come over.

Hang out. Ugh. Jisu's least favorite American phrase.

Yeah, I'm not doing anything.

She felt herself getting roped back in. Like she was slipping into a quickly moving pile of quicksand. But she didn't care.

"He can come over, but you have to keep the door open," Linda said. Jisu was prepared to give a whole explanation as to who Austin was and make up a project they had to work on, but none of that was necessary. When Austin arrived, Linda didn't even linger and hover over them after saying hello. Jisu and Austin walked up the stairs and to her room, with the door left open.

Only fifteen minutes ago, they had been texting, and now he was here, in her room, sitting at the edge of her bed. Fifteen minutes! Jisu felt thrilled, like she was exercising a new superpower. She also felt nervous all over again. Sure, they had been on top of each other and making out in his car, but that was a major leap for Jisu. And having Austin here in her bedroom felt like another exhilarating leap.

Austin leaned in for a kiss and most of Jisu's nerves melted away. It felt familiar and comforting. Like falling into a big, comfy couch and never wanting to emerge from it.

"Want me to close the door?" he asked. He must have noticed her eyeing it since he got here.

"No, Linda explicitly told me to keep it open. It's the one rule she has when boys are over." Jisu leaned back on the headboard, still nervous and somewhat grateful for Linda's house rule. There was nothing wrong with pacing oneself.

Austin crawled up next to Jisu and also rested his head against the headboard.

"So, what are you doing for Christmas? You flying back to Seoul?" he asked.

"No, actually," she started. Jisu wished she could tell him about everything that was going on. With Euni, with her parents, all of it. But a part of her knew that she wasn't going to be happy with whatever response or reaction she got out of him. "They're flying to San Francisco."

"That's awesome! You can show 'em all the cool spots I've been showing you." Austin looked at her and smiled.

"What are you doing over break?" Jisu asked.

"Just working at the restaurant. It gets crazy busy this time of the year." He put his hand on her knee. "I probably shouldn't have left my shift, but then you texted." Austin moved his hand up Jisu's thigh. She moved it back down to her knee. She didn't push him away completely.

"I want you to meet them."

"Who?"

"My parents. I want you to meet them."

Austin stilled. Jisu let the silence between them expand. She was going to let him talk first.

"Jisu… I don't think that's a good idea." Austin sighed and shook his head. Like he'd known this moment was going to come. As if he'd been here before.

"Why not? We've been hanging out, we like each other—"

"I know. And that's all true. But your parents? That's like kinda serious."

"I met your uncles!"

"Okay, that's different."

"How is that different?"

"I'm not one of those fancy Korean guys who's going to inherit a company or whatever kinda person that your parents are trying to set you up with. You think they'd really want to meet me?"

Jisu couldn't believe herself. She was practically begging Austin at this point.

"Well, what if they do?"

"Jisu, I'm not going to meet your parents."

Jisu felt like an idiot. Austin Velasco never did anything he didn't want to do. She never should have texted him.

"I think you should leave," she said.

"What?" Austin didn't budge from the bed. "Are you serious?"

"Yes. I am." Jisu got up and pushed her door open even wider.

"Fine." Austin snatched his jacket from her bed. "They probably need me back at the restaurant anyway."

He stormed off. Jisu let out a deep sigh and fell back onto her bed. The pillow he'd been leaning on smelled like him. Like a mixture of the ocean, frying oil and expensive shampoo. Jisu groaned and pushed the pillow off her bed. She hadn't thought it was possible, but she felt even worse now.

She took her phone out and pulled up Austin's name. *So much for go-with-the-flow.* She scrolled all the way down his contact page. She didn't hover for even one moment. *Delete Contact.*

DATE NO. 17

NAME: **Han Samuel**

INTERESTS:
Rugby, Lacrosse, Middle Eastern Studies

GOALS:
UN Translator

JISU: Hold up. *How* many languages do you speak?

SAMUEL: Three fluently. Working on the fourth. But I can read and write easily in all four. And this semester I'm going to try to learn a fifth.

JISU: That's insane!

SAMUEL: It's literally the only talent I have. I'm completely useless otherwise.

JISU: Okay, well, it's a very impressive and rare gift. What are the four that you speak?

SAMUEL: English, Korean, Spanish and French. I'm trying to tack on Italian, which is a lot easier than I thought.

JISU: Adding on a fifth language. Sooo casual.

SAMUEL: No really! I'm not even faking any modesty here. Once you master one Romance language, the others come to you really easily. So after Italian, I want to try to learn Portuguese.

JISU: You are like the ultimate overachiever. I don't think I've ever met anyone who spoke more than three, at most. So, you want to work in linguistics or translation?

SAMUEL: I'm not completely sure yet, to be honest. But I think I want to work in the UN.

JISU: That makes a lot of sense!

SAMUEL: Yeah, and I'll get to travel to all the countries.

JISU: Have you been to France, Italy or any of those other countries?

SAMUEL: Oh, yeah, plenty of times.

JISU: Plenty?

SAMUEL: My family likes to travel. It's how I got a knack for languages in the first place. I was born in New York and then spent a few years in Paris when my dad used to work there. We moved to San Francisco when I was ten. So by then I was pretty comfortable with English, Korean and French.

JISU: Wow, are you traveling then for the holidays?

SAMUEL: No, that's actually the one time we stay put in the Bay Area. Everyone else is flying on the holidays, so we just avoid it and stay put.

JISU: So not only do you travel often, you travel when others usually don't. That must be so nice! And there's no better way to learn a language than to be surrounded by it.

SAMUEL: That's so true. Pretty much all my nannies taught me how to speak a different language.

JISU: All your nannies? How many did you have growing up?

SAMUEL: One for each time we moved until I didn't need one anymore. So just like three or four. Are nannies not a thing in Korea?

JISU: I don't think so? I certainly didn't have one and didn't really need one either. I was just an only child, so—

SAMUEL: I'm an only child, too! But both my parents were working, so...

JISU: Both my parents work, too. I guess they have very different jobs.

SAMUEL: I'm gonna grab the check—I got this.

JISU: Oh, thanks! Should we split it?

SAMUEL: Please. Don't worry about this. Or any of the ones after. I got this.

JISU: Thanks, Samuel! Wait. Is tip included?

SAMUEL: Hmm? No, I left a tip.

JISU: This is just a dollar. I should have some extra bills on me if we want to leave a cash tip.

SAMUEL: No, no, it's fine. We just got coffee. Literally all they're doing is just pouring drinks.

JISU: Um, I got a fancy cappuccino and you got a flat white.

SAMUEL: Yeah, exactly, it's just coffee. What, are you feeling generous because it's the holidays? C'mon, let's go! I'll give you a ride home.

JISU: Wanna meet me outside? I'm going to go to the bathroom real quick.

SAMUEL: Okay! Sounds good.

JISU: (To herself at the table) Two, three, four, five. I wish I had more singles. This should cover it.

18

Mr. and Mrs. Kim had rented an entire house at the top of the hills for their two-week stay in San Francisco. The view overlooking the city was stunning, and the air was good for Haraboji. With his physical condition, they wouldn't be able to get around the city much, so at the very least they could enjoy all of San Francisco from above.

Jisu rang the doorbell to the Airbnb. The owners of the house had decked it all out in holiday gear. The front lawn was covered in lights and a beautiful ornate wreath was hanging on the front door. Mr. and Mrs. Kim swung the door wide-open and embraced their daughter immediately. Jisu nearly burst into a fit of tears.

Crying? Why am I crying? It hasn't been that *long.*

She'd been away from Seoul for only a few months, the equivalent of any summer camp, but it had been a difficult few months.

"Aigoo, my Jisu! Don't cry!" Mrs. Kim exclaimed, getting a bit emotional herself. She took the corner of her apron and dabbed Jisu's face first and then her own. Mr. Kim hurried them both inside, away from the brisk winter winds.

Hers were bittersweet tears. Although Jisu was relieved and thrilled to see her family, thoughts of Euni and Min lingered in her mind. How were her dear friends spending their holidays in Seoul? Euni had sent her a few messages and photos, letting her know she was recuperating at home. But it wasn't the same as sitting next to her, talking face-to-face. Being there for her.

"Haraboji!" Jisu shouted and embraced her grandfather. She'd missed her parents dearly, but it was clear which of the three she'd missed the most.

"Careful, Jisu! You're going to knock Haraboji down!" Mrs. Kim chided as she ushered her father-in-law to the couch in the living room.

"That's all right." Haraboji waved Mrs. Kim off. He beamed at Jisu. "I'm just glad to see my granddaughter."

"The flight must have been so long and uncomfortable. Why did you come all the way here?" Jisu sat next to him. "I even told Umma that I wanted to go to Seoul like we originally planned."

"I told her you should come back, too! I knew you would miss your friends and Seoul, but of course your parents didn't listen to me," Haraboji whispered, as if they were trying to keep their alliance a secret. He was always on her side. He was the one at home who really saw her and heard her.

"And how could I miss an opportunity to see my Jisu! I hadn't seen you in so long. When you're old like me, even a week without your granddaughter feels like an eternity."

Jisu locked her arms around her grandfather's and they leaned against each other. Two peas in a pod, two generations apart. It felt like they were snuggled on the couch back in their apartment in Korea. Except instead of looking out the windows at Seoul, they were looking out at the Bay.

Despite her longing for Euni and Min, Jisu felt full and warm. She felt an urge to get up, grab her camera and photograph her grandfather on that couch, basking in the last golden rays of the day. But why ruin a good moment by trying to capture it? She stayed put, happy for once to play the participant and not the observer.

Outside, the sun began its daily descent into the horizon. Seoul was hours ahead. It was morning there, and Jisu wondered what Euni and Min were up to. She pictured Min prancing down the street with her headphones on, practicing the latest choreography she had learned as she made her way over to Eunice's house. She imagined the two of them walking to their favorite coffee shop and ordering hot chocolate—extra whipped cream for both—a special treat since it was the holidays. They were probably gossiping about everyone in their class. How many of the Daewon kids had already gotten into college early? Jisu saw herself walking down the street, turning the corner and stepping into the coffee shop. Euni and Min turning around, mouths agape, screaming and yelling. All three of them hugging each other.

We missed you so much!

I missed you guys so much, too! I'm sorry I ever left.

Don't leave us again.

"Jisu?"

It was Haraboji. He looked at her like he was waiting for her to answer a question.

"Sorry, what were you saying?" she asked, a bit flustered, hoping she didn't offend her grandfather.

"What are you thinking so hard about?"

"Just Euni and Min. I miss them a lot."

"Don't you guys Kakao and video chat and all that now?"

"Yes, we do. But it's just not the same. If you hadn't come

to San Francisco and we only got to video chat, it wouldn't be the same."

"No, it wouldn't." Haraboji smiled at Jisu sympathetically. "I know it's hard, but just a few more months and all this will be over. Your parents are doing what they think is good for you."

Jisu wondered if what her grandfather thought was good for her was the same as what her parents thought. Would it really have hurt to have her fly to Seoul? Wouldn't it have been easier to have one person fly than to have three people—one of them super old—fly in the other direction?

Seeing Euni and Min will make it harder for you to part with them again.

Switching up the time zones will mess you up with jet lag.

You can't afford to have trouble sleeping when you're back.

This is the most important time of the most important year of high school.

Mrs. Kim didn't have to actually say any of this jansori. Jisu could recite her mother's go-to advice off the top of her head. In the end, her parents were making the decisions for her sake, whether she wanted it or not.

"So, tell me, Jisu." Haraboji spread his hands. "What have you learned during your stay in America so far? Aside from the things you learn at school."

"Well…" Jisu thought back on the past several months of her life. She thought of everyone she had met. Kaylee, with her arms wide-open on the first day of school, Jamie and Tiffany seamlessly incorporating her into their diner outings, Hiba showing her around the city, Dave inviting her to his home so that Mrs. Kang could stuff her to the gills…even Austin, who'd taken her to his favorite places in town.

"The people," Jisu said. "When they accept you here, you just melt into their lives. You become one of them."

"And so are you one of them now?" Haraboji peered over his glasses.

Jisu thought of everything she'd done in the past few months. She had learned how to surf, helped children learn to ice skate and attended rallies, gallery openings and random town hall meetings to find inspiration and take photos; she had made new friends; she had even attended new seons and gone after a boy she liked. Although who's to say how he felt about her now...but still. Within the confines of being sent away to Wick, she had managed to live life as it came at her, as *she* wanted. For once, she wasn't meticulously mapping things out, weighing which friendships would be most beneficial down the line or comparing which hobby would be most effective for her college applications.

"I'm still me. Jisu, the girl from Seoul. But something about this place is changing me," she said.

"Do you have more pictures to show me?" Haraboji asked, but without the accusatory, concerned tone her mother usually took on. If anything, he seemed hopeful that Jisu had continued her passion for photography.

She pulled her laptop from her bag to show her grandfather all the photos she had taken in the last few months but hadn't sent him: Crissy Field, Dolores Park, Mission District and City Lights.

"I took my camera on a swing and almost fell off trying to get this photo! Do you see how the city looks like it's right underneath your feet? Like you're a bird looking down." Jisu zoomed in on the cityscape.

"You should see the way you light up when you talk about your photos," Haraboji said.

It felt good to be seen the way Haraboji looked at her. Jisu could hear her parents busying themselves in the kitchen. She'd share her photos with them, but she wouldn't show them everything. It would just be more ammo for them to throw back at her. *Where did you find all this time to take photos? Make sure you don't stay out too late. Don't take too many strangers' photos—what if they get upset and try to get into an argument with you?*

"I think doing more of this has made me happier. At least it helps with all the stress," Jisu said as she clicked through the rest of her photo library.

"Jisu-ya, I'm glad you continued. School, grades, college— that's all very important. I'm not worried about you in that sense. You're a smart girl. But you need to use this time to find out what you like, what you don't like, what drives you. Or else, what do you have?"

Jisu nodded. The affirmation felt replenishing. Like she was a wilting plant unaware of how parched she was.

"You know, I see a lot of similarities between my genera- tion and yours."

"Mine? Not Appa's?" Jisu asked. She looked over to her dad. Mr. Kim was on the phone, pacing up and down the hallway. Business call, she assumed. It was early evening here, mean- ing it was the start of a workday in Seoul.

"No, not your father's. My generation—before the war and even during it—we sought out what we wanted. We went into the world and made of it what we could. Maybe it was because we had no other choice—Korea was still a very poor country ravaged by war. But then came your parents' genera- tion. They are all very concerned with money and success." Haraboji looked solemn. "Their generation had to bear a lot of scars as we recovered from the war. It created a fierce deter- mination that helped the country get back on its feet. But now that's all your father and his generation is obsessed with. Mak- ing sure that his family is secure no matter what may happen."

Haraboji motioned to his son, inviting him to sit down with them. Mr. Kim held up a finger, promising to join them with his eager gesticulation.

"See?" Haraboji laughed, but Jisu sensed he didn't actually find real humor in the situation. "But, Jisu, I see that genuine curiosity in you. When you show me your photos or tell me about your new friends."

"I think I'm just not the bookish type," Jisu said sheepishly.

"No, no. Listen to your grandfather," Haraboji said, his tone more serious. "Don't ignore your passions. Don't ignore that voice in your head. You know, the one that talks with your heart. If you ignore something like that long enough, it'll eventually explode and just make a huge mess!"

"Okay, Haraboji. I won't," Jisu said obediently.

"I'm serious. Your parents have worked so hard to give you these opportunities. I know they're hard on you. And you are a good daughter. But you're not like them. You see the heart of the world and want to be a part of it. And the biggest tragedy will be if you find yourself years into a job that you don't even want. At the end of the day, all of us want the same thing for you. We want you to be happy."

Jisu let the words sink in. She must have heard a thousand iterations of *Your parents are doing it for you*, but this was different.

Mr. Kim got off the phone and walked into the kitchen, where Mrs. Kim was cutting up fruit and placing it on a plate. He hugged his wife from the back, kissed her on the cheek and sat next to her. Jisu watched as her father took another knife and helped her mother cut the fruit. They looked tired—a ten-hour flight would do that to you—but happy and secure. And Jisu knew what her grandfather meant. Of course Haraboji would be the one to hit her with the hard facts.

"Just a few bites to tide us over until dinner," Mrs. Kim said as she entered the living room with her husband, a full tray of fruit and Korean snacks in tow.

"But don't eat too much or you won't have an appetite once we get to the restaurant," said Mr. Kim. He had made reservations at a Korean BBQ restaurant downtown.

"Don't you guys want to eat anything but Korean food while you're here?" Jisu asked, even though her taste buds were just as homesick as her heart was for the motherland.

"We want to see if the food here holds up to the food back home. We need to make sure it meets our standards for our daughter!" Mr. Kim joked, just like a dad would.

Jisu nibbled at a slice of apple. There were other snacks, including chips and cookies that her mother had brought from Korea. She'd brought all of Jisu's favorites: shrimp chips, honey sweet cakes, Choco Pie and Pepero sticks.

Jisu broke open a box of Pepero, and the chocolate-covered cookie sticks immediately transported her back to lunchtime at Daewon High. Min always kept herself on a strict diet in hopes of achieving the ideal pop star's S-line figure, but her weakness was Pepero. She always had a box of them on her at lunch and shared them with Euni and Jisu.

Here. Take these away from me. I shouldn't be eating this, she'd always say as she finished off one slim Pepero stick with three big bites.

Min, the best way to not eat Pepero is to not buy them, Euni would tease her. And then the three of them would laugh and indulge. It only ever took five minutes for them to finish off a box.

"Jisu-ya, are you feeling okay?"

Mrs. Kim cupped her daughter's face in her hands and looked at her with concern.

"I'm fine," Jisu said, her mind returning back to the present. "I'm happy you guys are here. I just really miss home."

"I know, I know," Mrs. Kim said. "Just a few more months and this will be over. Be strong, my Jisu." She pushed a slice of persimmon onto Jisu's plate. "Eat this, it's perfectly ripe and delicious."

"Yes, make sure you eat some of the persimmon," Mr. Kim

chimed in. "I just read somewhere that they're excellent for your immune system. Gives you a real boost."

Jisu obediently lifted the persimmon slice to her mouth. As much as her parents' constant hovering annoyed her, it was nice to have someone take care of her this way. The persimmon was just as boldly colored as the sun that was setting outside, a bright shade that all other oranges and tangerines would envy. It was soft and crunchy at the same time. The flavor was sweet and honeyed. She thought of the persimmon Dave's mother had meticulously peeled and fed her.

"So, Jisu. How many are left?" Mr. Kim asked.

"How many what are left?"

"She's gotten nearly all of them in—eight, right, sweetie? And she's working on the last two over the break," Mrs. Kim answered. "UChicago and Harvard."

It was only a matter of time before the conversation went back to Jisu's college applications. UChicago and Harvard. Of course her parents would be happiest if she got into an Ivy, but they would be almost equally thrilled to see her go to UChicago. But these two names were going to hang over her head all winter break and weigh her down until the moment she hit Submit on the applications. All the pressure that Haraboji had managed to take off her came rushing back. The tidal wave was coming for Jisu and dragging her by the ankles into the deep sea of college application uncertainty. Not a great way to spend the holiday break.

"No matter what happens, our Jisu will do great. Wherever she goes," Haraboji said authoritatively, like he was marking the end their conversation.

"Aigoo, your Haraboji has spent less than twenty-four hours here and he's already been infected with that foolish American optimism!" Mrs. Kim retorted.

But Jisu was not annoyed by her mother's words. That foolish optimism, the willingness to simply do what you can and trust the universe to handle the rest, it was neither American nor Korean. It was simply who she was. And Jisu saw now, in the old man sitting across from her, where she got it from.

The Kims and Murrays were hit with the strong smells of onions, garlic and marinated meat the moment they stepped into the restaurant. By the time the two family units made their way to their table, Jisu knew that all the scents had seeped into every hair strand and the fabric of her sweater. Getting KBBQ automatically meant having to smell like your food for the next few hours until you washed your hair and clothes. But it was always worth it.

"It smells amazing in here," Mandy said as she marveled at the plate of raw meat and vegetables that the servers immediately placed on their tables. They cranked up the gas and lit up the grill at the center of the table. Linda's motherly instincts kicked in and she pushed Mandy away from the table with a guarded arm.

"Have you ever tried Korean BBQ before?" Mrs. Kim asked.

"We've gone once or twice. There's a place on the other side of town that we've tried, but it's our first time here." Jeff opened the menu and traced his hand up and down the options. "But clearly you're the experts, so I'm going to leave the ordering up to you."

The Murrays and the Kims chatted away politely about their respective lives in San Francisco and Seoul. *And how did you guys meet? How long have you lived in San Francisco? How was the flight over? International travel can be so grueling at times, at least you're here long enough to make it worth it.* Mandy stared with her mouth agape as the servers quickly cut the slices of pork belly and placed them onto the grill.

If there was one way to briefly cure Jisu's homesickness, it was by eating the pork belly straight off the grill. Jisu lifted a still sizzling piece of meat with her metal chopsticks and gingerly placed it onto the perilla leaf that rested in her other hand. She added a smear of hot chili paste and some thinly sliced raw green onions. Then she wrapped it all up in a tight ball and ate it. The mash of the herbal leaf, pungent onions and marinated meat covered in flame-licked grease was heavenly.

Jisu's father spoke enthusiastically between bites, recounting some story to Jeff about a coworker who drank a little too much soju and embarrassed himself at the company party. Haraboji chuckled at each development of the story. Mrs. Kim was busy taking photos she could send to the Kakao group chat with her girlfriends.

The bell tied to the entrance door jingled when another group of patrons entered. Jisu glanced toward the door. She did a double take.

Was that...?

It was Dave Kang.

He was with his family, too. She didn't know why, but she hoped he didn't see her. It would be different if she was there with Hiba, Jamie or Tiffany. Or if he was there with one of his buddies, or even Sophie. But Jisu was out with her elders and he was with his, too. And nothing was more tedious than a gaggle of Korean adults making nice and trying to figure out who they knew in common and how many degrees they were apart in knowing each other.

"Oh, isn't that Jisu?"

Mrs. Kang spotted Jisu before she could duck and be hidden by the smoke. Jisu's gaze met Dave's. He smiled and waved. Jisu smiled back meekly. He was with a large group of people— cousins and other relatives, it seemed. Mrs. Kang shooed the rest of her family away and tugged Dave by the sleeve of his jacket toward Jisu and her family.

"Who's that?" Mrs. Kim nudged her daughter.

"Isn't that Dave?" Mandy whispered so only Jisu could hear.

But before Jisu could answer any of them, her mother had already flashed a welcoming smile and Mrs. Kang was already making a beeline to their table.

"Hey, Jisu," Dave said quietly as he ran his hand through his hair, like he was shy all of a sudden.

"You must be Jisu's family!" Mrs. Kang clasped her hands. She turned to the Murrays. "Both biological and host!" She gave Jisu a hug and extended her hand to everyone at the table. "I'm Mrs. Kang, Dave's mom. Jisu and Dave go to the same school. She was over the other day when they were working on a project. You have such a well-mannered daughter!"

"Jisu is very well-mannered," Linda chimed in. Jisu pulled a napkin apart in her lap. All of this attention was unsettling. Jisu's parents and the Murrays all got up from their seats to properly shake hands with Mrs. Kang. A simple hello, nice to meet you and goodbye would have sufficed. This whole overture of greetings was too much.

"Your name is Dave? Nice to meet you," Mr. Kim said as he shook Dave's hand. He turned to Jisu. "You never told us you were friends with such a good-looking kid. And Korean, too!"

Linda laughed and Jeff smiled at this remark. Jisu felt her face go beet red, just like her mother's whenever she had one sip of soju. She looked to Mandy for some comfort, but she was too busy piling pieces of grilled meat onto her plate. She looked at Dave but he was still looking down at his sneakers, probably feeling the same level of discomfort. When was this song and dance going to be over?

"Well, your daughter is such a nice young lady. I love it whenever she comes over. She has such nice manners. Some of these teenage girls just don't have noonchi, you know?"

"Noonchi? What does that mean?" Jeff asked.

"Tact and sense. But Jisu—she has a lot of noonchi." Mrs. Kang looked over at Jisu. "Jisu-ya, you can come over to ajumma's house, even when my son's not around. I'll make you Korean food when you get homesick for it."

"Thank you, that's very kind of you," Mrs. Kim said. "And as a mother, that makes me feel good to know someone's making her Korean food."

"Is your whole family out to celebrate the holidays?" Linda asked. "We heard this was the best Korean BBQ place in town and we wanted to take the Kims somewhere worthy."

"It *is* the best. And actually, we're out to celebrate something else—my son just got early admission to his top college choice. Harvard!" The joy in Mrs. Kang's voice was exactly what you'd expect to hear from a Korean mother whose child got accepted into Harvard: pure, unadulterated joy.

Jisu was surprised to hear the news. When had he found out? Everyone at Wick was dying to hear from their early-acceptance choices, and most shouted the news from the rooftops the moment they found out they got in.

Harvard? she mouthed at Dave, and gave him a look as if to say, *Why didn't you tell me?*

"Congratulations! That is a major accomplishment," Mr. Kim said. Jisu felt her mother's eyes on her. Mrs. Kim's gaze translated to, *You hear that? Harvard. Your American friend here was able to do it.*

"My boy is going to Harvard!" Mrs. Kang said, louder now. Some of the other customers turned to look at them.

"Mom, you really don't have to yell," Dave said through his teeth with a smile.

"What are you talking about? Jisu is still working on her regular admission applications. Early action must mean you're an especially outstanding student. If my daughter managed to get into a school like Harvard, I would be telling every stranger I passed on the street," Mrs. Kim said.

Managed to get in? She really never showed any faith in me, her own daughter, her only child. Jisu looked to Haraboji for help, but he had already checked out of the conversation and continued his meal. The elderly could do whatever they wanted. They were excused from having to participate in any social niceties.

Jisu could sense Mrs. Kim shifting gears.

"So, just how much time are our kids spending together?"

"I don't know, but every time Jisu comes over, I tell Dave how much better she is than the other girls he brings home."

Mandy choked on her water. Jisu wanted to choke on her food so everyone could stop talking.

"Other girls! Dave, you must be popular. I mean, look at how tall he is!" Jeff commented.

"No, no. He could pick up some Korean manners from your daughter. How can a girl be both so pretty and so well-raised?"

The more the adults prattled on, the more Jisu wanted to bury her head in the ground. Jeff and Linda returned to their meal, but her mother and Dave's mother shifted to Korean and continued chatting away. Jisu and Dave collectively rolled their eyes. They were being suffocated by an annoying, strong force of parental energy. Jisu wanted to die of embarrassment, but it looked like Dave wanted to die also, and that was comforting in its own weird way.

"Look, Mom, Auntie Kay is waving at us. We should go," Dave said, even though everyone at their table was still studying the menu and no one was motioning to them.

"Yes, we don't want to hold you up from your meal," Jisu said, following his lead.

"Aigoo, always so thoughtful, your Jisu," Mrs. Kang remarked to Mrs. Kim.

A major wave of relief washed over her as Dave and his mother walked to their table. If the small talk had continued any longer, she would've gotten indigestion.

"So?" Mrs. Kim looked at her daughter with a strange eagerness. "Anything you want to tell us about Dave?"

"Yeah, Jisu. That's the first I ever heard or saw of him," Linda joined in.

"You know everything there is to know. He's a friend from Wick. And he just got into Harvard. That's all."

Jisu wrapped a large piece of pork belly into another perilla leaf, shoved the whole thing in her mouth and hoped she wouldn't have to talk any longer about Dave and whatever ideas her parents now had about him.

DATE NO. 18

NAME: **Jang Jaeson aka Jason**

INTERESTS:
Tennis, Video Games, Law

PARENT OCCUPATIONS:
Economics professor; Architectural engineer

JASON: Deuce! Damn, Jisu. You're catching up. You're pretty good at tennis.

JISU: I took some lessons in Seoul. That was after I tried to take ballet classes for half a year…right before I took figure skating lessons like every other Korean girl who wanted to be like Kim Yuna.

JASON: Guess I should stop going easy on you, then.

JISU: Oh, is that your excuse for giving up the lead? That was out! Serve again.

JASON: That wasn't out!

JISU: It definitely was.

JASON: Okay, I don't think it was but I'll serve again. Can't go full-beast mode on you yet.

JISU: Are you saying I'm not a worthy opponent?

JASON: Not at all. It's just that I've been playing for like a million years. I'll ease into the game for you.

JISU: No. Play your best. I don't care.

JASON: You sure?

JISU: Yeah, I'm sure! If I'm going to win, it'll be because I actually beat you. Not because you let me.

JASON: All right. Somebody's competitive. Well, now I have the advantage point.

JISU: You still need to score one more to win the game.

JASON: Yeah, I know how tennis works.

JISU: Deuce again! See, I'm not so bad.

JASON: How many times have we tied up now?

JISU: Honestly, I'm losing count. Are you sure you're still not going easy on me? For someone who's been playing for a million years, I thought you'd be—

JASON: Advantage! If you keep yapping, I'm going to finish this game right here.

JISU: This game isn't over.

JASON: Game! I win. You sure about that? Hey, that was actually a good round.

JISU: It only got interesting when you decided to actually play.

JASON: You're kind of really competitive, aren't you?

JISU: After going to Daewon in Seoul and now Wick, it would be weird if I hadn't developed a competitive streak.

JASON: Fair enough. Everyone at my high school is crazy competitive, too. They're all trying to do a million sports or get an internship at Facebook while they're still in high school.

JISU: Water break?

JASON: Why, you feeling tired already? I've only just started. You said so yourself.

JISU: I'm not tired! Just need a breather. Also looks like you could use it, too. You're sweating an awful lot.

JASON: You know, the other times I've taken girls to play tennis on seons, it's never ended up like this.

JISU: Like what?

JASON: Like a legit game and full sets. With sweating and tiebreakers.

JISU: Oh, did you expect me to be all cutesy and ask you to teach me how to do a backhand? And then hope I'd be impressed by your years of tennis expertise?

JASON: Okay, *no*. Not quite like that.

JISU: But some version of that, huh? Okay, that was only the fourth game. Two more. I can still win this set.

JASON: Here—it's your turn to serve.

JISU: Yes! 15–0.

JASON: Love.

JISU: What?

JASON: It's 15–love. Not zero.

JISU: Oh. Right. I always forget that. Love means zero.

JASON: Whoever coined that was definitely a heartbroken cynic.

JISU: Yeah, and I bet they'd hate to see you try to use tennis to woo over girls.

JASON: Is that what I'm doing? Wooing you right now?

JISU: 30–love. Not if you keep letting me score like this! Where's your best at, Jason?

JASON: I am trying! This might be the first time I actually lose a whole set on a seon without meaning to.

19

*I*t was unfair how quickly holiday break came and went. The two weeks that Jisu's family was in town felt all too short. Haraboji and her parents were long gone, but the floor of Jisu's room was still covered with crumpled Christmas wrapping paper and gold ribbons. If she never picked them up, maybe it would still be Christmas and her family would still be in the same city with her.

Being apart from them for a few months had really made Jisu cherish her family's presence. She even spent New Year's Eve with them. Tiffany was throwing a party in her parents' basement as she did every year, but Jisu didn't even entertain the thought of ditching Haraboji and her parents on one of their final nights.

Are you sure? Tiffany had asked. *We're going to miss you!*

I think Austin's going to be there, Hiba had mentioned. *Would that change your mind?*

If anything, it only made Jisu double down on her decision. He didn't want to meet her family and didn't seem to want to spend much time with her either. Austin hadn't really reached out to Jisu over the break, except for random one-off texts that led nowhere and leaving the occasional prayer hands or heart-eye emoji comments on her Instagram posts. He wasn't ignoring her, but it was more like he was leaving small breadcrumbs of communication so he could pick things back up with her whenever it was convenient for him. Each breadcrumb chipped away at Jisu's icy, resolute determination to keep away from Austin. But it also gave her a twinge of chest pain each time. He wanted to see her, but not in the same way she wanted to see him.

On New Year's Eve, Hiba bombarded Jisu's phone with photos of herself, Jamie and Tiffany at the New Year's party, but for once Jisu was immune to FOMO. She rang in the New Year quietly with her family, the four of them snuggled on the couch, watching the countdown on TV. The next morning, Mrs. Kim made rice-cake soup as she did every single year. The moment Jisu lifted the spoonful of soup to her lips, took a sip and let the warmth of home cooking wash over her, she knew she had made the right decision.

The constant time Jisu spent with her family made saying goodbye more difficult. After they parted, a quiet stillness returned, like the emptiness of a home after all the party guests have left. But there was just one more semester remaining, and then Jisu would be back in Seoul.

Jisu groaned as she picked herself up off her bed. She heaved herself forward and forced herself to pick up the trash. Break was over. She had to get back on track.

At least all her college applications were now finally sent out and done. Jisu had saved Harvard for last. She'd given her best efforts, spent parts of her break embellishing her essay and adding letters of recommendations from her teachers at Wick to enhance her application.

When school resumed, everyone else also quickly sprang back into motion. Jamie and Tiffany weren't their usual social selves at lunch. Instead of floating from one table to another and catching up with everyone, they planted themselves down and revised each other's college essays. Jamie was armed with a purple gel pen and Tiffany with a red ballpoint pen.

"What are you circling so much?" Jamie asked. She looked at her essay in Tiffany's hand. "Seeing all that red ink is making me nervous, Tiff."

"Don't worry, I'm circling both the good and bad parts."

"There are bad parts?"

"Relax, girl. You said you wanted my notes, did you not?"

Watching Jamie and Tiffany bicker over final edits made Jisu feel better about being done. But a new nervous energy surrounded them...because all that was left to do was wait.

From the corner of her eye, Jisu spotted Austin. He made his way from group to group so seamlessly, like a free-flowing stream of water snaking its way down the mountain around all its curves. He looked so carefree. It was the exact opposite of how she remembered him last, sitting in her bedroom, resistant to the thought of meeting her family. Weren't they at least friends? Mr. and Mrs. Kim had met Hiba, Jamie and Tiffany during their stay. They'd even met Dave, however unintentional and embarrassing that whole encounter had been.

Jisu could call out to Austin. She knew he would waltz over, greet her warmly and act friendly in that unnerving way. As if they were simply passing acquaintances, and just friendly enough that expressing her frustration with him would make her look crazy. Jisu knew exactly what Jamie and Tiffany would say. *But he's so nice. It's not like he's ignoring you. Why are you annoyed with him?*

Jisu clamped her hands down and locked her eyes on her

friends. She concentrated on eating lunch and not looking up from her table. She'd hoped the break would come and go and Austin would be out of her system, like a bad stomach bug. But a part of her missed him even though he was *right there*. She wondered if he saw her, and if he wanted to come over and say hi. Maybe all he needed was a sign, a little bit of encouragement from her.

No. Austin Velasco was not the type to need encouragement. He would come over to talk to her if he wanted to. Jisu would not be the one to concede. She was resolute, but she also hated how much she wanted to see him.

"Hey!" Dave startled Jisu. This was the first time she'd seen Dave since they'd both had to witness their mothers' embarrassing small talk.

She was in the English literature section of the library, flipping through a copy of the *Oxford Book of English Verse*. School had been back in session for only a day, but she already had a test coming up next week.

"Shh! You're going to get us kicked out!" Jisu whispered. She'd spent one too many study hall periods at the library with Hiba trying not to break into a fit of giggles. Ms. Cole, the librarian, was always looking daggers at them.

"Hey, Ms. Cole!" Dave waved at the librarian as she pushed a cart of books past them. Instead of scowling like she usually did, Ms. Cole smiled. Of course Dave could win over even grumpy Ms. Cole.

"See? She loves me. We're good." Dave grinned. "Anyway, I've been looking all over for you."

"You were looking for me?"

"I was. Two things. One—I'm *so* sorry my mom was being so embarrassing the other night, yelling about Harvard and all that. I've never felt more humiliated."

"You have nothing to apologize for. Your mom was really excited for you! She's so cute—I love her." Jisu closed the book of English verse and walked down the aisle. Dave followed her. "If anything, *I* should be apologizing," she said. "I couldn't stop cringing every time my parents started talking. I swear to god they send me off on so many random dates and they're so desperate for me to date anyone at this point that they lose all sense of social norms."

"That's kind of the norm for Koreans though."

"Oh, it totally is. Korean moms are always overcomplimenting each other on their outfits, their kids, their husbands."

"Yeah, it's either that or backhanded compliments."

"Oh, my god, it's hilarious when ajummas go at each other with fake compliments. One time, in elementary school, this girl was mean to me. I didn't even tell my mom but word got back to her somehow. The next day, at pickup, she went over to that girl's mom and told her, 'Everyone has been talking about how bold and aggressive your daughter is. I only hope that kind of pushy unladylike behavior will serve her well in academics and life.' She actually said that."

"Okay, well, my mom hates my aunt—my dad's youngest sister. And every Thanksgiving, when we get together, she'll always tell her how 'plump and healthy' and 'well-fed' she looks. You know what that's code for. And my aunt won't even say anything back, because she knows not to mess with my mom."

"Your mom says that? But she legit seems so nice. I can't imagine her saying that!"

"Well, you know how they are. If they're on your side, you're golden. If not, well, good luck to you."

"Yeah, if backhanded complimenting were an Olympic sport, South Korean ajummas would win gold, silver *and* bronze." Jisu laughed, maybe a little too loud for Ms. Cole's liking, but she didn't care. The two of them walked to the front desk and Jisu checked out her book.

"Oh, and one other thing," Dave said. "We should figure out a time to meet one more time for the project."

"We got a lot done last time though. We're pretty much done, right?"

It was true. The last time they met up before the break, they had finished the PowerPoint presentation and gone over all their data. Mrs. Kang had made kimchi stew and steamed some homemade dumplings. It was easily one of the best meals she'd had in San Francisco, El Farolito burritos included.

"Yeah, but I figure we should go through it one more time and also practice doing the actual presentation." No wonder Dave had gotten into Harvard. He did everything until it was perfect.

"I'm free now, if you want to go through it? Might as well since we're in the library already."

"I can't now. Sophie's in the car outside, waiting for me."

"Sophie? Oh." Jisu felt defensive all of a sudden. Of what, she didn't know. She imagined basic Sophie sitting in the passenger seat, listening to basic music and checking her basic makeup in the mirror.

"Yeah, we're going to see the new Avengers movie."

"Fun!" Jisu forced the sides of her face upward.

"Let's meet up next week?"

"Yeah! Text me and we'll figure it out."

Dave left the library and Jisu let her smile drop. She wasn't jealous in any way, no. Jisu already had plans to see the Avengers movie with someone else. Sure, it was for another seon with a complete stranger via Ms. Moon, but Jisu had her own plans. *I bet Sophie's the type to constantly talk and ask questions throughout the movie. Does she even know who any of the Avengers are?* Jisu was just looking out for Dave. The way he looked out for her with Austin. It was in her own motherly way. Having Jisu look out for her son was what Mrs. Kang would want anyway. She clearly wasn't impressed much with Sophie either.

Jisu gathered her belongings and left the library. She turned her phone back on. There was a text message. Jisu could tell it was Austin. She had deleted him from her contacts, but she still recognized his number. And she hated herself for recognizing it.

Yo. You around this weekend? Starting to forget what you look like.

Starting to forget what she looked like? They were in the same room, eating lunch, just a few hours ago! If he wanted to remember what she looked like, he could've easily walked over and said hi.

But he had initiated contact. Jisu did feel a tiny rush of satisfaction. Maybe not saying hi to him during lunch had been the right move. Her thumbs hovered over the keyboard. Should she make him wait for a reply? Did she even want to see him? Thinking about Austin lately was proving to be more tiresome than pleasant.

Jisu's phone dinged with another notification. It was a Kakao message from Mrs. Kim.

Ms. Moon is emailing you a full schedule of your seons for this month. Don't forget to add them all to your calendar.

"Yes, Mother," Jisu said out loud as she swiped away the Kakao notification.

The screen returned to Austin's text message. Jisu looked at it for a moment. She put her phone away in her bag. Austin could wait.

DATE NO. 19

NAME: **Choi Henry**

INTERESTS:
Weight Training, MTV, Karaoke

PARENT OCCUPATIONS:
HR manager; Art gallery owner

HENRY: Look who decided to show up!

JISU: I am *so* sorry. I totally lost track of time. Usually I'm not so late. And then there was traffic on top of that...

HENRY: Ten, fifteen minutes—I totally get it. But a whole half hour? I really thought I was getting stood up.

JISU: Oh, my goodness. I'm really so sorry! I'm usually never late, I swear!

HENRY: I'm just teasing. Don't worry about it. We're here. Can I get you anything?

JISU: Oh, yes! Hmm, what did you get?

HENRY: Just a simple cappuccino. I might get another when I'm done with this one.

JISU: All right, then I'll do the same. So! Tell me about yourself. Harry, was it?

HENRY: My name is Henry...

JISU: Oh, gosh. I am really screwing it up today, aren't I? I'm so sorry Harr—Henry! Henry. I am the worst.

HENRY: Hey, that's all right. Just take it easy. You still seem a little out of breath. Did you run here?

JISU: Well, to save time, I thought I'd take an Uber. But then I got stuck in traffic. It looked like I was only a few blocks away from this coffee shop, so I decided to get out and walk over...but I totally misjudged. I think it was more like a full mile away.

HENRY: Maybe some coconut water or Gatorade would be better instead...

JISU: No! That's all right! It's all good! So, Henry.

HENRY: So, Amanda.

JISU: Amanda?

HENRY: Wait...are you not Amanda?

JISU: No, I'm Jisu...

HENRY: Definitely not Amanda Lim?

JISU: Trust me, I would love to be Amanda Lim right now so we could say at least one thing went right on this seon.

HENRY: But you look just like her. Here, take a look. Your—er, I guess Amanda's profile.

JISU: Wait, this is definitely my photo. This is the one I sent Ms. Moon. But this...

HENRY: See? First name Amanda. Interests include DJ-ing, saving Mother Nature and spoken word. Parents are school-teachers...

JISU: This is definitely not me. I mean, the photo is me, but it must have somehow gotten mixed up with Amanda's profile.

HENRY: So, somewhere out there, Amanda is on a seon with someone who thinks she's Jisu.

JISU: That's probably accurate.

HENRY: Wow, I don't think this has ever happened.

JISU: Should we just quit while we're ahead?

HENRY: Quit? No! I mean, you ran a mile to get here, right? You wait for your cappuccino and enjoy it. Why not?

JISU: That's true. I did practically run the whole way here...

HENRY: So, what does it say on your mysterious profile? I had such a completely different perception of you.

JISU: Yeah, you probably thought I was going to be some hippie who likes to read.

HENRY: I mean, if trying to save the earth makes you a hippie, I guess I'm also one then...

JISU: Oh, I didn't mean it in any derogatory way. I actually do think environmental issues are important...

HENRY: I am also bookish, which hopefully isn't an issue.

JISU: Not at all! I also try to read a novel or two whenever I can. I guess that was just a bad attempt at making a joke. I can promise you it doesn't say *comedy* under talents in my profile...

HENRY: Yup...

JISU: Yeah...

HENRY: So...

JISU: So, I think maybe I'll just ask for a coffee to go. This was clearly some minor snafu or glitch or something from Ms. Moon. I can email her and let her know.

HENRY: Uh, yeah. That sounds good. I can email her also. Well...it was nice to...meet you?

JISU: Yeah…hopefully we both end up having the best seon ever after this one.

HENRY: Ha, well, at least you have a sense of humor about all this.

20

Jisu had a sinking feeling as she logged in to the portal to check her application status. She had one new notification. How could one email feel so heavy with purpose and importance. That was probably how every email from Yale University felt. Jisu glanced over the school's email address. She didn't have to open it to know what it said. She just knew.

Yale was Euni's dream school. If Euni had to work as hard as she did to try to get into Yale, then there was no way Jisu would be following her there even if she did her absolute best. Jisu clicked on the message.

Dear Ms. Jisu Kim,

Thank you for your application to Yale University. The Admissions Committee has met and we regret to inform you that we are unable to consider your application further. Given the

*high volume of the applicant pool this year, it was inevitable
that several candidates with excellent credentials would have to
be denied...*

The letter went on, but Jisu didn't bother reading the rest.

She dialed her mother. Mrs. Kim could be at work—it was evening in San Francisco, and the start of the workday in Seoul.

"Hello? Jisu?" Of course she was available. From now until the last college notification came in, Mrs. Kim was going to be on call for her daughter.

"Umma, I didn't get in."

"Didn't get in where?"

"Yale."

Mrs. Kim was silent on the other end. Jisu didn't know which mother she'd be getting today: hypercritical or sympathetic. It was rarely both.

"Did they say why?"

"No. They probably sent out hundreds of rejections. They're not going to give each person a detailed personal letter."

"You got those personal recommendations in to them on time, right?"

So, she was going to be hypercritical today.

"Yes. I did."

"And it's a rejection. Not even the wait list?"

"It's what it says, Umma. I didn't get into Yale, but I'm not illiterate either." Calling her mom had been a mistake. This was the worst way to start off the day. In just an hour, Jisu would have to schlep her way to school and go about her day with this rejection hanging over her head. She wanted to change back into her pj's and crawl back under the covers.

"This is why I'm applying to non-Ivy schools, don't you remember?" Jisu said. "There was no way I was going to get into Yale. We both knew it. This was a waste of an application."

MELISSA DE LA CRUZ

"If you studied harder, you would have a better shot. At least get on the wait list," Mrs. Kim snapped back.

"I did study hard. That's what you don't get! Academics have never come easy to me. I'm not a good test taker. But I tried. I spent hours in hagwon, I did all the extracurriculars you signed me up for, I even left my friends and moved to a completely different country. You've *never* understood who I really am. You've never even tried to."

"Jisu-ya—" Mrs. Kim started. But Jisu had had enough. The rejection on her computer was bad enough. She wasn't going to let her mother double down on her.

"I'm hanging up, Umma. Goodbye."

Jisu could hear Mandy rustling in her room next door. She didn't care if Mandy had overheard her arguing on the phone. She cared only about what the nine other colleges would say.

At school the next day, Hiba did her best to offer words of encouragement.

"Well, Yale is a tough school to get into," she said.

"Thanks for stating the obvious, Hiba."

"Sorry… I'm not the best at giving pep talks."

"Probably because you never needed one in your life. I bet none of the kids at Princeton ever needed a pep talk."

"I haven't gotten into Princeton just yet."

"Psh." Jisu waved Hiba off. "You are getting in. I've never felt so sure of anything."

"Don't lose hope yet, Jisu. The first rejection stings the most, but you're still standing. You still have nine others to hear from. It's not like you're going to get rejected by all of them."

"What? I never even had that thought. Why would you say that?"

"Nooo. That's not what I meant." Hiba stumbled over her words. Finally, there was something Hiba wasn't good at: inspirational talks. "I just meant that you're clearly a smart girl, with good grades—Yale or not—and you're going to get into the best school for you."

"I love you, Hiba, but you would make the worst hype man ever."

Jisu and Hiba continued down the hall toward class. Hiba pulled at Jisu's bag when they turned the corner. She tilted her head and directed Jisu's eyes to their left. Austin was walking toward them.

"Hey, stranger," he said, friendly as ever. Jisu could swear she detected a hint of hesitation and uncertainty in his voice. Austin gave her a hug and Hiba discreetly rolled her eyes. "I've been trying to reach you. Did you not get my text?"

"Sorry. I've been…busy," Jisu said, even though since completing her college applications, she had more free time on her hands.

Austin looked at Hiba, like she might wander off and walk herself to class and leave the two of them standing in the hallway. But Hiba stayed put with her arms crossed. Jisu was glad. She could see herself easily getting swayed by the Velasco charm if her friend wasn't there to supervise.

"I have to tell you something," Austin said.

"What is it?" Jisu said as calmly as she could. Though she looked at him expectantly. A million thoughts swirled through her head. What could he possibly have to say? It wouldn't take a lot for him to make her day better.

"I'm going to San Diego State!"

It didn't take a lot for him to make her day worse either. All this time had passed and the thing he wanted to tell her was that he got into his top-choice college? On the same day that she got her first rejection? It was like pouring salt in the wound.

"That's great. I'm happy for you, Austin," Jisu said and tried her best not to reveal her smile as a wince.

"I mean, it's no Ivy League school, where you guys will probably end up. But I'm hella excited." Austin genuinely seemed so. Jisu let a part of herself feel happy for him.

"San Diego State is a great school," Hiba said. "Do you know what you want to do there?"

"Hell yeah, I do. I'm going to surf every day, all year round. The waves there don't even compare to the cold, choppy waters that we have here. Jisu knows. Right, Jisu?" Austin flashed her a knowing smile. That perfectly crooked smile. Would he ever take her surfing again? "But yeah, can't wait to catch some real waves. It's gonna be dope."

"I meant like what are you going to study there, but that's 'dope,' I guess," Hiba said coolly. She turned and gave Jisu a look like, *Really? This is the one you like? Of all the dudes*, before walking down the hall and turning into class.

Jisu braced herself for all the old, warm feelings for Austin to rush back, but they didn't. She looked at him. His black, wavy hair was tousled and unruly. It was as carefree as he was. She was still drawn to his face, just as she had been however many days ago when they had last been together and however many days before that when they'd been alone in his car at night.

But surfing? Really? That's what he was looking forward to most? Austin's let-it-be, laissez-faire attitude was starting to rub her the wrong way. There *should* be things that meant a lot to you. Things that you held close to yourself. How could someone cruise through life so detached from everything?

"When are we hanging out? I haven't seen you since…" Austin held Jisu's hand.

"Since I asked you to meet my family and you flat-out said no?" Jisu pulled her hand away from him.

"C'mon. You still bothered about that? I was working at the restaurant all break. And you didn't even come by. I missed you."

I didn't stop by because I never got an invite. If you missed me, you could've hit me up with one text, Jisu thought to herself.

"What are you doing tonight?" Austin asked.

"It's Tuesday. I'm not trying to stay out late."

"I never said anything about staying out. I could come over?"

"I'm going to be late to class. We'll figure something out. Just text me later. I'll actually respond!" Jisu walked away. She turned away from him and tried not to smile too hard. It was nice to have Austin be so eager to see her. She felt the pull of his charm, but noticed it was no longer as strong.

The phone rang and Jisu picked up as soon as she saw Euni's name flash across the screen. She was worried something bad had happened to her again.

"Euni? Hello? Is everything okay?"

"Jisu! It's so good to hear your voice." Eunice sounded like her normal, chirpy self. Jisu felt relieved.

"It's good to hear yours, too," Jisu said. "And you sound better. How are you?"

"I'm good. I don't have to rest for half the day anymore like the doctors told me to when I first got out of the hospital."

"That's amazing! And Min's being good?"

"Min's being too attentive. Honestly, it's a little suffocating." Euni laughed, and it sounded like a hearty laugh filled with energy.

"But, Jisu, I am calling because I have some news. Really good news."

"What? What happened?"

"I got accepted to Yale!" Eunice shouted. "I just found out and after telling my parents and you're the first person I called!"

"Oh. My. God. Eunice! That's amazing!" Jisu was thousands of miles away from Eunice but could feel her happiness radiating through the phone.

She'd had no doubt Eunice would get in, but after watching her work so hard for all these years, it felt good to see her friend thrive. It almost didn't matter that she herself had started the day off with a rejection from Yale—Jisu had known Yale was not going to be her school.

"All that hard work, Euni. You can relax and have fun now," Jisu said.

"I am so happy—you have no idea. I just wish you were with me. We should be celebrating together," Eunice said. She sounded breathless, like she had just run a quick mile. "How's all the college stuff going for you?"

"Well, it sounds like Yale got all their decisions out. I got a rejection from them last night."

"Aw, Jisu. That's just one. I did hear that they had way too many people apply this year. Plus, you're the one who said New Haven seems boring!"

Jisu laughed. Eunice was a little better at this than Hiba.

"Yeah, that's true. It's just my first rejection. I think that's why I'm so upset about it."

"You shouldn't be upset. You are a super smart and funny person. And you're so talented. My only talent is memorizing schoolwork and taking tests. Do you know how boring that is? Getting into Yale is going to be the best that those skills can do for me. I'm going downhill from here!" This was only the start of Eunice's big, burgeoning academic career—both of them knew that—but hearing her say otherwise made Jisu feel less small.

"Jisu-ya, listen to me. You're going to get into the perfect school for you and you will be so much happier there than at some stuffy Ivy that you don't like that much."

"Eunice, you've been an accepted Yale student for like two

seconds. You really don't need to trash-talk your own school for my sake."

The girls laughed. Eunice updated Jisu on all the Daewon gossip, primarily about who was now dating whom and which students had already gotten early acceptances to which schools. By the time they hung up, Jisu wanted to call Eunice back up again to chat with her for several more hours. Talking to Euni had made her feel more secure. The storm of anxiety that had been growing in her stomach had settled. For now. The waves of anxiety were prone to wash ashore anytime. She didn't know when they would hit her, but they would come back.

DATE NO. 20

NAME: **Kim Taehoon**

ROLE MODELS:
James Bond, Lee Minho

GOALS:
National Intelligence Service Investigator

TAEHOON: I can't believe they managed to get all these huge actors to be in one movie.

JISU: I know! I'm so excited. This is the exact movie I'm in the mood to watch right now. Actually...Taehoon?

TAEHOON: What's up?

JISU: I've had a hell of a day. I just got my first college rejection. And my best friend got into the school that rejected me.

TAEHOON: Shoot, that sucks. I'm sorry. Which school was it? Actually, you know what, you don't even have to tell me.

JISU: Yeah, and to be honest, I'm not really all that into dating and seons right now. I just want to ignore my phone for two hours and take a break from everything.

TAEHOON: Totally get it. School's driving me nuts, too. And I don't really care much about these blind dates. We're on the same page. Let's just watch the movie.

JISU: Sweet. Which aisle are we?

TAEHOON: Aisle G—right here.

JISU: Can you pass the popcorn?

TAEHOON: Yup—and I'm going to take some of those M&M'S.

JISU: Ooh, great, we didn't miss the previews. I love the previews.

21

*I*t was unofficial Wick tradition for all the seniors to make their way to Ocean Beach and huddle by a bonfire on the first long weekend of the year. Everyone drove to the beach in their hoodies, with their warmest blankets, to reminisce on the last four years they had spent together.

"I really don't see why I should go. I've only been going to Wick for a few months. I'm not really emotionally involved," Jisu said to Hiba as she fastened her seat belt.

She hadn't planned to go, but Hiba had pulled up to the Murrays' driveway and didn't stop honking until Jisu came outside.

"But you're still a senior at Wick. And it's not like you haven't made friends. Everyone's going to be there."

Hiba knew that there wouldn't be much for Jisu to reminisce about, but ever since the rejection from Yale, a dark cloud lingered over Jisu's head and refused to go away. She needed to get out of the house and get her mind off college.

The girls pulled up to Ocean Beach just as the sun was setting. The beach stretched on uninterrupted for miles. The wide expanse was so overwhelming, it felt like a tiny gust of wind would be enough to send someone hurtling several feet across the sand.

There was already a fire going and groups of people huddled around. The night sky quickly took over as Hiba and Jisu walked over from the parking lot to the sand.

"Jisu, you made it!" Jamie said as she flung her arms around her.

"We thought you weren't coming!" Tiffany joined in on the hug also.

"Hiba made me." Jisu shrugged. "I probably shouldn't even be here? I'm just going to be like an observer from the outside."

"Don't be ridiculous," Jamie said. "Some people were already asking if you were coming."

Jisu wanted to ask Jamie who specifically. She wondered if maybe Austin had asked about her. But she searched the crowd and didn't see him. It wasn't surprising. Austin either ran events like these or thought he was too good to be at them. If he wasn't making a show of tackling one of his buddies into the sand or handing out cans of cheap beer that somebody's older sibling got for them, he was probably off somewhere else, doing his own thing.

Jisu wandered toward the water. People were passing around old yearbooks and fawning over what they'd looked like years ago. The sight of the Pacific Ocean made Jisu emotional, the way it always did. She couldn't not think of Seoul when she stared out into the sea. Jisu took her flats off and dipped her feet in the water as the waves crashed and inched toward her.

The cold sent a shock up her spine. Jisu walked back to the group with her shoes in her hand.

"Did anyone bring extra blankets?" Tiffany asked. "We're running out of space."

"Oh, I brought one but I forgot it in my car," Hiba said. She was sitting right next to the bonfire and busy making s'mores with some of the others.

"I'll go and grab it," Jisu volunteered. Hiba tossed her the keys.

It was pitch-black by the time Jisu made the short walk over to the parking lot. There were no streetlights, just the full moon in the cloudless sky lighting the way. Jisu unlocked Hiba's door and searched the back seat for the blanket. It was so dark, it felt more effective for her to search with her hands.

She didn't know what made her look up. But when she did, she saw them through the back window. First she recognized his car. It was parked, and Austin was in the driver's seat. He was talking to whoever was in the passenger seat. Jisu couldn't make out her face from the angle she was crouched at. But she instantly recognized the situation for what it was. She knew it because, only a few weeks before, she had been that girl in the passenger seat, having a heart-to-heart with Austin.

Even in the dim light, Jisu could see and practically recite whatever line he was using on this girl. *I like you. I really like you.* Who was she anyway? Jisu leaned closer to the back-seat window and peered out of Hiba's car. She was no longer concerned with finding the blanket. She arched her head sideways to get a better look at the girl, but it was too dark to tell.

Who is she?

He put his hands on the girl's face and slid them down her neck. And then he went in for the kill. Jisu looked away and curled her knees to her chest. It was like a surreal out-of-body experience to watch someone else fall into the very trap you'd once fallen for.

It felt like someone had just gutted her. Heat rose to her face. She had to get out. She grabbed the wool blanket beneath her feet and jumped out of the car. She slammed the car door hard.

A little too hard.

From the corner of her eye, she saw the two of them turn. Jisu immediately regretted letting her anger get to her. She looked up and locked eyes with Austin. Kaylee was sitting next to him in the passenger seat.

Kaylee. Of all people.

Apparently, Jisu's approach to play it cool with Austin had driven him straight to the clingiest person he could find. It was a mistake. It was all a mistake. Jisu had never wanted to come to Ocean Beach in the first place. She'd never wanted to get tangled in Austin's web. She'd never even wanted to go to Wick. She'd never wanted to leave Seoul.

Jisu ran from the parking lot and onto the beach as quickly as she could. She just wanted to go home. She could hear Austin behind her and tried to walk in the sand as fast as she could, but he caught up with her.

"Whoa, hey. Slow down!" He reached out to her.

Jisu recoiled at his touch. She swiftly turned to face him.

"I thought you said Kaylee was clingy and annoying."

"Why does that matter? You're the one dating every Korean dude in town."

"What are you talking about?"

"Your blind dates. With the sons of power lawyers and execs or whatever. I heard Tiffany talk about them."

Was this why Austin was hot one second and cold the next? Did he think she was making power moves on him? It hadn't even crossed her mind to disclose the seons to him. They were just another chore assigned by her parents and all the guys ended up being her friends or people she never spoke to again.

"The seons? That's different. Those aren't really dates like—it's not the same as—"

"It's not any different and you know it," Austin said with brazen confidence.

He wasn't wrong, but he wasn't right either. Austin couldn't make Jisu feel like they were both playing games when he was the only person acting with that intent. Austin was affectionate, sure. He held her hand and told her he missed her, and every time he did, it made her insides do flips and jumping jacks. But he had kept her around as an option and quickly moved on when another interested party appeared. Jisu had wanted Austin and only Austin. She shook underneath her sweater. Her grip on the blanket grew tighter and she clenched her jaw as she glared at Austin. She clutched at her chest defensively—it felt like someone had knocked the wind out of her lungs. Like she had just sprinted several miles to reach this realization.

"You're mad at me," Austin said, his tone a touch softer now. But Jisu wasn't having it.

"I'm not mad at you," she said. "I'm mad at myself for wasting my time with you."

Jisu stormed toward the bonfire. She kicked her feet in the sand with each step.

"Yay, Jisu's here with the blanket—"

"Hiba, we have to leave," Jisu said sternly. "Now. Please."

Hiba seemed to read the panic and anger on Jisu's face and got up immediately, without questioning. Austin was still standing by the beach entrance.

"C'mon, Jisu," he said with that cocky look on his face. Like he thought he could smooth things over. But Jisu stared icily ahead as they walked past him. Hiba glanced at them both. The tension was impossible to ignore. She probably had a million questions for Jisu, but now was not the time. Hiba charged forward and led Jisu away.

Jisu thought of Mandy's magazines and all the stupid rules. "Signs Your Situationship is Turning into a Relationship."

You're always trying something new together.

You laugh a lot. He walks you home.

He texts you often.

He introduces you to his family.

All those stupid quizzes, rules and margins. It was all so unnecessarily complicated, and it didn't have to be so complex. If two people found that they liked each other, why couldn't they simply be together? Who dictated these inane rules, and who decided to go along with them?

"So, want me to drop you off at home?" Hiba asked.

"Yeah. Please," Jisu whispered.

She pulled her hoodie over her head and stared out the window, thinking about the girls who'd come before her and the girls who would come after both her and Kaylee. There were some things that you shouldn't take on and then discard on a whim. At least with the seons, she knew what was on the table. Nobody was hiding a secret hand. If anything, the entire business of seons was a little too candid. But it was better than dealing with this. What was the point of involving real emotions? It only made a mess. An ugly, unbearable mess.

DATE NO. 21

NAME: **Song Alan**

INTERESTS:
Young Musicians Orchestra,
Policy Research Institute, Pre-Medicine Club

PARENT OCCUPATIONS:
Luxury hotel chain owners

JISU: Nearly every seon I've been on in Seoul was at a fancy hotel and everything in America has been super casual. This is the first time I've been to a hotel in San Francisco. I thought you guys were all low-key!

ALAN: I actually am low-key…it's just my parents who aren't. They own this hotel and think it's a good way to show off and impress my dates.

JISU: Well, it's really nice. And very tasteful. I'm sure it makes a great impression.

ALAN: Ha. So far, the reactions have been all good.

JISU: All right, let's cut to the chase. Were you born and raised in the Bay Area? Which high school do you go to? What's your dream college? What do you want to study—

ALAN: Whoa, whoa. Let's take it one step at a time.

JISU: Eh, might as well get it all out and over with, right?

ALAN: I don't think I really get what you mean…

JISU: Okay, I'll just go first. My full name is Jisu Kim. I moved to the Bay Area last fall for my senior cram year at Wick.

ALAN: Nice. How do you like San Francisco so far?

JISU: It's beautiful. Definitely a different vibe than Seoul in a million ways, but mostly I like how chill everyone is. And I love how close I am to the ocean.

ALAN: Yeah, I have some family in Korea. It's so much fun when I go there—it feels like ten times more of a busy city than San Francisco does. There's just *so much* going on all the time there.

JISU: What do you do outside of school?

ALAN: I'm in my school orchestra. I play the trumpet.

JISU: Trumpet, nice. I don't play any instruments. Mostly spend my time with my cameras.

ALAN: Photography—that's cool!

JISU: I like it. It's fine. Have you gotten accepted into any colleges yet?

ALAN: No, playing the waiting game, just like everyone else.

I don't have a dream school that I've been dying to go to my whole life—unlike some other people at my school—so I just sent applications out to a handful of places.

JISU: I submitted applications to ten schools. I've already gotten rejected by one, which probably takes me down a notch as an ideal client for Ms. Moon, but still waiting to hear from others. What do you want to study in college?

ALAN: Jisu…

JISU: Yes?

ALAN: Is it just me or does it feel like we're checking off a list of first-date questions…?

JISU: Isn't that the point of all this? Of all of these seons?

ALAN: We could also actually get to know each other… It doesn't have to feel like a job interview.

JISU: Really, because sending Ms. Moon my résumé and waiting for her to accept me as a client—none of that feels like a job interview. I don't know how many seons you've been on so far, but you should know that it's all business. Everyone's doing it just to make the most lucrative business transaction they can get.

ALAN: Cynic.

JISU: Excuse me?

ALAN: You're a cynic. That's what it should've said on your one-sheet under About Me.

JISU: You actually read those things? They're useless fluff.

ALAN: Did you really just scoff at me?

JISU: No, I didn't.

ALAN: Yes, you did.

JISU: I'm just being honest.

ALAN: No, Jisu. You're being rude.

JISU: *Excuse* me?

ALAN: Yes. You're being rude. Look. I'm not naive about the purpose of these dates. All of our parents want us to find the ideal match within the same income bracket. I get it. It's shallow. But you've got an awful attitude and you're making an already not-ideal situation worse. I don't know if you just went on one really bad seon or if you parents made you split up with someone you like—

JISU: That's none of your business. And neither of those things happened.

ALAN: Well, whatever. I know it's none of my business and I honestly don't care. But you shouldn't be rude to someone, even if you don't like them.

JISU: Whatever...

ALAN: No, not whatever. I don't care if you think you're above this. You can still have some basic human decency.

JISU: I don't think I'm above this. I'm not above anything. It's just…

ALAN: What? You can tell me.

JISU: I hate the transparency of all this. People are always sizing each other up anyway. Why do we have to hire Ms. Moon and be so blatant about it? And also…

ALAN: And also?

JISU: I'm sick of going on seons with strangers and people I barely know. Meanwhile, in real life, I get strung along by someone I actually know and like… You know what? Never mind… You don't want to hear any of this.

ALAN: Honestly? I gotta say it's the least unpleasant part of this whole date so far.

JISU: Ugh, you're right. I am going through a bit of a rough patch.

ALAN: These seons can really suck. And bring out the worst in everyone.

JISU: Wow, you really think I'm that awful?

ALAN: I wouldn't say awful.

JISU: You literally told me my attitude was awful.

ALAN: I got a little heated, yes.

JISU: I'm sorry, Alan. For being such a grouch. These dates are so much more stressful than you think they're gonna be.

ALAN: I know, it's like dating and standardized testing combined. You have to have all the correct answers to get the best score.

JISU: Yeah...

ALAN: Don't take it all too seriously. It's not that serious.

JISU: Easier said than done, Alan. But you're right.

22

"So…you want to tell me what happened back there?" Hiba finally asked.

They were halfway back to the Murrays', and Jisu had been quiet the whole time. She replayed every moment she'd spent with Austin in the past few months and searched her memory for any incriminating evidence. But it was useless. His routine was well oiled and perfected over time. He had done nothing wrong. At least technically he hadn't. The player always came out unscathed. It was only the unsuspecting victim who was left in shambles.

"Austin was making out with Kaylee in the parking lot," Jisu finally said. "Just like he had with me."

"Kaylee? That thirsty bitch. Want me to text Jamie and Tiffany?"

"To do what?"

"I don't know, scare her or something."

"What? Are we in the mob? And Jamie and Tiffany are our hit men doing the dirty work?"

"Ahem. Hit *women*."

It almost felt too soon for Jisu to be laughing and she was still entirely miserable, but talking to Hiba like this was helping.

"No, Kaylee's not the issue here. If anything, we should pull her out of the trap she's about to step into. I just feel like such an idiot."

"Don't. Austin is a player. This is what he does."

"Exactly. You warned me. All of you! And I ignored it."

"Yeah, but it doesn't make it right for him to do that. To you or to anyone. It's okay to be mad, Jisu. But don't blame yourself. *He's* the snake."

Hiba was right. Jisu felt it in her bones how right she was, but it didn't make her feel any better about the situation. It didn't matter how blameless you were—getting duped like that was an experience that could only be described as *miserable*.

"Besides," Hiba said. "You deserve someone who's on your level. Austin's cute, yeah, but what does he really have going for him? He just wants someone vapid who will praise the ground he walks on. That's just not you. You have your own life, your own interests. You deserve someone like you."

"What about you, Hiba?" Jisu asked. "You deserve someone like that, too. Anyone on your radar?"

"No." Hiba sighed. "But now that all this college stuff is nearly over, my mom has been really on me to meet with some of her friends' sons. And I don't want that."

"You don't?"

"All the Lebanese boys here just stay in the Bay Area. They come back right after college and open up their dentistry or their business or whatever and repeat the same lives their parents had. It's so predictable. I don't want that."

"Maybe I should tell Ms. Moon to expand her business and she can find someone for us at whatever colleges we end up at."

Hiba pulled up to the Murray household.

"If she does, you have to give me a glowing recommendation."

"Hiba, when have you ever not received a glowing letter of recommendation?"

"Hmm. Yeah, I can't think of a time." Hiba laughed.

Jisu got out of the car. She felt like a wet towel wrung completely of emotions and was ready to collapse into bed.

"Don't beat yourself up so much about Austin," Hiba shouted out the window. "He's not worth it!"

"You're ruining my life!" Mandy shouted and slammed her bedroom door shut.

Another tween tantrum. Yikes. Mandy had been on her best behavior lately. What could have possibly happened during the short time Jisu stepped out?

"Jisu." Linda looked surprised to see her standing in the foyer. "You're back early." She spoke with an affected calmness, which only made whatever situation was happening seem that much worse. "I just put the kettle on the stove. Want to join me for tea?"

It was an invitation for tea, but also an invitation to get involved and chime in on whatever drama had unfolded between her and Mandy. Jisu wanted nothing more than to trudge up the stairs to her room and slip into bed. But Linda looked especially stressed.

"Sure! I'll have some chamomile. Trying to go to bed early tonight."

They walked into the kitchen, past the office where Jeff was on the phone as he always was.

"How was the bonfire?" Linda asked.

"Fine… I just got tired and Hiba was tired, too, so we left

early," Jisu said. "Is Mandy okay?" *Enough about my issues, Linda. Let's cut to the chase and get to the Mandy drama.*

"Oh…yes. She's a bit upset. Jeff just got promoted, you know. We all found out today."

"That's great!"

"Great, yes. But they want to move him to the Dallas office. Hence…" Linda threw her hands up and motioned upstairs. "Hence all the commotion you just witnessed."

"How soon would you guys have to move?" Jisu asked. She started growing concerned herself. What would this mean for her?

"We don't know yet. We're trying really hard not to pull Mandy out of the school year and wait until the summer," Linda said. "And of course we don't want to put you out either." The kettle on the stove started to whistle.

Great. Jisu had left Ocean Beach to escape one dumpster fire only to walk right into another one.

"Of course we would make sure you'd be all set before we even left. That is when we even figure out when we're moving," Linda reassured her. But her words only made Jisu more nervous.

"I think I understand why Mandy is so upset," Jisu said. "Being uprooted from all your friends and your whole life can be really painful."

"I know, but what can I do?" Linda looked just as exhausted as Jisu felt. "We're just trying to do what's best for all of us."

Jisu walked up to her room and wondered how many more days, weeks or months she had left in her bedroom. She couldn't be uprooted again. No. Moments ago, she was upset about a stupid boy. Now she was worrying about making sure she had a place to live.

Jisu could hear Mandy sobbing through the wall. She walked into her room. The floor was littered with wrinkled-up tissues.

"Hey." Jisu sat next to Mandy on her bed and gave her a hug. "It's gonna be okay."

"No…it's…not." Mandy sobbed between each word. "My life…is…over!" She continued to cry hysterically.

"At least you'll be moving to another city and not an entirely different country like I did, right?" Jisu said. But her attempt to be playful and lighten the mood only backfired and made Mandy cry even harder.

Jisu remembered how she had sobbed her way through Incheon Airport last fall. Poor Mandy. This was not going to be an easy move for her, but she'd eventually get through it.

"There, there." Jisu handed Mandy another tissue. "Let it out. Let it all out. You'll feel better."

DATE NO. 22

NAME: **Kang Philip aka Phil**

INTERESTS:
Hospitality, Fashion, Traveling

DISLIKES:
Germs, Bad Tippers

JISU: Okay, so we've established that we both like traveling.

PHIL: Except for your last flight from Seoul to San Francisco, where you cried during the whole flight.

JISU: Not during the *entire* flight.

PHIL: You did say you cried for at least eight out of the ten hours it took to get here.

JISU: I'm starting to regret telling you that.

PHIL: Really makes it hard to believe that you actually like traveling.

JISU: I was being forced out of my city and away from my friends! How else could I react? Also, no one actually likes the literal traveling part of traveling. It's walking around the city, going to museums, eating good food and meeting new people that makes traveling fun.

PHIL: No way. This whole time I thought people were saying that they loved sitting in a bus for hours in traffic. I mean, that's *my* favorite part about traveling.

JISU: All right, what is an actual pet peeve of yours?

PHIL: Hmm. When people don't wash their hands.

JISU: Ew. Like when they go to the bathroom?

PHIL: You'd be disgusted and shocked—well, maybe not shocked—at how many dudes do their business and just walk out the bathroom.

JISU: Bleh.

PHIL: Yeah. I wash my hands before *and* after. I might be a bit of a germophobe…

JISU: Better that than the opposite.

PHIL: True. I also hate people who tip poorly. It drives me crazy. I have a friend who always leaves the bare minimum tip whenever we order delivery. I work as a waiter during the summer, so if people don't tip well, I judge them.

JISU: Oh, my god, poor tippers are the worst! I once went on a date with a guy who left a dollar tip. We had fancy lattes and he left *one* dollar. One!

PHIL: Jesus, I don't think you can even call that a tip.

JISU: No, it definitely wasn't. I waited for him to look away and make his way out before I grabbed the few singles I could find in my purse and left it on the table. I felt so bad.

PHIL: Well, you did the right thing. Did you end up seeing that guy again?

JISU: God, no.

PHIL: You know, I'm always curious about what kind of guys I'm up against with these seons. That makes me feel a *lot* better about the competition.

JISU: Do you think of this as a competition?

PHIL: Jisu. We're Korean. We think of everything as a competition.

JISU: Ha, that's true, I guess.

PHIL: Why do you think we're on this seon? We're the horses at the racetrack and our parents are in the stands, placing bets.

JISU: Oh, my god, Phil. That's so dramatic.

PHIL: They're out there, waving our one-sheets in each other's faces as we run around the track.

JISU: Wow, you've really thought this metaphor through, haven't you?

PHIL: I have! It's basically my college essay.

JISU: No way.

PHIL: Yes way.

JISU: So you wrote about how suffocating and controlling your parents are? How is that going?

PHIL: I'm two for two, so I'm batting at 100 percent. Still waiting to hear from three more colleges, including my dream school, but I'm feeling pretty good.

JISU: That makes me so jealous. I've only heard from one school and I got rejected. I knew it was coming, but it stings. At least until I get my first acceptance.

PHIL: What do you want to study?

JISU: Sociology. Photography. I don't know. I hate that question.

PHIL: Why?

JISU: Because I don't know what to do, and the more people ask, the more I feel like I should know the answer. Even though deep down I know it's okay that I don't know. You know? Or do you have your whole life figured out?

PHIL: Definitely not. But I think I want to do something in hospitality.

JISU: What does that actually mean? Hospitality? People have told me I should look into that also.

PHIL: And you still haven't looked it up?

JISU: Hey, I'm concerned with getting into college first.

PHIL: Okay, let's say you're throwing a big party.

JISU: What kind of party? Big? Small? What's the occasion?

PHIL: You're already asking the right kinds of questions. I get why people are telling you to look into this.

JISU: So working in hospitality just means knowing how to put together a good party?

PHIL: Kinda. Think about what a good host of a great party is like. She's mindful of her guests, she makes sure everyone's happy and entertained and that all their needs are being met. It's about keeping everyone happy and making sure they have a good time.

JISU: So what about it do you like? Why are you drawn to it?

PHIL: I've always liked socializing. The most interesting and fun part is knowing all the people you've gathered into the room and watching them all get to know one another. It's like a little social experiment.

JISU: Like controlled people-watching.

PHIL: Yes, exactly!

JISU: I love people-watching.

PHIL: Right, you did mention liking photography.

JISU: Yeah, but I'm not like an official photographer. I wouldn't know what to do if you stuck me in a studio. I don't even know a thing about lighting—I usually just shoot outdoors and go with my gut.

PHIL: Well, that's a legit form of photography. Sounds better to me even. And probably the best way to people-watch.

JISU: It is! It's actually a lot of fun. I totally lose track of the time when I hit the streets with my camera.

PHIL: That's what we should do next. You can teach me how to people-watch with a camera. For our next date. If you want.

JISU: I'd like that actually, yeah. We should do that.

23

"**I** timed it and that was just a little over fifteen minutes," Dave said.

Dave and Jisu were practicing their IS presentation. After weeks of gathering all the photos and relevant data, they had finally completed their project. Except Dave, ever the perfectionist, insisted on running through it over and over again.

"That's good! We did it," Jisu said as she eyed the clock. They had spent the last half hour at the library in the media room.

"No, we have to keep it at fifteen minutes or right under it. Or else Mrs. French will shave off some points."

"I don't think she'll really knock us for going over by a few seconds."

"One point can make a world of a difference, Jees. Come on. I'll cut down on giving different examples of nonprofits and businesses. And you don't have to describe all the photos in such detailed length." Dave clicked through each slide and carefully read each one for any spelling errors.

"Dave," Jisu said. "You're already going to Harvard. I'm the one who's only gotten rejections so far."

"Exactly—every point counts!"

It wasn't that Jisu was phoning it in. The presentation was complete and they had practiced countless times. Maybe Dave was trying to kill time. But he could do that with his friends, so why stick yourself in the library? If Jisu were Dave, she'd relax and take things easy for the rest of the year. But then again, maybe that's why he was going to Harvard and she was still waiting to hear back.

Dave queued the presentation back to the first slide. He handed Jisu the clicker. He really did want to do another round. Was he always this much of a perfectionist? Or maybe he was trying to avoid someone. Sophie, maybe? The mere thought stirred something inside Jisu. Suddenly her brain perked right up, as if she'd taken a giant swig of coffee. Had the two of them gotten in a fight? No, no. Jisu stopped herself from hypothesizing crazy scenarios. It wasn't any of her business.

"Okay, fine. I just need to leave soon so I can go home and get ready for my seon."

"How many of those have you been on?" he asked. "Are they super formal and awkward, or do they feel like real dates?"

They had briefly talked about Ms. Moon and the match-making service, but Dave had never asked as many questions about it as he did now. Was he or would he soon be interested in seons? Were these questions someone asked if they were happy with their current relationship? Jisu waved away thoughts of Dave and Sophie and whatever conflicts she was trying to project on them.

"Just a handful since I've moved here. It's whatever, honestly."

"So they've all been duds?"

"Yeah, there have been some really bad ones. But they make for funny stories, so at the very least there's that."

Jisu thought back to some of the disastrous seons she'd been on. She really had done it all. Everything from getting into a shouting match to literally falling asleep on a date.

"Except for one," Jisu said, thinking about Philip Kang. When she'd sat down for their date, she had forgotten what number he was. She'd expected another hour wasted with a stranger she'd have zero interest in. But for the first time, that was not the case. The seon came to an end, and Jisu was sad to part ways.

"Really?" Dave asked.

"Yeah, actually, my second date is with him today. Which is why I'm trying to get out of here!"

"What made the date with him different than the others?" Suddenly Dave seemed more invested in Jisu's dating life than in the presentation projected on the screen behind her.

"Umm. He was nice." Jisu clicked through to the revised slides. If she wanted to get home and change in time before seeing Philip, they had to wrap things up soon.

"Nice? Is that all it takes for someone to win you over?"

"Well, it's one way in! Kindness is underrated." Jisu clicked through a few more.

"What else?"

"What else what?"

"What else do you like about this guy... What's his name?" Dave was asking an awful lot of questions. But Jisu didn't mind. She'd noticed that sometimes people who were in long-term relationships loved living vicariously through those who weren't.

"We like the same things *and* we dislike the same things. That goes a long way. His name is Philip."

"Philip... I don't know how I feel about that name." Dave

scrunched his face. "You really want to date a guy named Philip?"

"What?" Jisu laughed. "What's wrong with the name Philip?"

"It sounds a bit too…prissy. And a little bit self-important." Dave raised his head up into the air. "Hello, my name is… Philip." He spoke with a terrible aristocratic, posh accent.

"He goes by Phil!"

"Meh, that might be worse," Dave teased.

"None of it really matters though," Jisu said.

"What do you mean?"

"Well, even if Phil and I really hit things off, it won't matter because I won't be in the Bay Area anymore in just a few months. It's not like I'd be coming back here over college breaks."

Jisu turned on the lights and the sudden brightness stung her eyes.

"Yeah, I guess I never thought about it that way," Dave said. He looked a little disheartened. "But it's not like you'd *never* come back to the Bay. Unless your plan is to cut off all contact with everyone from Wick?"

"Yeah, Dave, I'm also going to fake my death and steal someone else's identity," Jisu said. "But seriously, after being uprooted from Seoul and knowing it's all going to happen again when I go to college, I'm trying not to take anything too seriously."

"So you're actually *not* taking this Phil guy seriously."

"I do like him, but I'm also not going to be upset if it doesn't go anywhere, you know? I'm not going to get involved in anything serious unless it really means a lot to me. With guys, with friendships, with everything."

"I don't know… It sounds like this guy has made the most lukewarm impression on you."

"Stop! You're going to ruin the date for me before I even

get there!" Jisu threw the clicker at Dave. He caught it and flipped through the rest of the slides.

"I don't think we really need another run-through. Aren't you tired of staring at this?" Jisu asked as she looked up at the projector screen.

"No." Dave looked at her. "Not at all."

DATE NO. 23

NAME: **Lee Edward aka Eddie**

INTERESTS:
Social Entrepreneurship, Banking,
International Justice Mission

ACCOMPLISHMENTS:
United States-Korea Business Council Internship

EDDIE: You can just call me Eddie, by the way.

JISU: Okay! So, Eddie.

EDDIE: So, Jisu.

JISU: What was the last movie you saw?

EDDIE: Hmm. I don't really go to the actual theater often…

JISU: Oh, me either. I usually watch whatever's on Netflix or Hulu. So, what's the last thing that you watched then?

EDDIE: You're going to think it's boring.

JISU: I won't!

EDDIE: I wouldn't blame you if you did. It's about Watergate and the whole scandal during the Nixon presidency.

JISU: I learned about that in US history! That was *wild*. In Korea, we don't get that in depth into American history when we're doing global studies, but I'm glad I learned about that.

EDDIE: Yeah, it's actually interesting, right?

JISU: Wait, I think I know what movie you're talking about. We watched that movie in class and it was like the best thing. The movie was so long, we spent two entire class periods watching it. *All the President's Men*. It's like a super old-school movie.

EDDIE: That's the movie-movie. It was pretty good. But the real thing is better.

JISU: Real thing?

EDDIE: The documentary. It's on Netflix. I had the flu a couple weeks ago and I couldn't do anything but rest in bed. So I watched a million documentaries.

JISU: You watched documentaries. In bed. When you had the flu?

EDDIE: I know. It's super lame.

JISU: No, I don't think it's lame! I think it's more like a feat. Documentaries are like visual class lectures. I'd probably fall asleep.

EDDIE: This one was really good. Actual interviews with the real Woodward and Bernstein. Real footage, pictures and documents.

JISU: What else do you watch? Outside of Ken Burns.

EDDIE: Ken Burns is a genius. But that's a whole other conversation. And I won't bore you with that. I like *Anderson Cooper 360*. Chris Hayes's show is good, too. Also Rachel Maddow.

JISU: So basically news shows?

EDDIE: Yeah but those are all my favorite hosts right now. And *The Daily Show*, of course. Sometimes I'll even check out what's happening on C-SPAN.

JISU: C-SPAN?

EDDIE: Yeah, it's like…hmm… I actually don't know what the Korean equivalent of it would be. Basically, it's a network that televises a lot of the federal government procedures. It's public affairs programming.

JISU: Oh…sounds…really informative.

EDDIE: It's pretty dry, but every now and then something crazy will happen. Basically, *The Daily Show* takes all the interesting parts and puts it on their show.

JISU: Gotcha. But you watch both *The Daily Show* and C-SPAN?

EDDIE: I find them both interesting enough. I'm more interested in global affairs, so it's cool when they air their news conferences or general assemblies.

JISU: Interesting…

EDDIE: I'm totally boring you, aren't I? God, why am I talking about C-SPAN? How did we get here?

JISU: No, it's okay! International studies is one of my favorite classes in school.

EDDIE: Yeah, but in school. Not, like, in life. We probably shouldn't even be talking about school. We should be getting as much of a break from it when we can.

JISU: So, do you want to go to school in DC and move there? Sounds like that city would fit you the best.

EDDIE: I did apply to some schools there, like Georgetown, American and GWU. But we'll see. Living in DC would be great though. I could probably actually attend the actual public hearings that I've been watching.

JISU: That sounds…thrilling?

EDDIE: Yeah, actually! For me at least!

JISU: I'm glad you know what you like. I'm still trying to figure my own thing out.

24

"Jisu!" Hiba yelled as she ran down the hallway a couple weeks later. It was early March, and college decisions were coming in. Jisu hoped Hiba had good news.

"What's wrong—did something happen?" Jisu asked. Between Hiba's wide eyes bulging out and her quick, rapid breaths, Jisu couldn't tell if she had just received good or terrible news.

"*Something* happened. Something *big*." Hiba took a deep breath. "I received my decision from Princeton last night and—" Hiba let out a tiny squeak "—I got in! I got into Princeton!"

"Oh, my god, Hiba! You did it!" Jisu hugged her friend. They screamed and jumped up and down with the same enthusiasm as someone who finds out that they just won the lottery. Except, this feeling was better. Hiba had worked hard for this moment. It felt better than good. It was rewarding.

"What about you? You hear back from any place yet? I heard the rest of the regular Harvard admission decisions went out."

Jisu wished Hiba hadn't asked. They could've continued to revel in her success. But her question cut right through the celebratory mood.

The rest of the Harvard decisions had gone out, and Jisu had received her notice through the online portal yesterday. The subject was short and succinct; her heart had sunk when she saw it.

But it wasn't a rejection.

Dear Jisu Kim,

In the last few months, the Admissions Committee at Harvard College has had the challenging task of reviewing applicants from one of the strongest applicant pools that the college has seen in years. At this time, we are pleased to offer you a position on our wait list.

Should you wish to accept this spot, please let us know by April 17. In May we will be reviewing the wait list and will then determine whether students from the list will be admitted…

Wait list. One half of Jisu had been relieved, but the other half was frustrated. More waiting? She was tired of waiting. *Take me in or cut me loose. Pick one. Pick me.*

But when she'd called her parents to relay the news, they'd been surprisingly positive.

"It's not a no!" Mr. Kim had said as cheerfully as he could. Jisu could imagine her mother was not as pleased, and her father was doing what he could to prevent the two of them from getting into a shouting match.

"Your father's right. You can keep trying. It's not over, Jisu," Mrs. Kim had said as encouragingly as possible.

"I got wait-listed," Jisu said to Hiba.

"Oh…" Hiba searched for the right encouraging words. "Well, it's better than nothing! And it means you still have a shot."

"Does it?" Jisu asked.

Waiting felt like a delayed no. Jisu wanted it to be over. She wanted all of it to be over. She was only a few feet from the finish line, and so many of her friends had already crossed it. It felt like the universe was playing a cruel trick on her and was moving the finish line farther away.

"Yes, of course! You should ask some of your teachers from your old high school for letters of recommendation and send them. You gotta send them all this extra stuff to sway them," Hiba said. "Plus, I'm sure you'll receive acceptances from other colleges rolling in any day now."

"Yeah…I guess." The thought of putting in even more work after all she had done felt daunting.

"You want a ride home?" Hiba offered.

"No, I'm good. I need some air. I'm gonna go for a walk."

Jisu loved her friends, but they were all so much more accomplished than her. Euni and Hiba deserved all the success they could get—they worked so hard for it. But sometimes, it was hard being friends with overachievers.

Jisu stepped outside. While there were players in practice mode on most of the fields, the football field remained empty. She climbed up the bleachers and tried to empty her mind. She felt trapped in college purgatory and there was nothing she could do to wiggle her way out. Jisu leaned back and stared at a passing airplane. She took her camera out of her bag and snapped a few photos. She watched it soar through the empty sky until it disappeared.

Her phone dinged and vibrated. It could be Hiba sending an encouraging text, Euni and Min chatting away, Ms. Moon checking in about her last seon or her parents providing unsolicited academic advice. The phone felt heavy in her pocket. Jisu wanted to throw it across the bleachers and onto the empty field. But she checked her notifications instead.

It was good seeing you the other night. Wanna watch the new Star Wars movie this weekend?

Phil. Somehow a stranger she had gone on one seon with was the most consistent thing in her life right now. But stability in any form was welcome.

She looked back up at the sky and out to the fields and searched for something to stare at. The players on the soccer field dispersed and some of them walked off the field while others kicked a ball around. One walked in her direction. Jisu peered through her camera lens to get a closer look.

It was Dave.

He waved at her as he paced forward. His forehead was shiny with sweat and there were grass stains on his shirt. He looked tall and triumphant, like he'd just won a hard-fought match. *Click.* Jisu snapped his photo.

"What are you doing out here?" Dave hopped up the bleachers and joined Jisu in her row. Jisu's nerves acted up as he approached. She came out here to clear her mind, but Dave's presence was fogging it all up again. Her brain was like San Francisco the morning after a rainstorm—foggy and muddled.

"I'm just trying to clear my head," Jisu said as she snapped a few more photos of the seagulls circling above them.

"Everything okay?" Dave asked.

Everything wasn't *not* okay, but it wasn't good either.

"All my friends are moving ahead in life and I'm stuck on a stupid wait list. Everything is *perfect*," Jisu said. "Plus there's a chance I might have to move again before the school year is even over."

"Really? Move where? Are you leaving Wick?" There was a twinge of worry in his voice. It caused a twinge in Jisu's heart and sent a shot of nervous excitement through her body. Chills ran down her arms through the tip of her fingers. Jisu placed her hand on the seat and could've sworn she felt a small electric shock.

"I don't know yet. My host family might move to Texas, but they're trying to figure out how to stay here through the school year for their daughter...and for me, too, I guess."

"You can't leave Wick," Dave said. "It would throw everything off...with college apps and stuff."

"Everything in my life was thrown off when I got on a plane and left Seoul. Dave, I'm really happy for you and all, but the Harvard early action is a million times more lax than what I'm going through now. You have no idea."

"Not entirely. You're making it sound like I'm some Disney princess leading a charmed life."

"You mean you're not a Disney princess?" Jisu laughed. "You don't have tiny birds and rabbits wake you up in the morning and help you make your bed?"

Down below, the remaining soccer players walked off the field and back into the school building.

"Practice get out early today?" Jisu asked.

"Yeah, coach had a family emergency and cut it short. His mom's been sick, so he's been in and out. She's super old, but I still can't imagine it's easy to see your loved one like that. I really hope everything's okay." Dave straightened his back and sat up. "But enough of my depressing talk. How's your boy Philip? You go on that second date with him yet?"

"I did actually. It was fun."

"What did you guys do?"

"We walked around and went to Dolores Park."

"That sounds boring," he said. The quick judgment from Dave was shocking. It was so out of character for him that Jisu was actually taken aback. She looked at him, a bit confused. He met her gaze and inched forward. Her heart quickened and she retreated an inch back as she straightened her spine. Jisu fumbled through her bag.

"It really wasn't! I brought my camera and he even took some photos. He's not bad. There wasn't that much chemistry, but he's kind of an interesting dude actually." Jisu was rambling and she was talking so breathlessly and fast, her words were falling on top of each other. *Stop talking so much!* Two sides of her brain were fighting: one was making her chat nervously and the other was begging her to shut up. Jisu took her phone out and glued her eyes to the screen. Still, she could sense Dave lean over to her and close in on the already small amount of space between them.

"Actually, he texted me just a minute ago. He wants to meet up again." She rushed through her words again. *Stop talking! Shut up!*

Dave peered over Jisu's shoulder as she texted Phil back. The entire left side of her body tensed up as Dave leaned closer and closer. Her muscles strained despite her best efforts to be chill.

"Third date! What are you guys gonna do?"

Jisu looked up from her phone. Dave's eyes were looking right into hers now. She felt like she would implode if she didn't look away, but she couldn't break her gaze.

"We're watching a movie. The new Star Wars," she said.

"Sitting next to each other for two hours and doing nothing?" Dave leaned in even closer now. His lips were so close to hers, but Jisu didn't move away this time. Could he sense how fast she was breathing? Could he hear how much faster her heart was beating with each passing second? "That sounds… boring," he said.

Dave closed the sliver of space between them and kissed

Jisu. In the split second when their lips met and their faces fell into each other's, it felt right.

And then Jisu remembered who they were. She was the single girl going on a third date with Phil this weekend…and Dave was Sophie's boyfriend.

She yanked herself away. Dave looked just as shocked as she did.

"You shouldn't have done that. You— I— We—" Jisu stammered. She picked up her bag and bolted.

"I'm sorry. Jisu, wait!" Dave called. But she'd already rushed down the bleachers and was running off the field.

That was a huge mistake. What was I thinking? What was he *thinking?* In that one moment, Dave had flipped their friendship upside down. How could he do that to her? Austin, Dave—American boys were all the same. They were all players in a game. A game that only benefited them. But Jisu knew Dave. And that wasn't who Dave was. So why? Why did he do it?

DATE NO. 24

NAME: **Kim Hyunwoo**

INTERESTS:
Military History, Fencing

DISLIKES:
Laziness, Sleeping, Neckties

HYUNWOO: Jisu?

JISU: Hmm? What?

HYUNWOO: I was just asking if you'd hit up any of the famous local food spots since you've been here.

JISU: Oh! Sorry. I'm just a little out of it today. I didn't get a lot of sleep last night. Umm…good food that I've had so far. Hmm…

HYUNWOO: If you haven't already gone to El Farolito—

JISU: I've been there! They have such good burritos.

HYUNWOO: Right? I always get the stewed chicken one.

JISU: They're so large. But *so* good.

HYUNWOO: So some of the Wick kids have discovered it.

JISU: Um, I think people from Wick have been going there for some time now. Last time I was there, I was with...

HYUNWOO: You were with...?

JISU: Uh, just some friends. Just friends. Which high school did you say you went to again?

HYUNWOO: Marin. We compete in the same league.

JISU: Do you play any sports?

HYUNWOO: Yeah, soccer in the winter and lacrosse in the spring.

JISU: One of my really good friends plays lacrosse and soccer! He's pretty good. He's good at everything he does. It's kind of maddening.

HYUNWOO: Huh?

JISU: Oh, nothing. So...have you been on a lot of seons?

HYUNWOO: Not that many. I was actually dating this girl for two years. We broke up several months ago.

JISU: What happened?

HYUNWOO: Nothing bad. We just wanted different things.

And I think we both knew it was going to happen sooner or later, especially with college coming up. Honestly, we could've ended things sooner, but you just get so comfortable.

JISU: Would you have done something sooner if you met someone else?

HYUNWOO: Maybe? I guess I won't ever know because that's not what happened.

JISU: What if your ex had kissed someone while she was still with you? That would still make you mad, right?

HYUNWOO: Of course! If we're still together, then yeah. Why do you ask?

JISU: It just happened to a friend of mine, and it's all our friend group has been talking about.

HYUNWOO: She cheated on her boyfriend?

JISU: Nooo. She didn't. She doesn't have a boyfriend, but this guy who has a girlfriend kissed her. But we think that he and his girlfriend have stayed together so long because they're "comfortable," like you said.

HYUNWOO: That's still cheating.

JISU: Yeah, I guess that's true.

HYUNWOO: If he's going to be so forthcoming about his feelings for your friend, he should be forthcoming about his lack of feelings for his girlfriend first.

JISU: Yeah…you're right.

HYUNWOO: You must really want your friend to end up with this guy, huh?

JISU: Um, not really, no.

HYUNWOO: It kinda seems like you do, the way you're talking about them.

JISU: No, it's not even a big deal. Plus I don't even know if she'd want that. He's the one who made the move and surprised her! Anyway…what were we talking about?

HYUNWOO: Dating…burritos…

JISU: I meant to ask you, a native Bay Area guy. What's the highest vantage point in the city? I'm trying to take some aerial shots. As much of a bird's-eye view as I can without using a drone or my feet lifting off the ground.

HYUNWOO: Well, there's Lombard Street, the obvious one.

JISU: Already gone there.

HYUNWOO: Then there are the parks. like Mount Davidson, Bernal Heights and DP.

JISU: I've been to Bernal Heights Park! My friend showed me the swing there and my knees got all wobbly because I got scared of the heights. I was nervous, but he was so chill the whole time…

HYUNWOO: Yeah, anyone with a fear of heights won't do well in this city. You're either on a steep road or a steep hill in the park.

JISU: I'll just go back to those spots and maybe I'll get over my slight fear of heights.

25

*H*e shouldn't have kissed her, because he had a girlfriend. He also shouldn't have kissed her, because she hadn't known how much she'd like it. And now she knew. She'd liked it. A lot.

It had been a full day since they'd sat together on those bleachers, and Jisu still couldn't stop thinking about Dave. How right his kiss had felt. Even though she knew it was wrong.

But butterflies in her stomach aside, thinking about it made her mad each time. It was *wrong*. What he did was wrong. Sophie was still his girlfriend.

And Jisu and Dave were friends. Why did he have to ruin things between them like this? Why now? Now that Austin was fully out of her system and she was well on her way to establishing something consistent and normal with Phil?

Jisu stared at her laptop screen. For the past hour, she had been trying to draft an email to her old teachers at Daewon to ask for recommendation letters. But she was too preoccupied with the events of the last twenty-four hours.

Focus, Jisu. Focus.

She shut her eyes and tried to clear away any and all thoughts of Dave. Getting off the wait list was her priority. Boys were a distraction. She could deal with them later. She opened her eyes and placed her hands on the keyboard, like a pianist about to tackle a concerto.

Dear Mrs. Han,

How are you? I hope you've been well. I'm writing from San Francisco, where I've been attending Wick-Helmering High School for the last few months since I moved here from Seoul…

She was just a few sentences into drafting the email when her phone dinged. It was Phil.

We still on for Star Wars tomorrow?

Ugh. Boys always seemed to text at the most inconvenient times. It was their extra sense, like they could smell it when you truly wanted to stop thinking about them. Jisu did feel bad for getting so annoyed. Phil had done nothing wrong. But sitting in a theater next to him for two hours and doing nothing was the last thing she wanted to do. He was nice, but that was it. It wasn't worth getting distracted by *nice*. She needed to focus. Jisu hadn't yet heard from UChicago, so the least she could do was try her best to get into Harvard, even if it was by the skin of her teeth.

Hey, Phil, I really liked spending time with you but I've been swamped lately with schoolwork and trying to get off wait lists. I think I need to take a break from seons and dating in general. I'm sorry and I hope you understand.

It was a white lie. Jisu knew that she would continue to go on seons as long as Ms. Moon continued to send her parents an invoice. She could withstand an hour or two making small talk with a stranger. But she couldn't go down the long path with one when she knew in the long run that it wouldn't work out. She especially couldn't do that to Phil, who had been nothing but nice. It was better to cut him loose now than to find herself in an emotional gray area several dates later.

Jisu put her phone facedown on her desk. Ever since Dave had kissed her, a messy ball of anxiety had formed in her stomach and grown daily. It expanded every time she thought of the endless seons Ms. Moon had lined up for her. It poked her in the sides whenever she thought of the colleges she had yet to hear from. It kept her up at night when she remembered Dave's face close to hers, his lips touching hers…and then remembered Sophie immediately after.

But closing the loop on Phil helped chip away at her nerves. It was one less thing to worry about. Jisu turned her attention back to the email she was writing.

I'm excited to share news that I have been wait-listed at Harvard University. My guidance counselor at Wick has advised me to obtain letters of recommendation from past teachers to help me get off the list. I would greatly appreciate if…

Ding. Another notification. Now what? It was an email from Ms. Moon.

Your seon with Shim Bongsoo is confirmed for tomorrow. Just a note that this cannot be pushed like a few of the other

ones you have tried to reschedule. Barry is a family friend and your mother has asked me to make sure this seon happens.
Below, you will find the address of the location...

Jisu rolled her eyes and confirmed with Ms. Moon that yes, she would dutifully show up to the seon. She returned to her original email. It was going to take her all day to draft this. Her thoughts wandered briefly again to Dave. What was he up to now? Did he feel guilty? Or regretful? Was he going to tell Sophie that he had kissed someone else? And that it was *her*?

It didn't matter what he was thinking. Jisu shouldn't care.

DATE NO. 25

NAME: **Shim Bongsoo**

INTERESTS:
Aviation, Judo, Fishing

PARENT OCCUPATIONS:
Auctioneer; Realtor

BONGSOO: Have you had any plastic surgery?

JISU: Excuse me?!

BONGSOO: Oh. Sorry. I didn't mean to offend. I thought it was pretty common in Korea.

JISU: I mean…people get plastic surgery. But you can't just ask that. We literally just met. And it's not like nobody here does it. Half of your friends' moms have gotten Botox. I guarantee you.

BONGSOO: Really?

JISU: Yes, really. If you can't tell and they still look young and like they're aging "gracefully," that probably means they have a really good doctor.

BONGSOO: But don't a lot of girls in Korea get procedures done? Like even at a young age? One of my cousins in Seoul got double-eyelid surgery for her high school graduation present.

JISU: Yeah…that is a thing. And I know some girls who got that too…but that doesn't mean that *every* girl in Korea gets her eyelids done.

BONGSOO: You don't have monolids though…

JISU: Not all Koreans have monolids! You don't! Did *you* get plastic surgery?

BONGSOO: What? That's a crazy thing to ask. I'm a dude.

JISU: You do realize…plenty of guys go under the knife, too, right?

BONGSOO: Really? In Korea? They do that, too?

JISU: Not just Korea. Look at your own state. Drive down six hours to LA or even right here around San Francisco. More people have had plastic surgery than you think.

BONGSOO: Wow. I had no idea. How do you know so much about this?

JISU: I don't know… It's not like some big secret. You're the one making grand assumptions without knowing anything.

BONGSOO: To be fair, South Korea is kind of known for plastic surgery. And most Asian countries do uphold certain Western beauty standards.

JISU: So you just assumed that every girl, including me, fits into that trope and has had surgery? And I know what the Korean beauty standards are, Wonho. I'm a woman who actually grew up there. You don't have to explain it to me.

BONGSOO: I'm not explaining anything. I'm just saying what I know.

JISU: Sure.

BONGSOO: Would you ever think about…?

JISU: Getting plastic surgery? Are you saying that I need it?

BONGSOO: No! No, oh, my god. Not at all. I'm just curious to hear from your perspective. Given all the pressure you and your friends must face whenever someone gets their eyes or their nose or lips done.

JISU: Let's…let's talk about something else.

BONGSOO: Yeah.

JISU: Umm.

BONGSOO: What do you think about potential reunification of North and South Korea?

JISU: Really? Of all the topics you could've picked to talk about…

BONGSOO: What if both sides just agreed to open up the borders and let families see each other now and then? I really don't get what all the beef is. Germany got over it. I'm sure they can figure it out... So many families were split up by it, and it's so tragic. They deserve to see one another before it's too late.

JISU: You do realize it's not that simple...right?

BONGSOO: What?

JISU: Never mind...

26

"Guess what I just did." Tiffany sat down on the grass and joined Jamie, Hiba and Jisu for lunch.

"Did you finally figure out how to do a reverse French braid?" Hiba asked.

"What? No. I officially said yes to UC Davis. I'm officially enrolled!"

"Congrats, that's great, Tiffany!" Jisu said.

"They already have their fall course schedule available and I started looking through it. And I'm thinking about how I want to set up my dorm room—"

"Can we please stop talking about college for once?" Jamie interrupted. "It's literally all we've been talking about every lunch period since school started. I'm *so* sick of it."

Jamie had just gotten rejected by NYU, so her resentment was understandable. Jisu knew exactly how she must feel. Remaining static as your friends zipped past you at a hundred miles per hour. In the last few days, she had received acceptances from her safety college choices—Vassar, UMichigan, the New School, UC Riverside. All perfectly reputable and highly respected schools. It had calmed her nerves, but a few important colleges remained MIA, including UChicago. And all she could do about Harvard in the meantime was continue to send whatever glowing reviews and letters she could garner from old tutors and teachers.

"Ooh, I know something we can talk about," Tiffany said. Her eyes lit up and she leaned in like she was about to tell them a big secret. "Have you guys heard about Sophie Bennett and Dave Kang?" she continued. Jisu froze as her heart skipped a beat. She waited for someone else to inquire further. None of her friends at Wick knew about what happened on the bleachers that day.

"No, what happened?" Jamie asked.

"Apparently, they broke up," Tiffany said.

Hiba gasped. "But they were together for so long!"

"Jeez," Jamie said. "Something bad must've happened for them to split up."

Jisu felt like a bus had run over her, backed up and run over her again. She wanted to clutch her stomach and keel over. Nothing good was going to come out of that kiss with Dave. It didn't matter how much she'd secretly liked it. Jisu was responsible for the end of one of Wick's most beloved couples.

"So, apparently Sophie was caught making out with a kid from another high school. It was at a Marin party, so it was someone from there." Hiba and Jamie stared at Tiffany with their mouths agape. Jisu's breathing became short and little black spots started to cloud her vision.

"What was Sophie doing at a Marin party?" Jamie wondered aloud.

Jisu was dying to ask more questions. Had Sophie gone off to find another boy to make out with for revenge after finding out about Jisu and Dave? Or had it happened completely separately? Jisu clamped down her tongue and tempered her curiosity.

"Poor Dave. How could Sophie do such a thing?" Hiba looked concerned.

If they only knew. Jisu wanted to tell Hiba she had no reason to feel sorry for Dave. That he was just like the rest of the guys. Acting without thinking, without meaning, without restraint.

"But she wasn't cheating! Apparently, they broke up months ago. Right before Christmas." Tiffany's voice rose and fell, and Jisu thought she might actually pass out. This was the biggest bit of gossip all semester and Tiffany was telling it the way an actor would deliver a dramatic monologue. Jisu had to make a real effort to not collapse onto the floor. Her limbs were losing every bit of strength. *Keep it together, Jisu!* "They were going to pretend they were still together for the rest of the year so that they could win prom king and queen."

"Yikes, then that makes it really obvious," Jamie said.

"Makes what really obvious?" Hiba asked.

"That Dave is the one who broke up with her, and it was Sophie's idea to pretend stay together through prom. Do you really think *Dave* cares about being prom king?" Tiffany said.

"Yeah, that was definitely not a decision they made together," Jamie said as she chewed through the last of her baby carrots. Jisu hadn't even touched her lunch.

"Apparently she practically begged him to pretend they were still a thing," Tiffany said. "She must really want the prom queen title. But that's all over. Word's out."

Jisu was utterly floored. So Dave *hadn't* been acting reckless. He'd been…real. Jisu's heart beat faster and faster. Her gaze darted around the field searching for him. It felt like a heavy fog had lifted from her feelings. The clarity was overbearing.

She revisited the memory of them on the bleachers. A part of her was relieved that she could now freely and fondly think of that moment. She hadn't hated the kiss at all, but the cir-cumstances had made her pull away, run off and be cold. Jisu felt awful all over again, but for different reasons now.

"I can't believe none of you guys knew about this," Tiffany said. She turned to Jisu. "Especially you."

"*Me?* Why me?" The tiny black spots reappeared in her line of vision. Only, they were large blots that threatened to take her out. Did Tiffany know about her and Dave somehow? She really did always have the latest tea on everyone.

"You guys seem like hella close friends, and you're always hanging out."

"Oh…no. I had no idea." Jisu tucked a strand of her hair behind her ear, her hand shaking ever so slightly. She packed her untouched lunch back into her bag. She had to find Dave. They hadn't seen each other since she'd run away from him as fast as she could—it was likely strategic avoidance on his part.

And then she spotted him leaving the cafeteria. He was alone. This was her chance.

"Dave!" Jisu said as cheerfully as she could, trying not to sound too overexcited or out of breath. Maybe if she pretended nothing drastic and embarrassing happened between them, he would pretend also.

But there was no pretending. Dave didn't even say hi. He simply stopped walking and stared at Jisu.

"Um, I haven't seen you around—" she started, feeling a warm glow radiating from her cheeks.

"I'm right here. Do you need something?" Dave said. His tone was entirely devoid of warmth, like a long, cold win-ter night.

"I wanted to apologize for the other day and how I ran off—"

"Are you all set for the presentation tomorrow?"

"What?"

"For Mrs. French's class."

"Oh…yeah, I'm all set."

"Good. Me, too. I'll see you in class tomorrow."

Dave walked around Jisu and continued on down the hallway. Each stride he took was like a dagger to her heart. A wave of dread washed over as her as she watched him walk away and realized that her chance was gone. It had been gone the moment she backed away on those bleachers only two weeks ago.

DATE NO. 26

NAME: **Moon Alexander aka Alex**

INTERESTS:
National Honors Society, Architecture, Polo

ACCOMPLISHMENTS:
3rd Place International Design Competition

ALEX: On a scale of one to ten, one being the least satisfactory and ten being the most satisfactory, how would you rate your experience with Ms. Moon?

JISU: Uhh. I don't really know.

ALEX: How many of these have you been on?

JISU: I lost count, honestly.

ALEX: Really? And none of them stuck so far? What's like a ballpark figure?

JISU: Hmm…more than twenty. You might be my twenty-fifth or twenty-sixth date.

ALEX: Interesting. And how were the matches—were they all misses?

JISU: No, no. Not all. I mean, there were some bad ones who were the complete opposite of what you'd expect from their one-sheet. Others, I just didn't connect with.

ALEX: And your interactions with Ms. Moon—how are those? Do you give feedback, does she solicit it?

JISU: You're asking a lot of questions.

ALEX: Guess I might as well be honest here…

JISU: Yes, that's kind of important on a first date.

ALEX: That's the thing. This isn't a first date.

JISU: It's not?

ALEX: No. Maybe I should've led with this. I work for a match-making start-up. But instead of the usual dating apps, we're trying to create a more human matchmaking experience modeled after the old-fashioned services.

JISU: Like what Ms. Moon is doing.

ALEX: Exactly! So I'm doing some reconnaissance.

JISU: Wow. Is your name even Alex?

ALEX: Ha, good one. Yes, it is. It's not like I'm working for the CIA.

JISU: Are you really in high school, then?

ALEX: Well, I'm eighteen. But I dropped out of high school. It's no longer that impressive to drop out of college and pursue a career in tech, you know.

JISU: How did Ms. Moon even take you on if you're a high school dropout?

ALEX: Well, first I created a super-convincing profile.

JISU: Yeah, I came here thinking I'd have to have something to say about design and architecture.

ALEX: Those were my actual interests when I was still in high school. I probably would've gone down that path and studied all that if I'd gone to college.

JISU: You probably still could.

ALEX: I know I could. Everyone gives you an average of three to five years tops to make it in the tech world. I've been in it for one, so I can still decide to go to college before hitting the legal drinking age and shrug this whole thing off as a "gap year" experience if it goes south.

JISU: And is that also what you told Ms. Moon?

ALEX: No way.

JISU: So, what fake identity did you put together to convince her, then?

ALEX: This is going to be slightly embarrassing. But do you remember that Korean movie *The Lost Boys* that came out when we were kids?

JISU: Oh, yeah! They called it the updated Korean *Goonies*, right?

ALEX: Yeah, well. That's me. I played the lead character.

JISU: What? That's not possible! That kid was crazy famous. And then he couldn't handle the fame, so his family pulled him out of the limelight. He just disappeared after that...

ALEX: Yeah, because he moved to San Francisco with his parents to have a normal childhood.

JISU: Nooo wayyyy. I loved that movie!

ALEX: Yeah, so did Ms. Moon. So she approached my parents as a fan. We both know I don't meet her requirements, but I think she's just happy to claim me as a client.

JISU: And now you're using her to get ahead.

ALEX: Hey, that's how it is. In Hallyu, in tech, even in matchmaking. People are only hiring her to get ahead. Under the guise of romance.

JISU: Yeah, not even much of a guise either, to be honest.

ALEX: So, what do you think makes a good matchmaking service, then?

JISU: That's the tricky part. It's not really a formula you can discover and use on everyone. Because everyone's so different. And the frills—the one-sheets, the fancy cafés and restaurants—none of that matters.

ALEX: So what matters?

JISU: I think, at the end of the day, it just comes down to the two individuals who sit across from each other. Two personalities that spark and click. If anything, that's the timeless formula, right?

27

"And in the last few slides, we'll show how it all comes together with the Wick motto," Dave said. He looked at Jisu and motioned her to move on to the next slide.

It was the first time he'd actually looked at her during the whole IS presentation—the first time since he'd walked away the day before.

"Head, Hands and Heart. The three elements of the Wick motto. The Head represents the political ideals and movements that Jisu and I worked to publicize better through this project."

Jisu and I. It was difficult to focus on presenting to the class when there were unresolved issues between them. Or at least for Jisu, they felt unresolved. For all she knew, Dave was done talking to her once the presentation was over. But at least in the moment, he was being civil.

"For example, the first labor union rally we attended had a modest attendance. The purpose of the rally—the Head matter—was the issue of unionizing. Which leads to the Hand."

It was now Jisu's turn to talk.

"The Hand represents the actual work and technical skills that go into exercising these political and cultural ideals, like unionizing and getting more people to vote. These images were posted across social media. They not only embody the ideals, but also the technical data we mined to determine how and when to post them for maximum impact."

"Wow, some of these photos are really great," Mrs. French interjected as Jisu went through each image on the projector.

"Jisu took most of them," Dave said.

Was that a compliment? He was stating a fact, but also giving her credit. Jisu turned to him and tried to give him an encouraging smile, but he ignored her. Maybe it wasn't an olive branch.

"And the last part of the Wick motto—the Heart," Dave continued. "For this project, the Heart symbolizes our personal passions, which determined the kinds of events we attended and researched."

"I picked the *Feminism in the Digital Age* art show at The Lab, and Dave picked the labor union meetings and rallies," Jisu said and concluded the presentation.

Despite the tension between them, they had done a good job of passing the ball back and forth and completing their project without issue. Jisu turned to the last slide. *The End.*

"Good work!" Mrs. French said. "Jisu, you should send this presentation to the schools that have you wait-listed. It might help."

Jisu nodded and followed Dave back to their seats. The next duo queued up and started their presentation. The class moved on, but Jisu had a hard time paying attention. Their big project was over and there was no longer any reason for them to talk to each other, unless she could salvage things.

"That went really well!" Jisu leaned to her left and whispered toward Dave's direction. He seemed not to hear. "And we didn't even go over fifteen minutes," she said. "All the practice was good for something."

"Yeah. Hopefully Mrs. French gives us a good grade," Dave said before quickly turning his attention back to the front of the classroom.

Jisu also turned to the front of the classroom, exhaling with defeat. She sat mere inches away from Dave, but it felt like a million miles. Jisu liked him. She always had. Despite however he felt about her now, was their friendship really so weak that it couldn't withstand one bout of miscommunication? Was this the end?

No. Jisu wasn't going down without a fight.

"I didn't know about you and Sophie," she said to Dave. She didn't care if anyone else heard or if Mrs. French had to shush her from the front of the classroom.

Dave kept his eyes forward. But he was listening, she could tell. He tilted his head toward her when she spoke.

"I didn't know I could offend someone so much," he muttered back.

"I wasn't offended. I was just shocked. I thought you and Sophie were still together." Jisu wished he would at least face her.

"I would've explained if you let me. But you just ran off. I don't know what I was thinking."

Jisu slumped back into her seat. She felt helpless, like a deflated balloon. How else was she supposed to react, then? And she was here now, apologizing. Why couldn't they at least go back to where they'd been before? Friends.

"What are you doing after school today?" she asked.

"Nothing."

"Wanna go hang at DP?" Jisu asked as casually as she could manage. Maybe the approach was to gloss things over.

"Jisu." Dave turned to her finally. "We're done with the project. There's no reason for us to hang out anymore."

Her shoulders dropped and she blinked rapidly to contain the sudden burning sensation in her eyes. His words cut deep. They were the final blow to whatever remaining pride she had left. Was this how he'd felt when she'd run off? Was he doing this on purpose—to show how he'd felt? But how could he be mad at her? She hadn't known what had happened between him and Sophie—he had never disclosed this.

"I mean," Dave started. "I'm not going to force you to hang out with me. I don't want you to feel like you have to."

Dave looked nervous, and he kept his gaze on the ground, by her shoes, like he was too nervous to look up at her. Maybe he was afraid he'd jumped the gun too early. He really had. But he hadn't screwed everything up. And maybe all he needed was a sign.

"Are you going to Tiffany's party this weekend?" Jisu tried her hand one more time.

"I don't know. It depends." He finally looked up at Jisu. "Are you going?"

"Yeah, I'm going. It'd be crazy to miss it," Jisu said. "You should go!"

Dave nodded his head, but he didn't say anything.

Jisu was out of things to say. She turned her attention back to the presentation happening in front of the classroom. She stared straight ahead as calmly as she could, but she felt rattled. In her mind, she was flashing the biggest green light and waving the largest GO sign at Dave. She wanted him to see it. Was he seeing it?

DATE NO. 27

NAME: **Lee Yongi**

INTERESTS:
Comic Books, Gaming, Woodworking

PARENT OCCUPATIONS:
Investment banker; Pediatrician

YONGI: Who would you say is your favorite superhero?

JISU: Hmm. I like Batman.

YONGI: Same! He's a superhero without mutant, crazy powers. He goes above and beyond for Gotham.

JISU: I mean, the whole wealthy-billionaire thing and having a fancy butler that does tricks doesn't hurt.

YONGI: Ha, that's true. Still, he's my favorite above Superman, Green Lantern and all those guys.

JISU: Oh, I also really like Wonder Woman.

YONGI: Of course. I knew you'd say that.

JISU: Say what?

YONGI: Wonder Woman. Every girl I know says that.

JISU: What's wrong with liking Wonder Woman? She's a badass.

YONGI: It's just so…expected. You really don't like any other character? You just *have* to pick her? And no one really picks Catwoman or Supergirl either.

JISU: Isn't Catwoman a villain?

YONGI: Originally, yeah. But she's more like antihero. She's not perfect, but you root for her.

JISU: Yeah, I know what the definition of an antihero is. And technically, she's an antiheroine.

YONGI: There we go again with the politicizing.

JISU: I'm not overtly politicizing anything. I'm just stating a fact.

YONGI: Okay, but choosing Wonder Woman as your favorite superhero of all time isn't a political choice?

JISU: You're saying it's only political when I happen to pick a female character. It sounds more like you're the one putting political meaning into it.

YONGI: I'm not. I just think it's interesting how every girl I ask says she loves Wonder Woman.

JISU: Well, if there were more female superheroes, then we wouldn't be having this conversation. But then again, if there were more female superheroes, that might annoy you.

YONGI: What? No, that wouldn't bother me. Just as long as they don't stop making Batman movies just to make more Wonder Woman movies.

JISU: Exactly my point.

YONGI: What do you mean?

JISU: You can't say you support more female superheroes if you're not willing for Marvel or DC to make space for them.

YONGI: Then to echo what you're saying, you can't have Wonder Woman and other female heroes take up all the attention. Then it's unfair for the male superheroes.

JISU: You're acting like things have been perfectly equal between men and women. They haven't. That's why when a female superhero gets any bit of attention, it's going to feel unfair even though it's not. You ever think about how what you perceive to be normal is someone else's oppressive reality?

YONGI: "Oppressive reality"—really? We're talking about comics.

JISU: We're not *just* talking about comics, Yongi.

YONGI: Well, whatever. Also, Batman and Wonder Woman are part of the DC world, not Marvel. DC and Marvel are so different.

JISU: Ugh. I know that.

YONGI: Did you really though?

JISU: Yes. But believe whatever you want. I really don't care about convincing you either way.

28

It was the first time in ages that Jisu had slept in on a Saturday. Not sleep in until 9:00 a.m. and then do a tiny bit of homework before lunchtime. More like sleep past noon until every cell in her body felt completely restored.

The last few months of Jisu's life had become an emotional roller coaster and the ride was finally coming to an end. The night before, Jisu had done a face mask, applied various fragrant creams to her skin and sprinkled lavender oil onto her pillowcase to ensure full slumber. Putting her phone on Do Not Disturb and turning off all the alarms felt like a luxury, and she made a mental note to do it more often.

The next morning, when she woke up at half past noon, it wasn't because anxiety or a panicked dream startled her awake. It was from the afternoon sunlight that spilled into her room. And when Jisu woke up, she felt ready to tackle whatever life was going to throw at her, however easy or difficult it was.

Still half awake, she reached for her camera and took a few photos of the sunlight and shadows that hit her bedroom walls. She eventually rolled out of bed and made her way downstairs.

"I was getting a little worried," Linda said and offered a smile. She was reading the paper and drinking a cup of coffee at the kitchen table. "I almost went in to check if you were still breathing."

"Just catching up on sleep." Jisu let out a yawn and stretched her arms out. "I feel like I've been barely functioning for the last few weeks."

"I'm glad you got some rest. You've been working so hard." Linda nodded toward Jisu's laptop. "You just got a notification on your computer. Maybe some of that hard work has paid off."

Linda pushed the laptop toward Jisu. Jisu flipped it around. She hadn't logged out of the application portal, and there was an email from the UChicago Admissions Office. Her heart started to beat rapidly and she ran up the stairs and into her room just as quickly. Jisu closed the door behind her and ran to her desk. She took a quick breath before clicking on the email.

Dear Jisu,

Welcome and congratulations on your acceptance to the University of Chicago.

   Earning a place in our community of scholars is no small achievement, and we are delighted that you selected UChicago to continue your intellectual journey.

Jisu let out a scream before she could even finish reading. It wasn't a rejection. It wasn't a wait list. UChicago wanted her, Jisu Kim, as a student!

Mandy rushed in without knocking, looking worried. "What happened, what happened? Are you okay?"

Jisu was too excited to speak. She jumped up and down and showed Mandy.

"Oh, my god, congrats, Jisu! You did it! This is amazing!"

"I have to call my parents!" Jisu picked up her phone and dialed them immediately. Her excitement kept growing. She didn't even pause to consider the time difference like she usually would. *Who cares if it's 3:00 a.m. or 8:00 a.m. there? They won't mind.*

"Jisu? Is everything okay?" Mrs. Kim answered, sounding equal parts groggy and concerned. Maybe the news could've waited just a few hours.

"Everything is *amazing*, Umma. I just got into UChicago!" Jisu shouted. She heard her mother gasp and then rustle her father awake.

"UChicago, honey. UChicago!" Mrs. Kim said. "Jisu-ya, that's so great. We all know how hard you've worked."

"Congratulations, Jisu!" Mr. Kim shouted in the back before clearing his throat. He sounded half awake, as well. But they both were ecstatic for her.

Much to Jisu's relief, they made no mention of her still being on the Harvard wait list. She wondered if she was more excited about going to Chicago instead of Cambridge for the next four years. Better to attend somewhere that immediately welcomed you instead of pushing your way into a school that wasn't sure.

"Enjoy this moment, my Jisu! You deserve it!" Mrs. Kim said. "Your Appa and I won't tell your Haraboji. We'll let you call him. Actually, you should just try him now. You know how he's always up so early. I'm proud of you!"

All this hard work was worth it to hear those words from her mother. The acceptance was only sweetened by her parents' approval.

Jisu dialed her grandfather.

"Jisu! What a wonderful way to start my day!" Jisu was already in a great mood, but hearing her grandfather's voice lifted her spirits even more.

"Haraboji, I have some great news." Jisu was so happy, she was nearly giggling to herself. Haraboji probably could tell because he was starting to laugh, too.

"What's making you so happy, Jisu?"

"I got into UChicago!" Jisu said.

"Wow! That's where you've been wanting to go, right?" Chances were her grandfather didn't fully understand which college was ranked high and which school was good for what. He only remembered that this was the school she wanted.

"Your parents really outdid themselves by sending their only kid across the ocean to study at a completely new school," Haraboji said. "But you still did it, Jisu. And I am so, so proud of you."

"Thank you, Haraboji." Jisu was surprised at how choked up she was getting. Her grandfather's words stirred something in her. She was filled with joy and happiness when she heard the news, but talking to her grandfather made her feel strong, like she really could do anything.

"I can't wait to celebrate with you, Umma and Appa when I get back," she said.

"I can hardly wait either."

It was a day filled with emotional phone calls. Jisu wanted to keep going. She wanted to call everyone she ever met in life to tell them she had gotten into a great college. A college of her choice. Was it too early to call Euni and Min? Jisu sent them a Kakao message anyway.

Hey guys* call me when you can. I have good news!

Jisu's phone started ringing the second she put it down. Euni was requesting a video chat. That was quick.

"What are you doing up so early?" Jisu was surprised to see not just Euni but also Min up and awake. They were dressed and outdoors. It was still dark outside in Seoul. "Did you guys sneak out and go clubbing? You said you'd wait until the summer so we could all go together!"

"What? No!" Euni laughed.

Jisu could see clearer now that they were wearing sweat-pants, leggings and headbands. Min grabbed a hold of Euni's phone.

"Guess what? Euni is a morning person *and* a runner now." Min looked exhausted. "And she's making me go on early-morning runs with her."

"Min, it was your idea!" Euni shouted from behind her as she stretched her legs.

"No, I said that you should start exercising more to maintain your health. Not like this!" Min pulled her hoodie over her head and groaned. "I already get my cardio in through dance class. You think I need to do this, too?"

"It definitely won't hurt though," Jisu said. "All that stamina will help you belt those high notes *and* get the choreography done."

"I guess." Min rolled her eyes. "Here, Euni, take your phone back. I need to stretch also."

"So what's the good news, Jisu?" Euni asked.

"Well." Jisu couldn't stop smiling. "I got my acceptance from UChicago today!"

Euni and Min both exploded with shouts and cheers. The three of them ran and jumped about.

"UChicago?" Min asked. "That's one of the really tough ones, right? It's supposed to be harder to get into some Ivy schools, isn't it?"

Min could've been playing dumb. She could've also been

hyping Jisu up. But hearing her talk about her future college this way was rewarding and made her feel accomplished.

"It's an amazing school." Euni beamed like a proud parent. "Jisu, I'm so happy for you! This means I get to visit Chicago!"

"And I'll visit you in New Haven!" For once, thinking about the future didn't fill Jisu with dread.

"By the way, what's going on with that guy Dave?" Min asked. Euni nudged her in the ribs, maybe a little too hard.

"Ow! What?" Min clutched her sides and glared at Euni.

"Can you just let her have her moment?" Jisu heard Euni whisper to Min.

"What? I thought *that* was what she meant when she said she had good news." Min scratched her head and looked back at the camera to Jisu. "Is he still being a jerk?" Euni nudged her again. "Ow!"

"Euni, it's fine," Jisu said. "He's not a jerk. He never was."

"But he cheated on his girlfriend! I don't care how good-looking or nice he is to you. That's just a bad omen in general," Min started to say.

"So turns out he didn't." Jisu wondered if she had the energy to really get into all the details. She didn't want to undo all the effects of the peaceful rest and good news from earlier.

"What do you mean?" Euni asked. "Spill!"

"Apparently he already broke up with his girlfriend months ago, and they were just being low-key about it."

"So he's not a cheater—he's just like a really upstanding, noble gentleman?" Euni said.

"Yeah, what are you waiting for, Jisu? Lock it down!" Min was now jogging in place and properly warming up, as if all of Jisu's news from SF had given her a boost of energy.

"I don't know. I completely misunderstood, and now he's being distant. I missed my shot. And I tried, too! If he even really liked me that much, we would've made amends. I don't think he even wants to be my friend anymore." Saying it all out loud made it seem more real, and Jisu felt disheartened all over again.

"Okay, so let me get this straight." Min took charge of the phone and commanded Jisu's attention. "This guy is cute, going to Harvard, comes from a nice Korean family that you *already* get along with and has already made a good impression on your parents that one time he met them."

"And more important, you actually like him!" Euni shouted from behind Min.

"Yeah, not to get all Ms. Moon on you, but you can't give up on this one." Min spoke as she did what looked like lunges to Jisu.

"But also, Jisu, if he's not chasing you either, then he's an idiot. All of his family and school qualifications aside," Euni said. "You have any chance of running into him outside of class? Like when you guys can actually talk?"

"Tiffany's throwing a party tonight at her house. It's a party for the seniors. I think he's going to be there...unless he's trying to avoid me."

"He's a man-child if he doesn't go to a senior class party just to avoid you. So if he isn't there, forget about him. But if he is, just talk to him," Euni advised.

"I already tried though! He wants nothing to do with me."

"Okay, but how soon after the whole messy incident did you try to talk to him?" Min asked.

"I don't know...it was a week or so after."

"Jisu, if I've learned anything from all the dance competitions I've aced, it's that there's nothing more fragile than a guy's pride and ego. He needs time to lick his wounds. And then he'll come around."

Min wasn't one to always dole out good advice, but what she said made sense. Maybe Dave just needed space.

"Well, even if I get to talk to him at the party, I won't have that much time. I have to leave early to go to a seon."

"You're still going on those?" Min asked. "I thought you were done after number twenty-five."

"No, Ms. Moon is still keeping them coming. I have one this afternoon, which will be twenty-eight—I counted—and then one after Tiffany's party, unlucky number twenty-nine."

"Back-to-back seons in one day? Damn, Jisu. Are you sure you're not the player here?" Euni joked.

"I'm not invested in them. They're just a way to kill time," Jisu said.

"Spoken like a true player," Min said. She was doing jumping jacks now.

"All right, Jisu. Min and I need to actually go on our run. Let us know how everything goes. And congratulations again on UChicago!"

The girls blew each other kisses and hung up. Jisu wished she could go on an excruciating 5:00 a.m. run with them.

She looked at the letter from UChicago on her computer and the adrenaline rush surged through her veins all over again.

Guess who just got accepted into UChicago!

Jisu sent off a text to her Wick group chat with Hiba, Jamie and Tiffany.

HIBA: OMG!

JAMIE: Amazingggg.

TIFFANY: Yesss. GO, JISU. Can't want to celebrate at my party tonight!

With each ding and celebratory response, Jisu's heart doubled in size with joy. She was excited to see all of them later.

If only she could just cut through seons twenty-eight and twenty-nine.

Jisu's fingers hovered over her screen. She wanted to text Dave and tell him her good news, too.

Maybe it was the rush of excitement from the acceptance combined with the bountiful support and adulation from her parents and friends, but thinking about Dave made Jisu's heart race faster. He was a Korean guy her parents had been impressed with, and she'd been quick to resist any romantic notion of him because of this. But he was so many other things. He was kind and caring. He could impress you with how smart he was, but he never showed off. He was funny and could make you laugh. He walked around with drive and purpose.

Jisu wasn't going to text him. She was going to see him at Tiffany's party, where she would tell him about UChicago. And she would tell him how he'd made her feel: seen, heard, complete.

DATE NO. 28

NAME: **Park Jimin aka Jimmy**

ROLE MODELS:
Lionel Messi, Mia Hamm, Pele

PARENT OCCUPATIONS:
Korean literature teacher;
American ambassador

JISU: Who are your heroes?

JIMMY: Oh, this one's easy. Pele, Lionel Messi and Mia Hamm.

JISU: So you like soccer! Got it.

JIMMY: Ha, yeah. It's a little more than a hobby.

JISU: Nice. I'm really into photography, so I get it.

JIMMY: So, how's your senior year going? I feel like people are either super chilled out or hyper stressed during senior year.

JISU: Well, I'm definitely in the hyper-stressed camp.

JIMMY: Oh, no! Why? All the college stuff?

JISU: Yeah, pretty much. I've gotten into a few places—

JIMMY: That's great!

JISU: But I've also been wait-listed at a few other places. What about you? Super chill or super pressed?

JIMMY: Hella chill. I'm never pressed. Nothing can get me freaked out.

JISU: Really? Nothing? What if Lionel Messi got injured really badly?

JIMMY: He'll get the best doctors. He'll always get back up.

JISU: What if he died?

JIMMY: Okay, that's the grim. You're talking about the King of Soccer here.

JISU: You're getting upset just by the mere thought though. I think we've figured out your no-chill trigger.

JIMMY: I *was* pretty upset when the US didn't qualify for the last World Cup. That was bad. I'm pretty sure it broke my heart.

JISU: But South Korea participated that year.

JIMMY: Yeah, thank *god*. I've actually never been to Korea, but I *am* Korean. So it was nice to at least have a team to root for. Plus they all look like me, and that's kinda cool!

JISU: So how is everything "hella chill" for you right now? Even my friends who got into their dream colleges are still trying to keep up with class so their acceptances don't get rescinded.

JIMMY: The honest truth is that I got into Notre Dame, not based off my grades—which aren't even that bad—but based off my soccer-playing. I'm going to play my way through college. It's gonna be great.

JISU: That's cool. What do you want to study when you're at Notre Dame though?

JIMMY: Uh, I've never really thought about that. I think I wanna try to go pro if I can. So I'm really just focused on soccer.

JISU: Huh. You kinda remind me of someone I know.

JIMMY: Oh, do you know someone else who's trying to go pro?

JISU: No. And he doesn't even play the same sport.

JIMMY: What sport then?

JISU: Surfing. Is that even a college sport?

JIMMY: Probably not?

JISU: Yeah, he's just really into it. He only wants to eat, sleep, surf and repeat.

JIMMY: If I could just eat, sleep and play soccer, that would be the dream.

JISU: Yeah... I don't know if I feel that way about anything. I need my various interests.

JIMMY: Hey—do you have any plans for later today? You wanna get outta here? We can watch a movie or something at my place.

JISU: Uh, I can't. A friend of mine is throwing a party at her house and I can't miss it. Actually, I'm running a bit late and should be on my way already. It was nice meeting you though!

29

Jisu spent the whole time en route to Tiffany's strategizing how she would find Dave and talk to him. But none of it was necessary. He was the first person in her line of vision when she walked through the door.

He gave a benign head nod. They approached each other and met in the center of the room.

"Heard you got into UChicago. Congrats," Dave said, his tone a touch softer now. He gave her a high five. It was a friendly gesture, but not the one she wanted. "I was worried you weren't coming," he said.

Did he still care? Or was he just being nice to be nice?

"Tiffany would hate me if I missed out on this." Jisu searched the room for Tiffany. She'd prepared for this moment, to come face-to-face with Dave, but her stomach kept doing flips and it was difficult to look Dave in the eye.

It had never been difficult to look at him before.

"I know." Dave looked down at his feet. "I was being kind of a jerk in Mrs. French's class the other day. So I thought you might try to avoid me. I'm sorry."

He looked back up at Jisu. Suddenly she no longer felt afraid to meet his gaze.

"When I kissed you, it wasn't for any other reason than the fact that I like you. I'm crazy about you, Jees."

Jisu's heart beat, not faster with nervous anticipation, but steadily and stronger now with exhilaration. The rest of her body felt springy and weightless. Thank god for the wall she was leaning on—without it, she might have collapsed into a puddle of feelings. Everything he said was everything she was feeling about him, too. She took Dave's hand and locked her fingers with his.

"I wish we could be alone on the bleachers again. It would be different this time," she said.

"You mean, you wouldn't get all red in the face and storm off?" Dave teased. It instantly felt like they were back to normal. *Finally.*

"What if we just left this party?" he asked.

"First of all, Tiffany would hold that against me for god knows how long," Jisu said. "And also...I kind of have to ditch early anyway. I have a seon to go to...but those things don't mean anything to me! Honestly." Jisu tried to temper the growing knot of anxiety in her stomach as she waited for his reaction.

"Well, you know you're not the only one people are lining up to date. I have my own blind date to get to." Dave grinned.

Jisu stared at him, confused.

"It's a joke!" he said as he pulled her in for a reassuring hug. "Well, kind of. The second my mom found out I broke up with Sophie, she's been trying to set me up on a blind date. I'm just doing it for her."

"Do you know who your date is?"

"She's the daughter of a friend of a friend of my mom's... I think?" Dave put his hands together like a light bulb went off in his head. "When's your seon?"

"Soon. I actually probably have to leave in a few. I like to be early to these things."

"Mine's also tonight. We should ditch our dates and meet up later," Dave suggested.

"Okay, but don't be rude to your date! I always go in with an open mind. I mean, I know it won't lead to anything, but—"

"No! Don't be too nice." Dave put his hands on Jisu's shoulders. "I can't lose you to some rando."

Jisu felt light and weightless, like she could float off into the air and Dave's arms on her shoulders were the only things holding her down.

"There's no way that's going to happen. He's going to be my twenty-ninth seon. And any number with the number nine is my unlucky number."

Jisu got to El Farolito ten minutes early, in case her date showed up early, as well. She'd keep it to an hour or less, and then meet up with Dave. That was the plan.

"Steak burrito to stay, right?" the man behind the counter asked.

Jisu was a bonafide regular at El Farolito now. The delicious and overly stuffed burritos made it easy to keep coming back, but it had also become one of her go-to spots for her American seons. It was so nice to not have to meet at a fancy hotel lobby that was covered in Italian marble and lit by grandiose chandeliers. And each seon she had here chipped away at her bittersweet original El Farolito memory with Austin, the one who originally took her for burritos—and where she'd seen Dave with Sophie for the first time.

Jisu placed her order and slid into a booth, wondering what her date looked like.

Her phone vibrated. It was a text from Dave. Already?

So I just got to my date. And she is a total stunner. Might have to see where this goes...

What? This was a complete 180 from what he'd said just an hour or so ago. Jisu stared at her phone, confused.

"Also, I think twenty-nine might actually be your lucky number. Or not. You know, there's no such thing as cursed numbers, right?"

Jisu looked up. Dave was standing in front of her. Dave Kang. Her heart burst and expanded like a time-lapse of a rapidly blooming flower. Happiness overwhelmed her. It was so tangible, she could feel it in her bones. For a moment, she blacked out, but the rapid beating of her heart jolted her back to consciousness. *Dave* was her twenty-ninth seon. But how?

"I guess my mom's friend's friend knows someone you know?" Dave grinned and slid into the other side of the booth.

"No, that can't be possible. I'm set up through this profes- sional matchmaker, Ms. Moon. I had to send in an applica- tion to even be considered as a client and everything. It's not like a friend-of-a-friend scenario."

"Wait, Ms. Moon? That's the friend's friend that my mom mentioned." Dave laughed. "I bet she was just trying to be chill so I wouldn't freak out or get weird about working with some matchmaking service."

"I guess you're a lot more plugged in to the Korean com- munity than I thought." Jisu smiled. "Also, unlucky numbers are totally a thing. If you want to be a real Korean, you have to indulge in a bit of superstition."

"So what—does that still make me your unlucky seon then?" Dave asked.

Jisu laughed. She'd never felt luckier in her entire life.

MARCH 28, SAN FRANCISCO

> ### DATE NO. 29
>
> NAME: **Kang Daehyun aka Dave**
>
> INTERESTS:
> Debate, Environmental Science, Lacrosse, Soccer
>
> ACCOMPLISHMENTS:
> Soccer Team Captain,
> Early Acceptance to Harvard

JISU: You're technically my thirtieth seon. Because Austin counts as one, too, somewhere between seon fifteen and twenty.

DAVE: Can we not talk about that guy?

JISU: And you know what number thirty is, right?

DAVE: What?

JISU: It's considered the luckiest number in Korea.

DAVE: Really?

JISU: No! I just made that up. Wow, you really don't know anything about Korean culture.

DAVE: Oh, here we go again with that. I'm very Korean, you know. I even have a Korean name.

JISU: Really? What is it?

DAVE: Okay, we're gonna start this seon all over.

JISU: Hey, I'm Jisu.

DAVE: I'm Daehyun.

JISU: Korean name! But you're born and raised here?

DAVE: Yup, and you moved from Seoul not that long ago?

JISU: Yeah, my parents were obsessed with me getting into an American Ivy League school and decided it would be a good idea for me to become a last-minute exchange student and sent me across the Pacific to San Francisco. And here we are now.

DAVE: I'm not even going to try to relate. My parents want me to go to a good college and all that, but I can't imagine moving to a whole new country.

JISU: It hasn't been the easiest. But I've met people along the way who've made it worth it.

DAVE: This is gonna sound silly, but I actually feel a little nervous right now.

JISU: For real? It's like we're just hanging out!

DAVE: I know, but it's my first seon. Even just saying that makes it sound official and formal. And you're making me nervous. I even asked some friends for dating tips.

JISU: And what did they tell you?

DAVE: That kindness is underrated. And common likes and dislikes are key. Heavy emphasis on the common dislikes. So, you've been on a lot of seons, both here and in Seoul?

JISU: Yeah, but none of them have worked out…clearly. I did meet some cool guys and I'm actually friends with some of them. But there was never really that chemistry with anyone, you know? I love meeting new people, but I'm kind of over seons, to be honest.

DAVE: I bet the right guy could be the end of all seons for you. You seem to know what you want.

JISU: What do you want? What are you trying to get out of these seons?

DAVE: Actually, I have a girlfriend, which might really screw me up in the long run if I keep sneaking out. I'm only going on these dates to appease my mother. She kinda hates my girlfriend.

JISU: Oh, that's too bad. I actually thought this might go somewhere.

DAVE: Well, it was nice knowing ya, Jees.

JISU: Did you just call me Jees? You know, I hate nicknames. Especially when someone you just met assigns you one.

DAVE: Wait—for real? I've been calling you Jees forever, like since the first day we met. Why didn't you tell me?

JISU: Because I ended up liking it! I still don't like nicknames, but you can still call me Jees. No one else. Just you.

★ ★ ★ ★ ★

Author's Note

I first learned about seon (matchmaking) blind dates through my best friend from college who is Korean and whose parents set her up on several of these dates. She later married a great guy she met at a bar, on her own, and her parents couldn't be happier. While most seon dates are between college and post-collegiate couples, I thought it would be fun to set a YA novel within this traditional dating structure. However, in setting the seon practice in high school, as an author of fiction, I've taken some liberties with this practice. The story is not meant to be representative of the South Korean or Korean-American experience with a matchmaker, but a lighthearted romantic comedy set in a culture I am lucky enough to feel part of through my friends and family. Any mistakes or misunderstandings in the text are mine alone.

My dear sister-in-law, Christina Jiyoung Hwang, inspired this novel due to her own personal history of immigrating to the United States from South Korea, alone, as an international student when she was just a freshman in high school. Christina has been a sounding board and an enthusiastic supporter of this novel from the beginning, and I thank her for her generosity, good humor and keen eye for inconsistencies.

Acknowledgments

Thank you to everyone at Inkyard Press, especially my wonderful editor, Natashya Wilson. Thank you to my 3Arts family: Richard Abate and Rachel Kim. Thank you to all my friends and family, especially all the DLCs: Mom, Aina, Steve, Nicholas, Joseph, Chit, Christina, Seba and Marie; and my Korean sistahs, Carol Koh Evans and Jennie Kim (and her mom, JJ Kim, who's kind of like my mom, too!). Thanks to Mike and Mattie for putting up with all my deadlines. Love to all my loyal readers.